The Burned
Woman

The Burned Woman

=========/ ◆ /=========

EDWARD MATHIS

CHARLES SCRIBNER'S SONS
New York

Charles Scribner's Sons
Macmillan Publishing Company
866 Third Avenue, New York, NY 10022
Collier Macmillan Canada, Inc.

This is a work of fiction. Names, characters, places,
and incidents either are the product of the author's
imagination or are used fictitiously. Any resemblance to actual events or persons, living or dead, is
entirely coincidental.

Library of Congress Cataloging-in-Publication Data
Mathis, Edward.
    The burned woman/Edward Mathis.
        p.   cm.
    ISBN 0-684-19039-7
    I. Title.
PS3563.A8364B87   1989
813'.54—dc19   88-32912   CIP

            10 9 8 7 6 5 4 3 2 1

Printed in the United States of America

The Burned Woman

/ 1 /

The sounds penetrated faintly into the thick upper reaches of the green-canopied forest. Harshly intrusive, yet strangely harmonious in part, melodious bells and discordant drums intertwined in a cacophony that was at once pleasing and distressing to the ear.

Vine in hand, knife clenched firmly in my teeth, I crouched high above the hard-packed earth of a compound filled with dancing savages. Cool and fearless, I calmly gauged the rising blood lust of the howling mob below, feeling a pleasant tingling as my magnificent muscles swelled in anticipation of imminent action, tensing a little as the pounding feet came ever closer to the lovely maiden staked cruelly in the center of the clearing, luxuriant raven hair cascading, an ineffective shield against the salacious eyes and barbaric implements of the savage horde. A spear point flashed carelessly, a thin bright splash of red along a tender naked flank, and I was growling deep in my chest—hearing the horrendous clatter again, the strangely familiar, haunting melody that a part of me recognized yet refused to acknowledge—springing forward and launching myself into the air, beginning the long smooth glide that would drop me at her side, the chilling battle cry of the great apes spilling from my throat, bringing paralyzing terror to the uplifted, glistening faces below, bright shining wonder to the countenance of the hapless captive who—

"My God, what was that?"

I opened my eyes.

Susie sat upright in the bed, staring at me with wide, round eyes, the forgotten light from the bathroom outlining her upper torso with a soft hazy aureole, her dark tangled mane of hair bouncing and tumbling as her glance whipped from me to the bedroom door and back again.

"What was what?" I said groggily, still enmeshed in the heady excitement of the dream, the wild exhilaration sadly diminishing, regretfully fading like the pulsing warmth of a shot of good whiskey on a cold and bitter night. It was a familiar variation of a dream I had fairly often.

"That!" Susie exclaimed, instinctively gathering the sheet to her bosom as the sounds came again—the discordant drums and melodious bells of my dream, the doorbell and pounding fists. Some damned fool was trying to knock down the front door.

"Good lord, who . . . ?" Susie began, but I was already fumbling at the pile of clothing on the foot of the bed for my jeans, groping through illusion toward reality, fighting slumber-fog and alcoholic haze.

"I don't know who, but the damned house better be on fire!" I struggled into my pants, searched for my shirt, then said to hell with it as the pounding began again, punctuated by the tinkling chimes and a shouting querulous voice.

"You stay here," I ordered over my shoulder, glancing at the clock as I went through the door. Three o'clock. A faint stirring of alarm crept into the anger as I padded down the hall in my bare feet. Maybe the damn house *was* on fire.

I reached the entry hall and leaned to look through the peephole; the door exploded in my face, bouncing and rattling, clanging metallically as the bolts clattered in their sockets.

"Jesus Christ!" Fuming beyond caution, I twisted the deadbolt, clicked the knob lock, and yanked open the door.

I had one fast glimpse before I was shouldered aside: a pale contorted face framed with long golden hair, a flowing mustache, a spade beard, and a long thin nose. A crimson cape hung to his knees and a black sequined jumpsuit glittered with a thousand lights.

"Where is she?" the apparition bellowed, its bony shoulder plowing into my chest.

Caught off balance, I stumbled backward, ended up clinging by my fingertips to the doorjamb leading to the den. I hung there for a moment, feeling foolish, fighting mad. I fought for balance as I watched him look uncertainly around, then head for the hallway leading to the bedrooms, the cloak swirling behind him like a cloud of crimson smoke.

My clawing fingers finally found purchase; I jerked myself upright, wondering vaguely if I could still be asleep, this unlikely nocturnal invader as much a figment of my alcoholic dreams as the howling savages.

But the huge black shape that had slipped in behind the apparition wasn't a dream; he stood in the doorway smiling at me and shaking his bullet-shaped head, eyebrows cocked above big black eyes shot with blood.

"Chill out, man," he advised calmly. He had big square teeth that gleamed like white dominoes against black shiny skin, and an absurdly tiny nose that peeked insolently through the upper reaches of a thick furry mustache.

"Yeah, you got it." I yanked open the hallway closet and reached for the .38 hanging on the wall. I had it in my hand and was turning when he made a clucking noise behind me and huge twin pincers gripped my arms. I heard my gun clatter on the tile floor. Pain shrilled along my arms, then diminished rapidly as my nerves shuddered toward numbness.

He shook me gently. "Hey, what'cha wanna do that for?" He shook me again, not so gently. "Ain't nobody gonna hurt nobody," he added, releasing my arms and picking up the gun. He reached inside the closet and shoved it into its holster, then closed the door.

"What the hell do you want?"

"The Man come to get his lady," he said, and grinned at me again.

I glared at him. "What the hell—" I broke off as Susie's voice rang in the hallway.

"You'd better get out of here, Mickey Conrad, before Dan gets mad."

"Dan's already mad!" I yelled. I whirled and stepped into the hallway. "What the hell's this all about, Susie?" My arms trailed along beside me, dangling, tingling their way slowly back to life.

They were halfway down the hall, the weirdo trying to take her hands in his, her face crimson, dark eyes blazing. She jerked her hands away and clasped them behind her back.

"Stop it, Mickey!"

"But, baby," he said, a plaintive note creeping through the arrogance, "all I want is to make you my woman!"

Susie flicked a glance at me.

"Who is this asshole, Susan?"

The big black man breathed in my ear. "That's Mickey Conrad," he said, with the same reverence a devout Catholic might use to mention the Pope.

I looked over my shoulder, found his grinning face only inches above mine.

"You don't know about Mickey Conrad?" Amusement cavorted at the edges of his voice. "Where you been?"

"No, I don't know him. But you can damn sure bet I'm going to."

"Come on, baby. Don't you want me?" He was almost crooning, one thin hand reaching into her tousled mass of hair. She flipped her head away and the bony hand fluttered downward to cup her breast through the blue silk robe. She gasped and slapped his hand; I cursed and leaped forward.

But the black man was faster; his thick arms slipped around me again, lifted me off the floor. "Chill out," he said. "You can't reason with him when he's like this."

"Reason, hell! Hey, you! You touch her again—" But the rest of it was lost in an explosion of breath as the black man squeezed.

4

"Hey, man, I tole you, be nice."

Conrad turned toward us, his face annoyed. "Milo, can't you keep him quiet?"

"Yassuh, boss," Milo said, and the pressure relaxed. "Be cool, old man," he said, almost pleadingly. "I'll see he don't hurt your daughter."

I sucked for air. "She's not my daughter," I said when I could breathe again.

"Huh?" He was silent for a moment, then I felt his belly tremble. "You old sucker."

Susie was chattering in a low strained voice I couldn't understand. Her hands were doubled into small brown fists, and I had faced her stiff-backed menace too many times not to read the signs of unrestrained anger.

Her voice hissed to a stop and Conrad said petulantly, "Why did you run off the other night?"

She said something else I couldn't understand.

He made a placating gesture. "But, babe, think about it, London, Paris, Rome . . . Mickey can take you to all those places. Cars, furs, jewelry . . . you name it, sweetness. Mickey's not stingy with his women." He reached out to touch her shoulder; she snapped something and he jerked back his hand.

I moved and the oak beams tightened. "This is over. Finished. Get him out of here, or I swear I'll come looking for him."

Milo chuckled. "Don't do that," he said. "I get some real good money to see nothin' happens to that little shit."

"I'll go through you if I have to."

I could feel him shrug. He lifted his voice, his breath stirring the hair on top of my head.

"Mickey. She ain't his daughter, man. She's his woman."

Conrad really looked at me for the first time. The sallow skin above his beard pouched in amusement. He bared a gleaming row of perfect teeth.

"That's all right, I didn't think she was a virgin. Old fart like him, I don't expect he done it much harm." He

5

threw back his head and laughed, then turned to Susie for approval.

Her hand became a blur of brown; his head recoiled, only to meet the other hand whipping in from his left.

"Get out of here!" Despite the threat of hysteria that lay just beneath the surface, she radiated defiance and determination like heat from a burning building.

"You bitch!" He stared at her incredulously, one thin hand coming up to his cheek. Then his left hand flashed out and twisted in the front of her robe, his right poised, a bony fist with white gleaming knuckles.

"Mickey!" The black man's voice thundered in my ear. "Don't touch her, man!" There was no trace of servility now; it was a command, harsh, imperious, not to be disobeyed.

Conrad stood poised for a long moment, the muscles working in his cheek. He shoved her back against the wall. "Nobody does that to me," he whispered huskily. He poked a finger into her face. "I'm not through with you yet, lady. You can count on it." He was breathing hard, long shuddering breaths that rasped sibilantly in his throat.

"Turn me loose," I begged. "Just for two minutes—one!"

"Can't do that, boss," Milo said gently. "He's valuable property." His voice was mocking, dry.

Conrad stomped down the hall, his face a dirty shade of gray. He had long thin arms and his clenched fists swung loosely—until he reached me; then his right made a short quick trip and ended in the pit of my stomach.

Milo saw it coming and tried to jerk me backward, but the bony knob found its mark and all my breath and part of last night's booze spewed out of my mouth. A wave of paralyzing sickness followed.

"Dammit, Mickey!" The black man wrenched me out of harm's way. "Sometimes you're a sorry shit, man."

"I want her," he said sullenly. He rubbed his knuckles and looked at Susie. "And you take this weak old fart over me? You've got to be kidding me, woman."

6

"Old fart?" She was actually snarling. "He'd make ten of you any day, you . . . you . . ." Words failed her, her voice clotted with anger, trembling with infinite scorn.

He stared at her for a long sixty seconds, then turned to me with a harsh grating laugh. "She didn't say that the other night when I balled her," he said.

I could just make out Susie's face, and even through the shimmering pink haze it gleamed the color of old bleached bones, her eyes stretched to their outermost limits, dark with indignation.

"You're lying," she whispered. She turned the agonized eyes on me. "He's lying, Danny!"

Conrad laughed. "She's all right, but she needs a better teacher, a young guy like me who knows the score."

"Get out of here, man," Milo growled. "Now!"

Conrad shrugged, straightened the scarf looped around his neck. He pointed his finger at Susie again. "I'll see you later, babe." He moved past Milo out of my sight. "Let's go. This place is a cheap stinking dump."

We heard the door slam and Milo released me. I dropped to my knees and hugged my stomach tenderly. Susie rushed up the hall and fell to her knees beside me.

Milo walked around in front. "I'm sorry about this, man. You know how it is."

I felt Susie's hands on my head. "No, man," I mimicked, "I don't know. You tell me how it is."

"Don't believe everything he said."

My laugh sounded more like a gargle. "You with him all the time, Milo?"

"No," he said slowly, softly. "Not all the time. Even I got scruples."

"Then how do you know he's lying?"

Susie's hands fell away from my head. I heard a small smothered gasp.

"I'm sorry, ma'am," Milo said, and seconds later I heard the front door open and close.

/ 2 /

I went into the bathroom and washed the taste of vomit out of my mouth. I brushed my teeth and rinsed again and stared at my reflection in the mirror. Sagging a trifle at the jawline, the squint wrinkles at the eyes a little deeper than I remembered, the beginnings of a double chin, but other than that, not yet the face of an old man—an "old fart." I still had a full head of hair, speckled with gray, a reasonably fit body considering I drank too much, smoked too much, and exercised too little. I gave myself another critical look and resolved to stop smoking so much, to cut down on the booze, to eat less and initiate a rigorous conditioning program. But all that would have to wait until tomorrow, so I lit a cigarette and went into the kitchen for a beer. I popped the tab, drifted into the den and slumped in my favorite chair, a dull throbbing behind my eyes, my stomach still queasy.

Susie was perched on the edge of the couch, her face composed and pale, hands clasped in her lap, lowered eyes staring into the fireplace. A pose I knew well: anxiety overlaid with deceptive composure.

"You want to hear about it?" Her voice was barely audible.

"If you want to tell me," I said. "But you're under no obligation to me."

Her eyes flashed at me briefly, then dropped to her hands. "Do you know who he is?"

"Yes. I remembered the second time he called you his woman. I saw him on the Johnny Carson show. Can't say I liked him even then. He sounds a lot like he's singing through a nose full of snot."

"He's a pretty big star," she said, as if that explained everything.

"So's the sun, but I don't want it crashing into my house at three o'clock in the morning."

She raised her head. "You're really mad, aren't you?" Her lips puckered gravely. "I can tell. When you're really angry you always try to be funny."

That didn't seem to require anything from me, so I focused on my beer and cigarette, attacking each one in turn, trying not to let her see how pissed I really was.

"You don't believe that garbage he was saying?" Her gaze met mine, glowing hotly, held fast for a moment, ricocheted off my cheek. She had warm brown eyes, as compassionate as a mother's touch when they wanted to be, clear and penetrating when they didn't.

"It doesn't matter," I said.

She made a small smothered sound, her face suddenly stricken. "Damn you!" she said, choking on the words. "It does, it does!"

I was silent for a while and she sat crying quietly.

"Yes, Susan, it does matter," I said finally.

She wiped her cheeks on the hem of her robe. "Why are you so . . . why are you this way? You act as if you wouldn't care if I . . . if I slept around. I know you do care."

"You want to tell me what happened?"

"Don't you?"

"Don't I what?"

"Don't you care?"

"Of course I care."

"Then why do you . . . ?"

"Susan." I squirmed uncomfortably. "I don't, dammit, know why I do half the things I do. Or don't do half the things I should do. I can't lay it on the line the way you want me to, the way you do. I'm just not made that way. I can't escape the fact you're sixteen years younger than I am. Even more than losing you, I think it would hurt most to have you pity me, to

9

have you feel sorry for an old man who couldn't hack it anymore. I keep having the feeling that if you did sleep around you might find out I'm not nearly as great as you think, or pretend to think."

"You shut that up," she said passionately. "I don't pretend anything. I couldn't do that if I tried. I'm not devious enough for that, and you know it. I love you and you know that too. Just the way I know you love me. It's your damn dumb hang-up over the difference in our ages."

She turned her head away, not quite quickly enough to hide a grimace of frustration. But when she turned back, her features had softened.

"I don't think it *is* the age thing," she said. "Or our jobs. Or any of the stupid things we fight about." She paused and I saw something in her eyes that was new, something that scared me.

"Aren't we straying off the subject a little?" I said quickly. "What about this Mickey Conrad?"

She took a deep breath, and looked away from me. "I accepted Betty Mercer's invitation to go to Mickey Conrad's concert. The night you were in Houston. Her brother-in-law works for the promoter and he gave her five free tickets. She asked three of the other women from the station to go with us, and her brother-in-law fixed it up for us to go backstage and meet him after the show."

"Nice of him," I said, and watched her finely chiseled lips draw into an austere line.

"Yes," she said quietly, "I thought so."

"Go on," I said, and lit another cigarette.

"Well, we did . . . go backstage to meet him, I mean. And he invited us all to an end-of-concert party." She stopped and gave me a grim look. "How did I know it was out at his ranch and that it was going to be a . . . a pot party? Anyway, I was hoping I could talk him into an exclusive on-camera interview."

"Just pot, huh? Seems pretty mild for such a big star."

"Well, they did have some coke . . . and some pills . . . but you know how I feel about that stuff, Danny."

"I know. So you just had some booze."

"Well, I just couldn't stand around, could I? I nursed my first drink an hour before I had another one."

"Okay, so you got loaded?"

"Not really loaded, Danny. Just a . . . a little high." She smiled. "You know that only takes two or three drinks."

"Uh-huh. Then, lo and behold, the big rock star was there all of a sudden, telling you how lovely you were, wanting to show you his scrapbook . . ."

"No." She blushed furiously. "It was his paintings."

"Oh, my God, etchings! I thought that one went out with celluloid collars."

"Make fun if you want, but it wasn't funny."

"No, I don't imagine there was much laughing going on."

She looked at me reproachfully, nibbling at her lip, teetering on the verge of righteous anger. "Do you want me to tell you, or not?"

"I'm sorry. Go ahead."

"Well, he did have paintings, a lot of them. They weren't his, though, I don't think. I mean, I don't think he painted them the way he said. He wouldn't let me see them up close. As soon as we were in his . . . his bedroom, he started . . . he was all over me." She stopped to wet her lips again. "I was kind of . . . well, I guess flattered, at first. I even let him kiss me . . . once." She averted her head, stealing surreptitious glances at me from the corner of her eye. "You know, so I could say he had, I guess. I don't know why exactly, except I was pretty high." She paused. "He was really awful."

"You could have kicked him in the cajones."

She watched me carefully to see if I was being serious or not. She nodded finally. "I know. I could have, I guess, but I didn't want to cause a scene. I finally had to promise him I'd . . . I'd hang around after the others left . . . to get him to let me go." She took a deep breath. "He promised to talk about the interview, but as soon as I got back downstairs, I made Betty leave."

I shrugged. "No big deal that I can see. If that's all there was to it." I had unconsciously, almost automatically, slipped into the role of a suspicious husband with a stilted disapproving voice and a hearty scowl. She shifted on the edge of the cushion, her left hand fluttering to her throat. She made a valiant try for a smile, lips curving upward, then suddenly drooping. "All right. I've never lied to you. I'm not going to start now. He—he did have his . . . he did expose . . . himself. He kept trying to make me look at . . . him." She kept her voice light, made an effort to smile again, to give it humor it didn't have. But the glance she threw at me was filled with apprehension.

"And you hated it, huh? Yet you stood watching while he pranced around—if there was nothing more to it, why hadn't you told me about it?" I was being unreasonable and I knew it, but it didn't seem to matter.

"Because I know you," she said quietly. "I knew you'd make a big thing out of it. I'm telling you the truth, Danny."

"Sure you are. I believe you. Only I'm not the one making a big thing out of it. I think your boyfriend handled that very well."

"He's not—" She broke off abruptly and stood up. "All right. You've made up your mind. I know I can't change it, so it's useless to argue. But he wasn't abusive, Danny. He was crude and aggressive and conceited and in a way that made the whole thing kind of funny—"

"Yeah, I can see the humor."

"No you can't and maybe I can't blame you for that. He had no business coming here the way he did and I should have told you. I would have eventually. It's just that . . . that I didn't want to spoil last . . . last night." She stopped, a tremor in her voice. "It's been such a long time since . . . well, it *was* nice, wasn't it?"

"Yes, it was, Susan. It was great, but—" I stopped to light a cigarette, realizing abruptly that I had nothing to say, nothing that wouldn't hurt.

"But it didn't change anything? Is that what you mean, Danny?"

I hid behind the cigarette until the silence became too hard to handle.

"I don't think so. We made love and it was great but that was no surprise. Our sex life has always been terrific. We said we loved each other and that was no surprise either. But that doesn't alter the basic problem. You can't live with what I do, I can't live with your absences, and neither of us can do anything else. At least I can't do anything else. I'm too old, Susan. I'm too old to switch lanes. I've been on the slow track too long."

"That isn't true," she said, her tone gently argumentative. "You're not too old. You've been a cop and you have an engineering degree and you can fly a helicopter. How many men have your background?"

I snorted, twin jets of smoke pluming from my nose. "My degree is eighteen years old and I haven't flown a chopper for fifteen. My memory has a half-life on par with a rabbit's. With my background and a lot of pull I might be able to get a job as a mechanic trainee."

"You have money," she said, a note of stubbornness creeping in. "The income from your lignite coal money. You wouldn't have to do anything—"

"I'm forty-two, Susan, not sixty-two."

"You didn't let me finish. You wouldn't have to do anything until you found something you liked."

"What would you suggest?"

"Oh, I don't know. You're a smart man. You—"

"Yeah. Smart enough to know my limitations."

She made an exasperated sound and went back to her seat.

I stood up. "We just keep going over the same old arguments. I'm sorry. I can't handle this. Everything we do seems to represent a compromise for one of us. You're not cut out to

13

be the little woman, home and hearth and dinner at seven. Maybe I'm a chauvinist, or selfish, but right now I think that's what I need."

"I can do that, Danny." Her voice was low and uneven, oddly plaintive, her eyes dark and precative, burning at me with solemn intensity from the shadowed well formed by her tousled mane of hair. "I could stay home and be your wife."

"For how long, Susie? How long before you begin to resent it, resent me?" I crossed to the patio door and pulled the draperies, stood watching the muted glow of Fort Worth against the predawn Texas sky. Vague shadowy clouds hung low on the dim horizon, dark lurking invaders waiting to pounce.

"I think sixteen years are too many, Susan. Different values, different goals. Your life is all ahead of you. Mine is on the far side, winding down. You want rock concerts and dancing and bright lights, action, movement. I want peace, a mug of beer, a liverwurst sandwich, and an occasional unsavory cable movie."

I slid open the door and flipped the cigarette butt out across the patio, waiting for her to speak. When she didn't, after a moment I stepped through onto the concrete.

I found a seat on the redwood lounge and lit another cigarette, the air cool and crisp against my bare chest. I felt tired. Really tired.

She was right. The night before had been nice. Nice and wonderful. And for a few hours I had let myself believe that all was right with the world and the Roman empire, that it could be again the way it had been the first two years of our marriage.

Tranquillity. Euphoria. Illusion. Such is the power of romantic love, obfuscating everything: the first faint tremors of trivial contention, the tiny ripples of discontent.

Blithely oblivious. I had muddled on, confident that I had spanned the yawning generation gap, conquered the rift of inexorable time. Enlightenment came slowly, like sunrise on a cloudy day: the ship of love was listing, wallowing, settling finally into a trough of disharmony and dissension.

She wanted more of me than I was willing to offer; I demanded less than she had to give.

And along with the epiphany came another realization: I was a worn-out old plug wired to a fiery young filly, the race forfeit long before we left the paddock, our hoofbeats drumming out of sync, insouciant youth and middle-age paranoia teased in discordant rhythm. She was finding herself and I was losing what little I had already found. Inequities became wrongs, minor faults sources of indignation.

I was losing my battle with the bottle more and more often. She was spending more and more time away from home, taking on extra assignments, moving ahead in her career while moving further away from me. Some nights the only time I saw her was when I turned on the damn television news. Some nights I fell asleep before it came on.

I paced around the patio, swinging my arms against the chill that comes with descending day. Gradually I became aware of sounds, the coughing roar of a car motor, a slamming door. Somewhere a rooster crowed and a bellicose dog hurled a husky challenge at the vanishing slice of moon. Above my head the oak trees whispered among their branches, adding scope and dimension to my malaise, a creeping feeling of self-contempt and cold aching loneliness enveloping me like the cowl of a mendicant friar.

I went back inside. The den was empty. I closed the door softly and tiptoed quietly down the hallway to the bedroom door, taking care not to rattle the knob.

I needn't have bothered; she was gone. She had left a note. "I'll be at Janey's," it said.

/ 3 /

Sunday, I typed my report to Theodore Weincoff, something I had been dreading. He was a tall, dour man, taciturn and unbending. Stern and righteous, a member in good standing of the Moral Majority, he had hired me to find his daughter, six months gone and not particularly missed if I read his signals correctly. But her desertion had been an affront to his pride, his puritanical Christian ethics, and his standing in the community demanded that he make at least a token effort to return her to the fold.

I had found her easily. As simple as a twenty-dollar bill into the eager palm of my contact at the Social Security office in Fort Worth. She was where their records said she would be, working as a salesgirl at Walden's Department Store in Houston. She was also four months pregnant and deliriously in love with a roughneck from one of the oil fields. I had left her there, unaware of my existence, and now I was getting ready to demolish the code of ethics of the brotherhood of private eyes. I had done it before. I was going to lie to Theodore Weincoff, tell him his daughter had somehow successfully evaded the mechanisms of modern chase technology. I had a gut feeling it wouldn't matter to him all that much. Now he could be pious on Sundays and console himself that he had done all he could for his ungrateful wayward girl.

But, despite my rationalization, I felt a faint twinge of guilt as I hurriedly finished the report and crammed it into an envelope with my bill.

* * *

I drove into the edge of Dallas to Weincoff's small machine shop, only to learn that he was out of town on business. Relieved, I left the report and my bill with his secretary. Although I had charged him only for expenses, the flight to Houston, and a car rental, I felt, somehow, that I was cheating him a little. And maybe I was. But I could live with that.

Finding missing people, strayed, lost, or stolen, can be exciting, rewarding, or even sometimes fulfilling. But mostly it's dull, tedious work, filled with frustrations, and more often than I'd like it to be, sad. People disappear for all sorts of reasons, most of which are illogical, and in a great number of cases finding and returning them to the fold is in their best interest—especially the young ones.

But there are those who have good and cogent reasons for running away. Not that it usually solves anything. Human nature being what it is, people have a distressing habit of drifting unerringly into the same sort of situation or relationship they were running away from in the first place. A young girl will run away from a domineering, oppressive father, only to end up with a domineering, oppressive lover or husband. Or, just as likely, a domineering, oppressive pimp. A young boy will run away from parents who don't understand him, only to find a great big uncaring world out there that understands him even less.

But sometimes they find something better than they had. And as far as I was concerned, Lori Ann Weincoff had done just that. Not fame or fortune—but a man who loved her for what she was, and not for what he would like her to be.

And it's the lucky ones like Lori Ann that I walk away from, leave in whatever peace they've managed to find, with whatever love they've been fortunate enough to grab onto. There's damn little of that in this sad, sorry world.

So I become the judge and the jury; I invoke Dan Roman's law and release them to their fate, their chance at the brass ring, or the good life, or whatever the hell it is they're looking for. Sometimes when I'm half drunk and melancholy, cynically introspective and sadder than I want to be, I wonder about these few probationers, these recipients of Roman's largess, wonder about my own elusive motivations, my omniscient role as benevolent benefactor.

But later, when I'm fully loaded, truly omnipotent, it all becomes crystal clear: I'm God. And most of the time, I do a pretty good job.

On the way home, I stopped by the Midway City Police Department. Homer Sellers, captain of Homicide, my boss for a number of years and still my best friend, was gone as usual.

A big, shambling man, pragmatic, pugnacious, he was an impeccable friend when he wanted to be, obstinate and perverse when he didn't. He was moody and sometimes explosive, but as fair-minded as a cop ought to be. Over the years we had done a lot of drinking together, hunting, poker playing, and had even jousted for the same female a time or two. He was slovenly, and had a lot of disgusting habits when he was drunk, but he had a friendly smile, a generous heart, and was so honest it was painful more often than not. What else could you ask from a friend?

I traded gossip with his secretary, Mitzi, for a while, finally gave up on him and drove home and had a beer. I was bored and restless; the day stretched before me, endless and dreary.

I picked up a paperback Susie had been reading before she left. Jackie Collins's latest; a raw, sex-filled story about the glamorous world of rock stars. I made myself comfortable and tried to read it, washing down the straightforward, unimaginative sex with intermittent cans of beer. After an hour or so, I gave up. I built a sandwich out of French bread, pastrami, and ham and went out on the patio.

It was a cool, pleasant day, late October, the kind of lazy autumn day that makes you appreciate living in Texas. I dragged a redwood lounge into the sun and ate my sandwich and watched the big oak tree for my three resident squirrels. They've been there for years—always three. And I'm relatively sure they're the same ones because one of them doesn't have a tail. He came out of the nest that way. Either a freak of nature, a natural bobtail, or some old buck squirrel missed his grab at the tiny baby nuts and chopped off the tail instead.

The old males, given half a chance, raid the nests and castrate the young to eliminate future competition. Straightforward and sure, about as unsubtle as you can get. Given the world's current population explosion, it's a thought to ponder on.

I finally decided my furry friends were sacked out for a midday snooze. That sounded like a hell of a good idea. I dragged the lounge back into the shade, dropped it into a full reclining position, and did a little snoozing of my own.

Rowdy woke me up at four-thirty with a low, gruff, insistent bark that ceased as soon as I raised my head and looked at him beyond the chain link fence. He wagged his tail happily. A buff-and-white German shepherd, he belonged to my next-door neighbor, Hector Johnson, a retired Bell Helicopter engineer.

Hector was the nearest thing I had to a fan club and the nearest thing to Ichabod Crane I had ever seen. He had me pegged somewhere between an overweight Dirty Harry and a truncated Marshal Dillon and was convinced I led an exciting, adventuresome life, replete with beautiful women and exotic sex, with a smattering of bad guys lurking around to spice up the off moments.

I lit a cigarette and strolled over and talked to Rowdy. He raised huge front paws against the top rail and allowed me to scratch between his ears, dark eyes gravely avoiding mine, plumed tail waving in silent pleasure. As dignified and stately as a politician poised on the edge of greatness, he ignored the derisive comments of the chattering squirrels above our heads, rolling his eyes in disdain, only the rigid pointed ears betraying the atavistic yearning deep within the tawny chest.

I laughed and roughed the sleek muzzle, tweaked the cold

nose. "Forget it, old buddy. There's just some things a man's gotta put up with in this life. Noisy little critters and females. One of nature's little jokes."

Rowdy woofed dolefully as I crossed the yard and went back inside the house.

Five o'clock. Maybe Susie would be leaving the TV station where she worked. Maybe she'd be coming home.

But maybe not. Maybe she wouldn't be coming home at all. Maybe she had an early dinner date with one of the sleek, mealymouthed word jockeys who had been hitting on her from her very first day as a reporter. Maybe thoughts of me wouldn't so much as enter her pretty head except in musing retrospection, a twinge of guilt—

It was a melancholy notion; demoralizing. However deserved. I yanked up the phone and dialed Janey Petroski, Susie's best friend. She answered on the third ring.

"Hello." She stretched it into at least four syllables.

"Greta Garbo? Right?"

"Oh, hi, Danny." She chuckled good-naturedly. "I was expecting Leon."

"Lucky Leon. You pack more promise into that one word than most women could manage with a candlelight dinner and a massage."

She laughed again, delightedly. "Flatterer! Stop it, you'll turn my head. I'm conceited enough as it is."

It was my turn to chuckle. "And with good reason, babe. Boy, if you were only a few years younger . . ." I let it slide and listened to her heartwarming laughter. She was Susie's age and a great audience. She had an easy nature, a quick wit, and an understanding heart, and maybe some of that came from being too tall, too slender, and borderline homely— survivor tools most of the beautiful people never seem to need, or want.

"Susie's not here yet, Danny." She paused, still breathless from the laughter. "Anyway, if I had an ounce of loyalty in me I wouldn't even be talking to you. You rat."

"Rat? What did I do?"

"I don't have any idea, but I'll bet you do. She came storming in here this morning, scaring the daylights out of me, mad as a stinging hornet, crying, slamming stuff around and . . . and she wouldn't tell me a darn thing. Not one word." She paused again, breath rustling. "I had high hopes for last night, Danny." She ended on a plaintive note. "I told Susie she should—" She broke off. I heard the sharp hiss of indrawn breath as she realized she had set the bean pot spinning.

"You knew about it in advance, huh? Imagine that? Old dumb me. And here I thought all along it was spontaneous."

"It was, Danny—I mean, I'm sure it was. I—we—we—she—oh, dammit, now I've messed it all up!"

"No you didn't, Janey. We managed that ourselves. Or maybe I did. I'm just surprised that she'd go to the trouble."

"No you're not. You know she loves you. She's been miserable the whole time. She told me—"

"Don't tell me anything she told you in confidence, Janey."

"I'm not!" She sounded offended. "I'm not taking sides. I think both of you are dumb."

"Well, you know what they say: 'Most of the time you ride the horse, but sometimes the horse rides you.' "

She was silent for a moment. "What does that mean?"

"I'm not sure, but they used to say it a lot over in East Texas."

She made an exasperated sound. "Get serious, Danny. This is a serious thing. You and Susie are going to fool around and mess up your lives real good."

"I thought we already had. Maybe we're not trying hard enough."

"I'm going to hang up this phone right now!"

"Okay, but would you mind asking Susie to call me? I thought of a couple of names I haven't called her yet. You ever hear the term 'addlepated, wasp-butted sow'? Or—?" I hung up the receiver slowly, grinning, wondering if the strangling sound I had heard just before the dial tone had been laughter or indignation.

/ 4 /

I had a Hungry Man TV dinner at six o'clock. Beef and mashed potatoes, a fist-sized hunk of Italian bread. Green onions and sliced tomatoes. All of it washed down with beer. Not exactly gourmet fare, but it was fast and filling and only a little heartburn.

At six-thirty I decided she wasn't going to call and said to hell with it. At six-forty I picked up the phone and dialed Janey's again. It was busy.

At six-fifty I dialed again—still busy.

I dialed again at seven o'clock. It rang once and clicked.

"Hello!" Short and snappy this time. No sexy overtones.

"Janey?"

"Danny? Are you still trying to track down Susie? She's not here."

"Oh, well . . . maybe she stopped somewhere. To eat."

"That's not like her. I mean, she'd call, I think."

"She didn't mention going anywhere after work? Shopping? A movie, maybe? A . . . date?"

"No, but maybe she wouldn't have. She was still angry when she left. She didn't say two words to me. I told you that before." She was growing more agitated by the second. "But it's not like her to be inconsiderate."

"Easy, Janey. She's only an hour and a half late. A flat could explain it, car trouble, a bad toothache."

"Did you call the TV station?"

"No. I'll do that now. You just take it easy and try to think of somewhere she might have gone."

22

"All right, Danny, but she'd have called by now. I just have this horrible feeling—"

"Stay by the phone, okay? Call me." I broke the connection. I had to get her off the phone. Fear is contagious and just listening to her dolorous voice had taken its toll, a cold pocket of dread forming in my chest.

I automatically lit a cigarette before I picked up the phone again and dialed the station where she worked. A male voice answered.

"Susan Roman, please."

"Susie? I don't believe she's here. Who's calling, please?"

"Dan Roman. I'm her husband."

The voice chuckled. "Of course, Mr. Roman. Susie talks about you so much I feel like I know you. I'm Ray Tolliver. Susie's assigned to me at the moment, but I'm afraid she's not here." He paused. "I'd think she'd be home by now, though. That is, if the interview didn't run longer than she planned."

"What interview, Mr. Tolliver?" I felt the short hairs on my neck begin to lift.

"Why, Mickey Conrad. Didn't she tell you? You know, the biiiiig rock star." He chuckled again.

"She has a film crew with her, then?"

"Why, no, as a matter of fact, she doesn't. We were going to tape the actual interview here at the studio tomorrow. She was just going to run over the questions with Conrad. You know how these big stars are . . . afraid you might ask something that requires an intelligent answer." He ended with another chuckle.

"Jesus Christ!" Something flexed in my chest and a blinding atavistic rage flooded my senses.

"What?"

"Why in holy hell did you let her go alone?" I kept my voice down through sheer force of will, the current of anger so intense it was almost a physical force.

"What . . . I—I don't understand. Why shouldn't she go alone?"

"Didn't she tell you what happened Saturday night?"

"Saturday night? No . . . not that I recall . . . well, she did say something about dinner at that new dinner theater out on—"

Dammit! Of course she hadn't told him. Not as long as she thought there was still a chance for a legitimate interview, a chance to prove to herself and to me that the sorry antics of a stoned rock star mattered little to dedicated reporter Susan A. Roman in the relentless pursuit of truth, who would, if need be, become a martyr to the imperatives of her chosen profession. Dammit, dedication had its place, but there was a limit . . .

"Why . . . what happened Saturday night?" Ray Tolliver's voice had become softly seductive, a sympathetic friend, a nosy damn reporter.

"That son—" I chopped it off and breathed deeply. "Where is she? I mean, where is Conrad's ranch?" My face was tight and hot.

"Ranch? Why . . . well, maybe he calls it a ranch, but it's only four or five acres."

"Where?"

"Mr. Roman, is something wrong? Is there . . . ?"

"No. No, nothing's wrong. I just need to get in touch with her immediately. If you'll tell me . . ."

"Of course. Hold on a minute."

I lit a cigarette while I waited and discovered my hand was shaking. The hard aching knot in my stomach had fragmented, spreading rivulets of prickly heat along the pathways of my body. I thumbed irritably at a film of perspiration on my forehead.

"Mr. Roman? I have the address here. I also have the telephone number. Would it help if I called on another phone? See if she's still there?"

"Yes, please. Do that."

"Hang on."

He was back in less than two minutes. "Mr. Roman. They said she's gone. Left about fifteen minutes ago."

I felt a rush of relief so intense it was almost painful.

"Okay," I said, my voice dragging a little through a hot, dry throat. "That's fine. She should be . . . she ought to be home anytime, then."

"Uh . . . Mr. Roman. Was there something wrong in Susie's going out there? I don't . . ."

"No. No, it's all right, Mr. Tolliver. She was just an hour and a half overdue. I was getting worried, is all." My voice tightened. "She should have called."

"She did try to call someone before she left, Mr. Roman. She tried several times, in fact."

"Oh? Well, I appreciate your trouble, Mr. Tolliver."

"That's quite all right. It's nice talking to you, since I've heard so much about you."

"Yes, well, thanks again. . . . Oh, Mr. Tolliver, while you have it there handy, maybe you should give me Conrad's address . . . just in case."

"Well . . . okay, sure."

He read off the address and I wrote it down.

"Do you know where that is?"

"Somewhere north of the old turnpike? Along Elberfeld Road, somewhere in there?"

"Right. It's just west of Loop 820. The street runs into Elberfeld Road. You turn right and go about a mile. You can't miss it. Big wrought-iron gates, a ten-foot-high brick wall around the entire place." He chuckled. "Probably be a bunch of teenage girls hanging around the gates."

"Okay, well, thanks again, Mr. Tolliver."

"You bet. Glad to be of help. Come and see us, Mr. Roman."

"Thank you. Good-bye."

I hung up the phone and slumped back in the chair. I lit another cigarette and felt the stirrings of anger again. Dammit, she could have called.

"And I think he's got her out there at his ranch, Homer." I finished my recitation quietly, keeping my voice steadier than

25

I would have thought possible considering the state of my nerves. I clamped the receiver between chin and shoulder and busied my hands lighting a cigarette.

"Now hold on, boy. Don't go off half-cocked. Have you called all the towns between here and there?"

"I've called Fort Worth, Richland Hills, Hurst, Bedford, and I called Haltom City even though she wouldn't be that far west if she came up Loop 820. Nothing. I think the bastard lied to Tolliver. If she's not here by nine, I'm damn sure going to find out." I glanced at my watch. "That's fifteen more minutes."

"You're fixing to get your ass shot off," he rumbled. "How about here in Midway City?"

"No," I said slowly. "Jesus Christ! I didn't even think about here. I just assumed . . ."

"Yeah," he growled. "That's what I mean. How many other things have you assumed?"

"What do you mean?"

"She coulda had a flat, car trouble, had to be towed in."

"She'd have called Janey, Homer."

"Maybe, maybe not."

"She's no kid, and she's levelheaded about things like that. She knows Janey'd be worried. She'd call, Homer . . . if she could."

"Well, you just hold your water all the same. How long ago did you call Fort Worth?"

"It's been about an hour now. Why?"

"Well, if she did have a wreck they may have been working it when you called before. In that case they wouldn't have had anything on it yet."

"Okay, I'm going to hang up and call them again. If they can't tell me anything . . ." I let it fade away and listened to his exasperated snort.

"Dammit, boy, you listen to me for once! You don't go nowhere! You stay the hell where you are! Let me do some checking on my own. After all, I'm the one's a cop!"

26

"All right, Homer. You've got until nine-thirty." I hung up in the middle of his howl.

I dialed the Fort Worth police; the phone was picked up at the beginning of the second ring.

"Sergeant Peabody, please."

"Just a moment, sir."

I tugged a chair away from the kitchen table and sat down wearily. I took out a cigarette, then held it in my hand as a male voice came on the line.

"Sergeant, this is Dan Roman again. I talked to you an hour or so ago about a missing—"

"Yes, sir, Mr. Roman, I remember."

"I wonder if you could tell me if there's been any report?"

"Please hold on a second, sir. Let me just find that note with your information. . . . Here it is. Okay. The young lady's name is Susan A. Roman. I have all the information here, sir, but we can't file a missing person's report for twenty-four hours."

"Yes, I know that. I just wanted to check the accident reports during the last hour or so."

"Just a moment, sir."

Perhaps a minute later there was a click and his voice came on the line again. "All right, sir. Now, you wanted to check the recent accident reports, right?"

"Yes."

"I'm at another extension, sir. What was the area you were interested in again?"

"It would be Loop 820 and the Elberfeld Road area. Lucas White Road, along in there north to the Fort Worth line."

"I see," he said. I could hear the rapid rustle of paper. Then a silence long enough for me to light the cigarette. He came back. His voice had changed perceptibly. "What was that car she was driving again, sir?" There was a flatness in his tone that sent something plummeting to the pit of my stomach.

"A Toyota," I said hoarsely. "Silver, 1988 Tercel . . . license—"

"Not it," he said quickly, and I heard the sound of expelled breath. "There was an accident in that area. Only one automobile, a 1980 blue Chevrolet Corvette. Lucas White Road around seven-fifteen this evening . . . but you're not interested in that. No, sir. That's the only accident anywhere near that area. I've also checked all the accidents in Fort Worth the last two hours or so. No silver Toyotas involved." He hesitated. "I'd suggest you check the areas east of here, sir. Richland Hills, Hurst . . ."

"Yes, I will, Sergeant. Thank you very much . . . and you have my number if . . . if anything should come up."

"Yes, sir, I still have it. Good luck."

"Thanks, Sergeant."

I hung up and the phone rang before I could get my hand off the receiver.

"Dan?"

"Yeah, Homer?"

"Nothing here in Midway City. You check Fort Worth?"

"Yeah, they had a wreck on Lucas White, but it was a Corvette."

"Maybe you oughta check them mid-cities again."

"It's a waste of time. I know where Susie is."

"Dammit, you don't know any such thing. Uh . . . by the way, what did you say that bozo's address was?"

"Just a second. Here, it's—" I broke off, staring through my reflection in the bay window into darkness. "Huh-uh, I don't think so." I barked a short humorless laugh. "You planning to have one of your Fort Worth pals waiting for me, old buddy? Dammit, I thought you were my friend!"

"Hellfire, boy, I am! I'm just trying to keep you from gettin' your ass in trouble. You can't go bustin' in on people like . . . what the hell was his name?"

"Hah! Homer, you hear that noise? That was me going out the door."

/ 5 /

Despite Homer's protestations to the contrary, I knew exactly what he had in mind, and throughout the fifteen-mile trip the thought nagged at me that there might well be a squad car waiting at Conrad's gate. I hoped it would take the Fort Worth police a few minutes to run down the address. If they happened to have it in the computer, my goose was plucked and ready for cooking.

I found Elberfeld Road without any trouble, a narrow winding blacktop road that followed the line of least resistance over and around and through a series of small oak-studded hills and ravines. A mile from Lucas White Road I came to the corner of the yellow brick wall.

At least ten feet tall, capped with two strands of barbed wire, it angled off to the right in a dead-straight line and followed the curvature of the road ahead. A hundred yards over the next rise I found the gate.

There was no one there: no squad car, no teenage girls, not even a guard inside the small brick guardhouse to the left of the driveway. And, as far as I could tell, no lock on the gate.

I pulled into the driveway and nosed up to the gate. I got out and shook it; nothing happened, not even so much as a rattle. Electronically controlled from the house. That meant there had to be a way to contact them. I walked over to the guardhouse and looked through the window. A small black box was fastened to the wall under a sign that read "Press Button to Talk." I walked around to the other side, opened the door, and went in.

I pressed the little red button; the box crackled and popped. I waited a while and did it again, this time holding it down. Another half minute and the sizzling stopped. There was a click, followed by a hoarse guttural voice.

"If this is some of you young gals again, I'm gonna come down there and get me some of that tender white ass." The voice sounded black and vaguely familiar.

"Milo?"

"You got me, man, but I don't dig your voice."

"This is Dan Roman, Milo."

"Dan Roman? I don't know no . . . oh, yeah, man, now I got you. You looking for blood, man, you wasting time. The Man ain't here."

"I'm looking for Susan, Milo. Open the gate; let's make this easy."

"Hey, man, your chick ain't here. She's been gone . . . two, three hours, at least."

"I'll have to take a look. Open the gate."

"I can't do that. Come on, man, no jive, your lady's been gone away from here since about seven. I know, I let her through the gate myself."

"You're wasting my time, Milo. Open it, or I'm coming back with a whole damn truckload of law. You want that?"

"Won't do you no good. She jest ain't here, goddammit!" His voice had deepened perceptibly, resonated with a trace of alarm.

"You've got five seconds to decide."

"Aw, man! Why the hell won't you believe me? Why'd I want to lie about it?"

"Three seconds, Milo."

"Aw shit! Just hold your drawers. I'll be right down there."

I left the guardhouse and leaned against the grille of the Dodge station wagon. I could see the front of the house fifty yards from the road. A two-story colonial-style mansion, it had huge white pillars supporting what appeared to be a glassed-in porch across the entire front of the building. The grounds were well lighted by dusk-to-dawn lights cleverly spaced among giant elms and stunted oaks, and had the close-cropped, artificial look of a well-kept cemetery.

I noticed movement at the left corner of the house, and a few seconds later I recognized the canopied shape of a golf cart. It zipped down the curving driveway and I eased away from the Dodge and moved to the corner of the gate. I slipped the .38 out of its clip-on holster and held it along the seam of my Levi's. I was standing behind the square brick gatepost when the cart ground to a halt at the gate. I stepped into Milo's view, the gun held loosely at my waist.

"Step out of the cart, Milo."

His big square teeth made a white slash across the black glossy face. "Man, you shore do like to play with them guns. What'cha got that thang for?" He walked around the cart to the gate, stood looking at me through the ironwork, his expression somewhere between annoyance and amusement. He cocked big, scarred hands on his hips and looked at me curiously.

"You really believe your woman's in there, don't you?" He spoke quietly and distinctly, the guttural twang missing.

"That's right, I do. Either that, or he's taken her somewhere else. Either way, I'm damn sure going to find out."

"Well, she's not, I told you the straight of it. She left here around seven in that little silver car of hers. I let her out myself."

"Why so late? I understand she came here around two this afternoon. Five hours to run over a few questions? You're not getting through to me, Milo."

He waved a heavy arm. "Aw, man, you know. That asshole Mickey can't take no for an answer. He's finally run across a cute chick who won't roll over for him and it's eating his guts. Besides, I think the little shit really digs her."

I felt my face beginning to burn. "What are you telling me? Did he . . ."

"Aw, no, man. He didn't really do anything. Just come on

to her real heavy. You know what I mean. I was around the whole time. I wouldn't hold still for no real bad shit. Besides, he's just obnoxious when he's not doping. He's a conceited little prick, used to getting his own way. Big star, all that crap. Used to having the chicks crawling around just for a smell. Thinks he's the latest thing in cocksmen. Most the time he's all right, except when it comes to chicks."

"I'd like to believe you, Milo. But I'm going to see for myself. Open the gate."

He stared back at me, unblinking, his broad face bland and shining. He shook his head slowly. "Man, I can't do that. He'd fire me for sure. This ain't the best job in the world, but the pay's good and lots of fringe benefits. I just can't do it."

I stepped closer to the gate, laid the edge of the barrel on a cross member. "I think you'd better," I said softly, putting as much menace into my voice as I could muster.

He shrugged his shoulders and put on a lopsided grin. "You won't use that," he said quietly. "You ain't got the look. I been up against guns before. There's a look, a look a guy gets when he's ready to use a gun, and you ain't got it."

I looked into his steady black eyes for a long moment. Then I slipped the gun into the holster on my belt. "You're right. I'm not ready to use it . . . not yet. But if you're lying to me, I wouldn't bank too much on my expression if I were you."

"Hey, I didn't say you *wouldn't* use it," he said, his voice relieved, heavy with humor.

"Where is the great man?"

"I don't know. He's out honky-tonking with some twins from Texarkana."

"How come you're not with him? I thought you were his sheepdog."

"Man, that ain't nice. I got to sleep sometime. There's two of us. We kinda take turns." His grin came back. "Leakey's like you, he likes to play with guns. Gonna get caught one of these days, get his pecker in a tight hole."

I shrugged. "Well, we've come full circle. We're back to a carload of law." I turned on my heel and walked to the door of the Dodge.

"Hey, man! Hey, don't ... come here, man. Look, I'm gonna level with you. The little shit's got dope stashed all over that house. Lots of places I don't know about. The law starts nosing around, they're gonna find it sure. That's a bad scene, man. This Texas law is pure-D hell on dope, you know that."

"That's not my concern. I only want Susie. I'm going to get her one way or another."

"Awwww shit!" He jigged up and down in a frenzy of frustration and anger. "Dammit, man, why the hell can't you believe nobody? I'm telling you the truth! She's gone from here. Hell, I'll even go help you look for her!"

He gripped the bars of the gate, white scar tissue on his knuckles gleaming, his sweat-shiny face thrust forward earnestly.

I watched him calmly. "Open the gate, Milo."

We stared at each other silently; a full minute passed slowly in the warm humid night. Then the whites of his eyes flashed as he threw up his hands in despair.

"Okay, man. But it's gotta be fast. Okay? I'll take you through the damn house but it's gotta be fast. The Man happens to come back, it'll be my ass."

He disappeared from sight as he talked and seconds later the gates creaked and began to swing inward. He came back trotting; he leaped into the golf cart and backed it out of the way.

"We'll take your car. It's faster."

He was panting slightly as he climbed in beside me. Silently, gravel crunching under the tires, we drove up the curving driveway to the house.

It was a whirlwind tour. As thorough as I could make it, not knowing all the nooks and crannies of the house. It was not as large as I had thought. Seven bedrooms, all upstairs, the first floor taken up almost entirely by a huge combination living room, game room, and bar. A large kitchen extended across the rear and there was a small room beneath a massive stairway where Milo hesitated outside the door.

"This is my room, man," he said gruffly. "My chick's in there."

I studied his blank, unsmiling face for a heartbeat or two. "Okay, Milo, I believe you." Something surfaced briefly in his eyes, flickered, then went away.

He smiled. "No, man. Let's do it right." He swung open the door and I saw a chocolate-colored face with big brown eyes and pigtails staring at me over pulled-up covers.

"Hi, sugar, be right with you." He closed the door. "Okay, man, that's the drill. You've seen it all."

"No basement?"

He gave me a disgusted look. "No basement. You happy now?"

"No, I'm not happy."

We threaded our way across the huge front room toward the entrance. He beat me to the door, opened it, and stood watching me impatiently. I stopped on the glassed-in porch.

"Okay, she's not here. But she didn't come home and that means one of two things."

He cocked thick black eyebrows. "Accident?"

I shook my head. "No. We've checked that pretty thoroughly." I stopped and stared directly into his eyes. "Susie just wouldn't go off on her own unless something has happened. Something she's ashamed of. Maybe something she did herself and she couldn't face me with. Or maybe something that was done to her . . . and she still couldn't face me . . . not for a while, at least. Maybe because she was afraid of what I might do." I paused and smiled at him. "She knows me well, you see."

He held my glance as long as he could, then looked away uneasily. "I'm telling you, Mr. Roman, nothing bad happened to her here. I'll swear to that. I wasn't out of hearing distance all the time she was here. Man, he hassled her some, you know, but he didn't lay a mean hand on her. You got my word on that."

"Okay," I said, breathing deeply. "I'll accept your word that you *believe* nothing happened to her here. But if something did—" I broke off, feeling an old familiar constriction in my chest, a thickness in my throat. "But if something did, you tell him, Milo, you tell Mr. Superstar he had better start running. He's gonna need the head start. It won't help. Finding people is what I do best. But it might give him a little more time to reflect."

"Hey, man, that's pretty heavy stuff." He shifted his feet, watching me from the corner of his eye.

My face was hurting from the smile. "Right. Dying always is. It's final, too."

"Hey, man, come on," he said plaintively, "you don't want to threaten somebody's life like that. What if—?"

"It's not a threat, Milo," I interrupted. "It's a promise. In my business it's a law: you always keep your promise. Just tell him for me, Milo." I walked across the large porch. He closed the door and we started down the steps. We were at the station wagon when lights flashed from the direction of the gate and the faint sound of car tires on gravel drifted to our ears.

Milo cursed softly, bitterly, his eyes glaring balefully across the hood of my car.

"Tell him yourself," he snarled. "There's the son of a bitch now."

/ 6 /

The gray-and-black limousine drew to a halt a few feet behind my Dodge. I could see two faces in the front seat and at least three in the rear. I heard a murmur of voices and the front doors popped open. A man in a gray suit and flat, hard-billed cap stepped out and came toward me. He stopped a few feet away and stood watching me silently, his eyes flicking back and forth between me and Milo. The other one moved up the other side of my car, stopped, and glared at me across the hood. He was tall and heavy, wearing a western shirt with four-button sleeves and a flat-crowned, narrow-brim Stetson.

The rear door opened. Slowly, deliberately, Mickey Conrad climbed out. His gaze raked over me insolently, moved briefly to Milo before he turned to assist his companions.

Two blondes, alike as two grains of corn, skimpy dresses slit up the thigh and down the sides, plunging to their navels in front. And not a day over sixteen if I was any judge at all. Conrad murmured something; they went skipping up the walk to the house, honey-colored ponytails flying.

Conrad ignored me; he turned his attention to Milo.

"Milo, you let this creep in here?"

"Yeah, Mickey, I did. He's looking for his lady."

Conrad raised his head and looked at me, the strange shine I had seen before in his eyes. His lip curled under the bristling mustache. "What's the matter, old man, that chick run out on you?" He moved up to stand beside the man in the gray suit.

"No," I said, keeping my voice steady and even. "She's missing. This is the last place she was seen."

Without raising his voice or turning his head, he said, "Milo, you're fired. Get your stuff and get your black ass out of here."

Milo didn't move. "He was coming back with a carload of law. You rather have that with all that junk you've got in there?" His voice was aggrieved, but there was no trace of servility.

"Don't matter," Conrad said coldly. "You know the rules." He turned his attention back to me. "You really think I'd keep that black-haired chick here against her will? Mickey Conrad don't have to do that, man."

I smiled into his expressionless eyes, pale and cold as two chips of ice. "You'd have to do it with this one. That's the only way she'd let a faggot like you touch her . . . man."

He twitched enough to make the chains and medallions jingle on his chest.

It was an exposed nerve and I jabbed at it a little more. "We had a nice little laugh after you left the other night. She told me how you kept flipping it around trying to get it up." I smiled again. "She said something about a limp wet noodle."

That pulled his plug; he screamed a curse and flung himself at me. I stepped in close, let his right fist bounce off my wrist, his left slap me across the shoulder.

Taking my time and doing it right, I smashed my fist to the pit of his stomach, an inch or two below the dangling chains. Then I stepped quickly aside to avoid the mixture of air and spit and vomit that came whooshing out of his mouth. He slumped to his knees like wet cement, hung there for a moment, his hands scrabbling aimlessly at his gut. Then he coughed and gasped, sucked for air like a drowning man, white foam spewing from the corners of his mouth. He toppled slowly sideways, came to rest in the gravel, knees drawn high under his chin in a tight fetal knot.

There was a moment of intense, almost painful silence, then a curse behind me and I whirled to see the big stout man with a gun in his hand. He was leaning across the hood of my

37

Dodge, the gun extended before him, his left hand supporting his right in the approved TV-cop fashion.

I held my hands out from my sides. "Be careful with that thing, Mac."

"Don't move, bastard," he shouted, his hands shaking a little, his face dark with blood or shadow. I wondered if this was the first time he had ever pointed a gun at anyone—that worried me.

"Just take it easy," I said soothingly. "Fight's all over."

The man in the gray suit was kneeling beside Conrad, helping him to sit up. The rock star hawked and spat, trying to clean the mess out of his mouth. The gray-suited man offered a rumpled handkerchief and Conrad knocked it out of his hand.

"Milo!" He was almost screaming. "Milo? You want your job back, man?"

I glanced at the black man; he watched silently, a faint smile edging his wide mouth. He flicked a glance at me.

"It depends," he said.

"You bust this bastard up, man, and you got it! I mean really break him, put his ass in the hospital, mess up his face, man, you know what I mean!"

"Yeah, I know what you mean." He looked at me and the smile widened. "What do you think about that, Mr. Roman?"

"Whatever you think is right, Milo." I smiled a little myself. "Whatever you think you can handle."

His smile grew into a grin, and I knew he was thinking about the gun. Half his face was in shadow, the bright side lit with sardonic glee. He shook his head in disgust, turned, and headed for the house.

"Where you going?" It was the stout man. He had straightened, the gun dangling loosely in his hand, forgotten. His eyes followed Milo; I slipped the .38 out of its clip and held it down at my side.

"Get my stuff, man. I been fired."

I walked the few feet to the side of my car. I poked the .38

across the windshield. The big man started to yell something at Milo, caught sight of me out of the corner of his eye. He froze, then swiveled slowly toward me, his mouth still open, chagrin and fear pulling his face into a ludicrous grimace. He let the gun slide until he was holding the butt with two fingers.

"That's it," I said softly. "Just lay it on the hood. Nice and easy."

The gun rattled on the metal as he carefully followed my instructions.

"Now back away."

He did as he was told, almost eagerly it seemed to me, his round face sallow in the artificial light. I picked up the gun by the barrel and threw it into the waist-high shrubbery along the front of the house. "If I were you, pal, I'd leave it there." His head bobbed; he tried to look as if he were giving it some serious thought.

Conrad was back on his feet, one hand pressed against his stomach. The man in the hard-billed hat hovered over him anxiously.

I put my gun away and ambled over. Conrad's eyes were squinted, sunken, occasional murky flashes breaking through like glimpses of brackish water at the bottom of a pit.

"You want to tell me what happened this afternoon with Susie?"

"Nothing, man," he said after a while, sullenly. "She brought a list of questions for my approval. That's all. She left about seven o'clock."

"I understand you hassled her some. Just what does that mean . . . hassled?"

His slender fingers plucked nervously at his beard. "I don't know what it means, man."

"I'd suggest you think about it."

"Hey, man, you know you're trespassing."

"Right. And you call me man one more time and I'm going to break something."

His eyes popped open and he backed away a step. "Hey, m—fella, I don't know what you want from me."

"What happened today with Susie," I explained patiently. "I want to know if you touched her. I don't think that's too hard to understand."

"Hell no, ma— no, I didn't. What's the big deal if I had?"

"The big deal is, pal, if I find out you're lying I'm going to break every one of your goddamned fingers. Is that a big enough deal for you?"

He licked his lips, his eyes burning. He looked over my shoulder toward the big man. "Leakey! What the hell you standing there for? You're supposed to protect me from shit like this."

I grinned at him. "Me and Mr. Leakey have an understanding. He won't move from where he's at and I won't shoot him. I think that's fair."

The front door of the house opened and closed with a bang. Milo came down the steps carrying a suitcase, a suitbag draped over his shoulder. He walked up to Conrad and dropped the suitcase on the gravel. He held out a big pink palm.

"You owe me a week's pay. I'll take it now."

"You don't get shit, man. You didn't do your job."

Milo sighed. He stretched the suitbag carefully on the gravel beside the suitcase. He looked at Conrad and shook his head sadly. "You're something else, man." His hand snaked out and caught in the chains and twisted. He jerked Conrad forward until their faces were only inches apart.

"Listen, you bag of shit! I owe you, man. I owe you for all that boss-man shit you been dumpin' on me for a year. Don't push your luck." His other hand fastened in the waistband of Conrad's pants. "Now, do I get my money or do I drop your pants and show these fellers that teensy-weensy little dick of yours?"

Conrad waved frantically at the man in the gray suit, clawing at the chains choking off his air. Milo eased off.

"Pay him!" Conrad gasped. He pushed his fingers between

the chains and his neck and sucked in air. "Pay him, dammit!" He looked bedraggled and weary; it hadn't been one of Mickey Conrad's better nights.

The gray man whipped out a billfold. "How much?" he asked tersely, fingering a thick sheaf of bills expectantly.

"Nine hundred oughta do it," Milo said. "That'll take care of my termination pay, too."

Conrad threw him a baleful glance, thought better of what he was about to say, and fingered his neck lovingly. He adjusted the high, stiff collar on his yellow silk shirt and tugged at his trousers.

"Hey, man, thanks," Milo said, taking the packet of bills and counting them slowly. He stacked them, folded them, and put them in his front pants pocket. He looked at me and grinned. "Think I might hitch a ride out of here with you, Mr. Roman?"

"Sure. What about your girl?"

He shrugged thick shoulders. "She belongs here. She cooks for these assholes."

Conrad was watching us with hot, shiny eyes, his mouth a thin, mean line. He had regained his composure, his natural arrogance beginning to show. I had a sudden urge to hit him again. Instead, I turned back to Milo.

"Let's go."

The three men stood silently while we made the circle in front of the house. The moment we reentered the drive, Conrad began yelling obscenities. We reached the end of the lane, turned left. We had barely straightened out again when headlights flashed in my eyes and the revolving lights of a police car came over the rise ahead. I slowed and we watched the squad car brake and turn into Conrad's driveway.

"Man!" Milo said. "How'd they do that so damn fast?"

"They didn't. That was meant to be my welcoming party. They're about an hour late, is all."

He gave me a quizzical look, but I didn't bother to explain. Instead, I speeded up a bit. "That clown might be just mad enough to file a complaint on us."

Milo shook his head. "Don't sweat it, they don't want no law nosing around. Too much dope on the premises." He grinned. "Not as much as there was, though."

I paused at the intersection of Lucas White Road and Elberfeld Road. "Where do you live, Milo?"

"Dallas. You can drop me at a phone somewhere. I'll call my woman to come get me."

"May as well be my place. I'm only a mile from the Airport Freeway and it's easy to find." I hesitated. "Or, I could run you on into Dallas."

"No way, man. You got too much on your mind. I know how woman trouble is."

"She's probably at home waiting right now," I said lightly, the nagging apprehension that had been diverted by the fracas at Conrad's beginning to build again.

I could feel his eyes on me. "Yeah, I'll bet you're right."

We were silent for a while. I angled into Loop 820 North and found a spot in the buzzing traffic. We dipped under Highway 183 and a few minutes later went into the curve at Northeast Mall. The traffic thickened perceptibly and I kept my attention on the road.

Milo lit a cigarette with my dash lighter. He smoked for a moment before breaking the silence.

"What're you going to do now? If she ain't home, I mean."

"Look for her," I said tersely.

"Can't blame you for that. She's something else." He made a snorting, derisive sound. "She sure had his Lordship diddling himself. Probably the first time in years he'd heard the word no."

I glanced at him. "Sorry about the job."

His dark eyes flickered. "I had just about enough, I guess. Time to move on, you know? I fought my way through four years in the navy, come damn close to the title. Then I fought my way through four years of college. Now I'll just wait and see what comes along."

"Why did you work as a bodyguard?"

"Man, where else am I gonna make thirty thousand a year? I got a business degree. Just barely. Poor averages and looking like a black thug don't make for a good business career. In seven years the best thing I had was chief clerk in a shipping department. Fifteen a year, tops."

I turned the corner into my street and discovered that I had been holding my breath. I expelled it slowly. The house was deserted and quiet. I pulled into the driveway and sat looking at the dark windows. Milo had lapsed into silence. He shifted uneasily.

"I'm sorry," he said quietly.

The next morning I called Ray Tolliver at the TV station—just in case.

"I'm sorry, Mr. Roman, she hasn't come in this morning. Is there anything I can do?"

"No. Not unless you can think of somewhere she may have gone. Another interview, maybe . . ." I let it trail away.

"No, sir. I can't think of a thing. The interview with Conrad was the last thing for her day. Did you get to see him?"

"Yeah, I saw him. Didn't help a whole lot."

He was silent for a moment. "I don't know, Mr. Roman. I just don't have any idea where she could have gone." He hesitated. "You did check the hospitals, police . . . ?"

"Yes. Well, thanks anyway, Mr. Tolliver. Please let me know if . . . well, if she turns up there, or anything."

"I'll sure do that, sir. You bet."

I hung up the receiver and stared dully through the bay

window at the busy squirrels flashing up and down the limbs between their nest and the ground; storing acorns for the coming winter. Rowdy sat stolidly in a corner of the fence, watching. They sensed his helplessness behind the wire and teased him unmercifully, flitting a few feet in front of his quivering nose, venturing boldly along the top rail over his head. Finally he could bear it no longer: he rose to all four paws and marched away with stately dignity. One of the squirrels, the tailless one, barked derisively.

I wrenched my eyes away, feeling a sudden rush of desperate urgency, an overwhelming need to do something, anything, as long as it was movement, activity. I got up and paced restlessly, my head aching and hollow, my eyes tired and burning from a sleepless night. I lit another cigarette and glanced toward the bar in the den. Just one small one couldn't hurt; something to soothe my jangled nerves, help ease the tension that kept me on the cutting edge of panic.

I was halfway across the den before I brought myself up short. Just what I needed: a foggy brain on top of everything else. I went back into the kitchen and opened a beer. I took a sip and made a face. Beer is not a morning drink. I poured it into the sink and found a bottle of Pepsi. It was cold and wet and sweet. Not a hell of a lot better, but maybe the caffeine would help.

I drank half of it, dumped the rest, and called Homer Sellers again.

"Anything, Homer?"

He sighed heavily. "Dan, I know you're worried. Dammit, I'm worried, too. But you calling me every fifteen minutes ain't going to help none. Let me do my job. I'll let you know the minute—"

"It's been more like an hour," I broke in. "Put yourself in my place. I'm sitting here twiddling my fingers, my thumb up my ass, and she's out there somewhere, God knows what's happening to her, and you expect me to be calm."

"Yeah, I know." He was silent for a while, the line humming emptily.

"Homer?"

"Yeah, I was just thinking. Why don't you go out there? Drive around. There's a lot of hills and ravines along that stretch of road. Hell, she could have run off into one of the gullies. Be hard to see from the road with all that brush."

The thought sent my spirits plummeting, but it was something to be doing.

"All right," I agreed reluctantly. "I'll call you later."

"Just give us some time, boy."

"She may be running out of time, Homer."

I turned around in front of Mickey Conrad's gate, drove slowly back the way I had come, my right wheels on the narrow shoulder. I carefully scanned the brush-choked ravines and the shoulder as I passed. Once or twice I stopped and got out for a better look. In spite of the No Littering signs spaced along the road, the bottoms and sides of the gullies were strewn with refuse: cans, bottles, old tires, paper.

A mile from Conrad's gate I came to the cone-shaped traffic marker I had noticed on the way in. It was perched on the edge of the shoulder; the gravel around it showed signs of disruption, scuffed and scraped by some unusual activity. I had assumed it was the location of the accident Sergeant Peabody had told me about, but I stopped the car and walked over anyway, my heartbeat accelerating, my throat suddenly dry.

There was little to see: a ravine perhaps twenty-five feet deep, a fire-blackened circle thirty feet in diameter, a few skeletons of bushes, and scars halfway up the trunks of several nearby trees.

The blue Corvette, I thought, and wondered if anyone had been in the car when it burned. Almost in the center of the fire circle there were two medium-sized boulders, and perhaps ten feet from where I stood two faint tire trails angled down the steep slope of the ravine. Two additional trails, deeper, more easily discernible, came straight up the bank from the rocks, the marks left when the tow truck yanked the vehicle from its fiery place of death.

I walked over to have a look. No signs of braking; the car must have simply rolled over the edge. Or been pushed, I thought grimly. Despite the fact I was certain this was the site of the blue Corvette's accident, my stomach was rolling queasily, and a faint taste of nausea clotted my throat.

I climbed stiffly into the station wagon and drove to Loop 820; I found a phone booth at the edge of the liquor store parking lot and dialed Sergeant Peabody's number. A female officer answered.

"I'm sorry, sir, Sergeant Peabody doesn't come on duty until four-thirty."

"I'm calling about an accident that happened on Lucas White Road last night around seven. A blue Corvette—1980, I believe."

"Just a moment, sir."

While I waited, I watched the liquor store's customers flitting in and out of the swinging doors in a steady stream. Just like my squirrels, storing up for the long cold spell ahead.

"Could I have your name, sir?"

"Captain Homer Sellers, Midway City Police."

"Oh, yes, Captain. I have it here. A 1980 blue Corvette. One mile west—"

"Yes," I broke in brusquely. "I have the location. Was anyone injured?"

"Yes, sir. A Ms. Charlotte Ellie Wilkins, owner of the vehicle." She hesitated a beat. "She was DOA at John Peter Smith Hospital, sir. She expired when the automobile burned."

"You have a positive ID?"

"Yes, sir. Her father came down this morning and made the identification."

I expelled my pent-up breath slowly, my head feeling a little light.

"She was the only occupant?"

"Yes, sir, as far as we know."

"What does that mean?"

"She was the only one at the scene when our unit arrived."

"Was there reason to believe there might have been some-one else?"

"I'm sorry, Captain. I can't answer that question. Perhaps you should talk to the investigating officers." Her voice had become crisp and cool, tinged with impatience.

"Is there anything else, Captain?"

"No, that's fine, thank you."

"You're welcome."

I cradled the receiver and lit a cigarette. That was that. At least Susie wasn't at the bottom of a ditch dead, or wounded and dying. Something, anyhow. Damn little consolation, but a gruesome possibility eliminated.

I watched the solemn throng of customers for a few minutes longer, then went in and bought a half-pint of Wild Turkey. After all, it was afternoon and Susie hadn't burned to death in a car in a ditch; that was something to celebrate.

Although it was still daylight, the house looked dark and forbidding, emptier than it had ever seemed before. A maga-zine lying open to new spring fashions brought a tight hot knot to my throat, a pair of red shoes at the end of the couch a poignant reminder of Saturday night, the last time we made love.

And suddenly I was aching with longing, a desperate need to reach out and grasp that moment again, relive, if only fleetingly, that precious time before it was irretrievably lost down the cloudy corridors of memory; loneliness struck, a vicious numbing blow straight to the center of my being.

Standing in the middle of the den I upended the bottle of whiskey and drained it, slammed it into the fireplace in a burst of savage frustration. It clinked dully against the fire brick and fell into the ashes.

I stood shaking, gripped with a dull helpless rage, my mind stuttering with the frantic need to smash something, destroy, and in a choked, whispering voice I made myself a promise and a covenant with her: "If they've hurt you, baby, I swear to you, somebody's going to pay!"

Then I sagged, turned toward the bar, flinching at the whiskey melodrama in my voice, shrinking from the taunting knowledge of my helplessness.

Alone, almost penniless, certainly drunk, my father curled up and died fifteen yards from the door of a hunting cabin he and I had built on four hundred acres of southeast Texas land he had set aside for me when I was born, all that was left of a once prosperous cattle ranch. The rest had been swept away in a torrent of good whiskey and lonely drunken tears. My mother's unexpected death had set him off, awakened a susceptibility to alcohol only vaguely suspected. Shoulders hunched beneath the weight of an existence he could no longer bear, he had drowned his misery, then found a simple solution to his life by lying down and freezing to death a few feet from safety. A painless death for him, a nightmare legacy for me.

Along with the four hundred acres and bad dreams, he left me one other thing: a predilection for all things alcoholic. Not that I became a drunk, exactly, or had to have it on a regular basis. It's just that it dulled the glare a little, smoothed the ragged edges, muted the cacophony, filled up the lonely hours. On the other hand, alcoholics do shameful things like stashing bottles in unlikely places, sneak around to drink in private, black out for hours, sometimes days, in an alcoholic fog. They lie, cheat, and steal to get booze and likely as not end up going to meetings and confessing, pouring their hearts out to other drunks, or ex-drunks, who understand maybe, but aren't really all that impressed, since they have their own problems staying straight.

All of which proved beyond a doubt that I wasn't an alcoholic. I didn't hide my whiskey or my drinking, never stole a penny in my life, and never—not once—ever went to a damn meeting.

Homer Sellers settled himself more comfortably into the leather recliner-rocker. He tasted his scotch and looked at me over the rim of his glass, his florid face grim.

"You look like hell, boy," he said roughly, his tone bordering on contempt. "You better lay off the booze, get yourself straightened out. Looks to me like you're using Susie's disappearance as an excuse to—"

"Go to hell." I scrubbed my face with both hands, the two-day stubble of beard rasping, as irritating as his disapproval.

He grunted, stared at me with bright blue eyes. He bounced the rim of the glass off his lower lip, tasted it again, then set it on the table beside him.

"Always thought you had guts, boy. With all your other faults, I always admired you for your courage. Not the kind you suck up out of a bottle, neither." His voice was clear and cold, filled with carefully metered sarcasm.

"Lay off, Homer," I said wearily.

"You don't know that something's happened to her," he went on reasonably. "Two days. Maybe she just took off on her own. You've been giving her the short end of the stick too damn long, Dan."

"Don't you think I know it?"

"Did you call her grandmother?"

I shook my head. "No. Her grandmother's health is none too good lately. There's no way I could call her without giving it away. Better she don't know anything . . . until we do."

"How do you know? Maybe Susie went down there."

I glared at him in disgust, not bothering to answer. I got up and trudged to the bar, refilled my glass with vodka.

"Two days, Homer? Why haven't I heard? If she's been kidnapped, why haven't the sons of bitches called?"

"They do that sometimes. Raises the level of anxiety. Makes the victims easier to deal with once they've had a few days to think about the alternatives first."

I went back to my seat, stared dully out into the dying day.

I could feel Homer's eyes as I drank the vodka, his disapproval a palpable force in the growing dimness in the room.

"You think I should go to the media?"

"I dunno," he said. "There's two sides to that. Might help find her if she's hurt, maybe wandering around, her memory bad or something. On the other hand, if she has been taken, might make them panic—" He chopped it off abruptly and picked up his glass. Despite his phlegmatic manner, I knew he was deeply disturbed; he had known Susie even longer than I had, loved her almost as much.

"I can't believe anybody would kidnap her for money. She works for a living. I'm not a rich man. How much could they hope to get? It doesn't make sense."

"What does make sense today? And don't be so sure about the money. How much could you raise? A hundred thousand?"

"I could if I had to, yes. Twice that much if I had a little time."

He snorted. "Jesus Christ, Dan. There's people out there that'd kill you for pocket change. That guy in Dallas a couple of months ago? Held that banker's wife while the banker went to get the money? You know how much he wanted? Twenty-five thousand. That's all he asked for. Could have asked for a hundred just as easy. Done him about as much good, too. Caught the clown two hours after he got it." He took off his glasses and poked at the corner of his eye with a thick finger. "Don't count out ransom yet. You could hear anytime."

"You know what I think?" I said, the words dragging in my throat, thick and dry. "I think some nut's got her. Some crazy, sick son of a bitch . . ."

"Stop that shit!" he said harshly. "You're wrong, dead wrong. If that'd happened, we'd have found her car, wouldn't we?"

"The same thing applies if she'd been kidnapped for ransom. They wouldn't take her car." I rubbed fruitlessly at a small stabbing pain that had suddenly developed between my eyes.

50

"Dammit, we don't know what they'd do. No use us settin' here guessing about it, either." He pointed a finger at me. "And you better be cleaning yourself up, shave, take a damn bath. Lay off the booze. What if Susie come walking in right now? What the hell do you think she'd think? Tell me that."

I almost dredged up a smile. I waved my hand and took a drink of vodka.

"Just go on home, papa bear. I'll worry about me."

His eyes glowed with indignation behind the thick spectacles. "Don't flatter yourself, boy. Nobody's worrying about you. I gave that up a long time ago. You been wanting to be a bum the last ten years. . . . I think maybe you've about made it." His voice was as cold as his eyes, hard accusing cop's eyes that had never been directed at me before.

I felt a chill along my spine and realized I had to say something. I mustered up a sneer instead.

"Bug off, old man."

"I'll do that," he said. He walked stiffly to the door, vaguely ludicrous in too-tight pants and horizontally striped shirt. His big flat feet slapped on the hall tile and I opened my mouth to call him back, then closed it with a snap; nothing he could say right then would matter, and I had already said too damn much.

I watched his broad figure go through the door into the night and wondered vaguely about this miserable character flaw of mine, this dark perversity that made me drive people away at the times I needed them most.

It seemed only moments later when the doorbell began ringing and I turned away from the vodka martini I was building, thinking Homer had mulled it over and decided this childish game we were playing had gone far enough. I weaved a little on my way to the door, plastered a forgiving, if somewhat aggrieved, smile on my face.

The size was right—three inches taller than my six feet, almost twice as broad—but there the resemblance ended. Where

Homer slouched, hulking, this man stood straight and tall. Years younger. A shock of inky black hair tumbling forward almost to the bushy-browed black eyes that gleamed bright and shiny in the entry's light. He was dressed in worn denims and a quilted blue windbreaker; his wide shoulders tapered to narrow hips, bulging outward again as thigh muscles tested the blue denims. A weight lifter, I thought, seconds before he spoke lazily through a gap-toothed, faintly yellow smile.

"Mickey Conrad sends his regards," he said, pausing a beat to let it register, the smile compressing a bit as his shoulder dipped, telegraphing the punch already on its way toward the point of my jaw.

Another goddamned amateur, I thought, sliding my head to the left—almost enough—feeling his knuckles clip the end of my jawbone, the heavy thrust of his forearm against my neck as the unexpected miss brought him lurching the rest of the way through the doorway into the suddenly tiny entry hall. My head rang, but not enough to matter, and I locked my hands, leaned into him, and drove my right elbow into his short ribs. A quick, hard blow with a lot of my weight behind it.

He grunted, almost a scream, his own momentum and my blow carrying him face forward against the wall. Amateur or not, he had guts, and he was turning, the smile a murderous frozen grimace, goggle-eyed with the pain of his caved-in ribs, spittle flecking the corners of his mouth, thick arm sweeping in a backhand blow that would have taken my head off.

I weaved and ducked again, enough this time, and the oak beam of his arm whistled harmlessly through my hair, the violent momentum whirling him around, giving me time to slap him openhanded across an ear, lock my clenched fists, and smash my forearms across his shoulder near the juncture of his neck. He staggered, groaning, but stayed on his feet, one hand clamped against the ear I had savaged, the other pressed against his ribs. His eyes were still bright, flames licking in their depths with an unholy light, and I had the sinking feeling I had had my chances and muffed them.

I wound up and kicked him in the balls, watched him stand helpless for a second in openmouthed, exquisite pain before folding slowly to my terrazzo tile floor, the ear and ribs forgotten in this new white-hot agony.

I sighed deeply, as much in relief as for needed air. I squatted beside his head and pushed a hank of hair out of his blaring eyes. The deeply tanned skin had a curiously yellow tinge, like an unripened tomato after too much sun, the grotesquely distorted face an image of inexpressible misery.

"You work for Mickey Conrad, huh?" I asked.

His eyes rolled and he made an unintelligible sound.

"I didn't quite catch that, old buddy," I said. "Reckon you could speak up a little?"

His head rolled minutely: a negative.

"Okay, just move your head yes or no. That shouldn't take too much concentration. Do you work for Conrad?"

The shaggy head moved minutely again: another negative.

"You don't work for Conrad?"

His head started to roll, then bobbed: a positive.

"You work for one of Conrad's people?"

Negative.

"Hmm. What the hell are you, then? A groupie trying to suck up to Conrad?"

A moment's hesitation, then another negative.

I sat back on my heels and pondered a bit. A light went off. "If you'd succeeded in trashing my ass, would Conrad have given you a job?"

"Yeah," he said scratchily. "Yeah, that was the deal." He licked his lips and closed his mouth for the first time in five minutes, then opened it again to groan. "Goddamn, it hurts."

"It's supposed to," I said absently, thinking about Conrad, wondering at his motives. Revenge for the small indignities Milo and I had subjected him to? Or something infinitely more sinister? Something to do with a missing—

"Why?" I shouted the word, my voice as harsh and abrasive as I could make it.

53

His shoulders hunched, eyes squeezing shut, then flipping open to stare at me in startled fear. "I—I—he said he owed you for what . . . something you did to him. I don't know—he didn't tell me what." He studied my face for a second. "I swear to God." He was younger than I had thought, with long curling lashes, a fine grainless skin that was trying desperately to pale beneath the heavy bronze. His eyes had the pleading innocence of a puppy caught squatting over his latest mistake. "Please . . . I was just trying . . . I needed a job . . ."

I held his eyes with mine. "He said nothing about a girl . . . a woman?"

His head rolled. "No, no woman . . . nothing like that." A heavy vein throbbed in his forehead.

"What's your name?"

"Pete. Peter Berghoff."

"Pete, if you're lying to me . . ." I let it trail away, my voice as menacing as I could manage in the face of his obvious fear and the pain that radiated outward in palpable waves.

"I swear to God I'm not. I was just supposed to come here to . . . to rough you up . . . a little bit." He wet his lips again. "He said he has an opening for a bodyguard—"

I stood up abruptly. I stepped over his head, fastened both hands in the collar of his windbreaker, and began dragging him out the door. It wasn't easy.

"Hey, what—?"

"Shut up!"

I tugged him across the ground-level concrete porch and out into the St. Augustine grass. I released him and walked back toward the door.

"I'm calling the cops, Pete. It'll take them about three minutes to get here. If you're still here, I'll charge you with assault."

He wrestled himself to his knees, one hand still cupped protectively around his groin. "Hey, man, I can't walk. . . ."

"Then you'd better learn how to fly. You've got three minutes." I stopped at the door and watched his lurching three-legged crawl toward his car. I waited until one huge hand was reaching for the door handle on the ancient Ford parked at the curb.

"Give Mickey my best," I said, "and tell him I'll see him soon."

I waited until he was gone before I went back inside. I didn't bother calling the police, of course. Other than a small red spot on my jawbone there wasn't a mark on me, so they probably wouldn't have believed me after they got a good whiff of my breath.

I had a feeling the whole thing had been what Pete Berghoff had said it was: revenge. It had a choreographed air about it, the melodramatic flair of a sorry script with an inept leading man. But I guess they had no way of knowing that a bumbling, insensitive clod like me would rewrite their ending for them.

The telephone's shrill clamor yanked me out of a sleep that was neither deep nor restful. I woke up quickly, in a mild panic, the persistent ringing an ominous, alien sound. I rolled off the couch onto my hands and knees, hung there for a moment shaking my head like a bear with a bee-stung lip, disoriented and stuporous, hoping the noise would dry up and go away.

But it rang again, and again, and I reluctantly climbed to unsteady feet and fumbled my way to the kitchen extension. I glanced at the wall clock as I picked up the receiver: eleven forty-five.

"Mr. Roman?" The voice sounded young and vaguely familiar.

"Yes."

"This is Sergeant Peabody, sir, Fort Worth Police Department. You called me a couple of days ago about a missing Toyota. A 1988 silver Tercel?"

"Yes," I said again, the adrenaline beginning to flow, knifing through the sludge in my brain. "Have you found it?"

"Oh, no, sir, nothing like that. It's just . . . well, to be frank with you, Mr. Roman, I probably shouldn't be calling you about this, but . . ." His voice stopped for a second, then continued. "Do you remember the blue Corvette, sir? The one wrecked and burned? I was telling you about it as I recall—"

"I remember."

"It's probably just a coincidence, Mr. Roman. Probably has nothing to do with your wife's disappearance at all." He hesitated again. "But it *is* an odd coincidence that that color should show up . . . even though the detective on the case didn't think so."

"You've lost me, Sergeant. I don't understand what you're talking about."

"The silver color, sir. The same as on your wife's car. Traces were found on the right front fender of the Corvette."

"You mean paint from Susie's car was found on the Corvette?"

"No, sir, I didn't say that. The silver streaks on the Corvette's fender were from a 1988 Tercel. Like I said, it's probably just a—"

"But was it exactly the same paint as the paint on Susie's car?"

"I can't say that for sure, sir. There were several shades of silver used on Tercels in 1988. I was just going by what you told me. It could be the same paint."

"You say the detective knew about this?"

"Yes, sir. I pointed it out to him when he came by for the report. He didn't seem too impressed. He said there was no way of telling how long the paint had been on the fender, and that there were no signs of an impact on the road above the burned car." He hesitated again. "As far as they're concerned, she just ran the car over the edge."

"They could be right, Sergeant. I was out there the next day. There was nothing to indicate she even so much as touched the brakes."

"Well, maybe." He sounded faintly aggrieved. "But I thought it was . . . interesting."

"Yes, it is, Sergeant, and I appreciate your call. What did you say the name of the detective was?"

"Uh . . . Mr. Roman, if you don't mind, I don't think I had better tell you that. You can find out by calling downtown. I'd appreciate it if you didn't mention my name. I'm probably way out of line calling you at all."

"You got it, Sergeant. You never called. One thing: the girl who was killed, you said her name was Charlotte something-or-other?"

"Yes, sir, I can tell you that. It was in the papers yesterday. Charlotte E. Wilkins."

"Okay, Sergeant, and thanks again."

"Uh . . . Mr. Roman. Mrs. Roman, could that be the same Susan Roman on the news?"

"Yes."

"I thought so," he said emphatically. "I know her, then. That telethon they had a while back . . . I met her then. She's a nice . . . pretty lady."

"Yes, she is."

"Well, I . . . I sure hope she turns up okay."

"Thank you, Sergeant."

"Good luck, Mr. Roman."

"Good-bye, Sergeant."

I found the newspaper in the trash bag under the sink. A small story, less than a dozen lines, a follow-up story with a simple headline: ACCIDENT VICTIM IDENTIFIED. It listed her address, an apartment complex on the eastern edge of Fort Worth, and gave her age as twenty-seven. And, after stating that she had died in the fire that occurred after her automobile left the road and crashed in a ravine, that was all. Just another traffic fatality, less spectacular since there had been no gory multicar crash or mutilated bodies.

I dug out the Fort Worth telephone book and looked up the Oak Meadows Apartments in the yellow pages. A small crude map in the corner of their advertisement revealed the nearest major intersection: Highway 183 and Loop 820. Probably five miles from where she had been found in the ravine.

I opened a beer and went into the den. The TV was still blaring: David Letterman and a motherly old lady with a sweet shy smile; but she had hard cold eyes and was probably an ex-madam. I didn't want to find out; I cut her off in mid-sentence.

I drank the beer slowly and pondered the significance of what the sergeant had told me. As I was listening to him, the chilling thought had flashed through my mind that Susie might have been involved in the accident, panicked, and ran away. But that idea vanished as quickly as it came. She was much too honest and straightforward to do that. And even if she had, through some temporary mental aberration, some momentary lapse, she would have come running to me for help, for protection, just as she had always done.

The detective had been right. I had automatically scanned the area as I approached the wreck site. There had been no evidence of a crash of any kind, no tire marks, no hard clods of accumulated dirt dislodged from under the fenders, nothing. The woman had apparently lost control of the car and driven over the edge, had the misfortune to strike the rocks and puncture the gas tank. Sparks from the rocks or the engine would have done the rest. She could have been drunk, sleepy, nervous, or just plain tired. Any number of things. Mechanical failure on the car, a tie rod dropping loose would have done the job nicely.

But way down deep in my mind another scenario was forming, nudging gently at the periphery of my consciousness, begging for permission to enter, for equal time.

58

Reluctantly I opened the door and let it in, a variation of my previous script: Susie running late and driving fast, the hilly curving road, old and narrow and poorly banked . . . the two cars meeting, swerving to avoid collision, not quite far enough, scraping fenders, the Corvette losing control, diving over the edge, the devastating fireball . . . what would she do?

Cold reason, logic, and my knowledge of her told me she would have reacted characteristically—would have gone for help; not even considering the consequences of her act, responding automatically to her innate sense of responsibility and compassion for another human being in peril.

That was what my reason told me. But was it possible I could be wrong? Extreme stress, anxiety, can do strange things to people, generate irrational behavior patterns totally divergent from normal conduct. Could the sight and sound of the woman burning to death have thrown her into terror-filled panic? Caused her to run? Even as this heresy squirmed in my mind, chilling my blood, I was shaking my head vehemently.

No! Not Susie! Rebellious, petulant at times, obstinate at others, but never cowardly, never insensitive to the pain and suffering of others.

No. Susie, my Susie, could never do something like that. Could she?

"Just because you're pissed at me, Homer, doesn't mean I'm going to quit calling you."

"Never thought it would," he growled. "Just got out of bed, I suppose."

"None of your business." I sucked smoke from my first cigarette of the day and coughed. "I didn't call to argue with you. What have you found out—if anything?"

"No need to get touchy," he said mildly. "Nothing new. We had a couple of false alarms on the car. It would have helped some if you'd have had the license number handy, or at least told us the car was still in your name."

"That's for insurance reasons."

"I don't give a damn what it's for. We've been cussing the computer because it couldn't come up with a registration in Susie's name, and all the time it was in yours. If I hadn't finally figured it out, we'd still be fighting with the state."

"Why in the hell didn't you ask me?"

"How the hell could I? You've been gone or drunk the last two days."

"Bullshit! You were talking to me last night, and the day before. Why didn't you ask me then?"

He was quiet so long I finally prompted him.

"Well?"

"Goddammit! I can't remember every damn thing all the damn time!"

"It's reassuring to know that you're not perfect either."

"Anything else on your mind, boy? I'm busy."

"Yeah, there is. I found out there was a wreck on the route Susie would have taken to Loop 820. It happened just about the time she could have been passing the scene."

"The burned woman. Okay, so what? It wasn't her; she's been identified."

"I know that. I also found out there was paint on the right front fender of the Corvette . . . silver paint . . . from a Tercel 1988 model."

"How did you find that out?"

"Never mind how. Doesn't that seem like a hell of a coincidence to you?"

"Are you trying to say Susie may have hit that car, sent that woman over the edge of that gully? Then . . . run off?" His voice was ominously calm.

"No, Homer, I'm not saying that. It's just that it seems like a damn funny coincidence to me. The right time, the right place . . . just seems odd, is all."

I waited, lit another cigarette, and waited some more. I knew from experience he was running it through his mind, sifting the various possibilities the same way I had done the night before. Our minds worked much alike, and that was understandable; he had been my teacher for a number of years, a close friend for a great many more.

"Naw," he said finally. "Too much foam on that one, boy. Susie wouldn't do that in the first place, and in the second, why didn't they find evidence of a collision? Contrary to public opinion, cops ain't that dumb."

"Way I figured, too, Homer," I said gratefully. "But I couldn't trust my own instincts. I can't be objective about Susie."

"All the same," he said. "I'll look into it a little. May even run over to Cowtown myself. I need a little road time. I stay cooped up in this damn cell all the time."

"Be cool, Homer. My source is in a sensitive spot."

He barked a humorless laugh. "That's a switch, you telling me to be cool. Don't you remember, boy? I invented cool."

"Yeah," I said. "You invented bullshit, too."

"Why don't you mind your . . ." But he was already gone and didn't bother finishing it.

I had just finished showering and shaving when Milo called.

"How you doing, Mr. Roman?"

"Just fair, Milo, how about you?"

"I've been wondering, did you ever . . . did your woman ever turn up? I know it ain't none of my business. . . ."

"No, Milo, she hasn't. And I appreciate your concern."

"Wish I'd squeezed the boss's chains a little more the other night."

"Why, Milo? You said Conrad had nothing to do with Susie's disappearance."

"Yeah, that's right. But it was his fault she was there so late. If he hadn't been hasslin' her she'd been long gone. Maybe then nothin' would have happened."

"Yeah, but that's reaching a little. She was there doing her job. She knew how it would probably be."

"Maybe so. But that didn't give him no right to come on like he done. I can't believe I worked for him as long as I did."

"The money was good."

"Yeah, right. Well, I just wanted to hear . . . and to say that if you need me . . . for anything, anything at all, I'm available. I'm just setting around going crazy, pestering the old lady every chance she gives me. I mean it."

"I'm sure you do, Milo, and I appreciate it. But I've about run out of things to do myself. There's just nothing to go on, no leads, nothing. What little there is to do, the police are doing. They've got a call out on the car and her picture will be in this evening's paper. Until something turns up . . . there's just nothing more to be done."

"Maybe. Maybe not," he said. "When that paper hits the streets, I'll do a little circulatin' of my own."

I mustered up a laugh. "I'd appreciate anything you can do, Milo."

"You got it, man. I figger I owe you one. I'll catch you later, okay?"

"Thanks."

I finally ate some of Susie's whole-grain cereal with milk and sugar for breakfast, or lunch, since it was almost two o'clock. I spent the rest of the afternoon alternating between restless cruises around the backyard and short, bored sessions with the TV soaps. When it was finally time for the five o'clock news I settled down with a fresh beer and listened to the day's accumulation of cheery news: murders, fires, and assorted mayhem. The broadcast was almost over when Homer Sellers called.

"You had that shower yet?"

"Smell like a rose."

"Then whyn't you come on over here to the office. Got something I want you to look at."

"What?"

But the ornery, exasperating bastard had already hung up.

/ 9 /

Short, stocky Mitzi was standing by her desk, purse in hand, ready to go home. She gave me her usual smile and flirtatious wink.

"He's waiting for you, Danny. What in the world have you been up to now?"

"I'm not washing enough to suit him," I said.

She had a high, shrill laugh and it followed me into Homer's office. He looked up with a frown of annoyance, a wad of Kleenex cupped around his nose. He blew lustily.

"What's going on out there?" He grimaced and dropped the Kleenex in the wastebasket.

"Mitzi busted her garter belt," I said impatiently. "What do you have, Homer?"

He gave me a critical glance, grunted, and shoved something across his desk. "Take a look at these pictures."

Eight-by-ten glossies; two of them, creased down the center from being folded. Living color: a picture of a burned-out hulk of a car and another of a charred, almost unrecognizable form inside. Something flexed in my stomach, coiled tightly.

I glanced at him. "Where'd you get these?"

"I borried 'em," he mumbled around his cigar. "Tell me what you see."

I looked at them again; a car, undoubtedly the blue Corvette. I could tell that much from the shape. A large circle of fire-blackened stubble of weeds and brush, a few surrounding trees with burn marks on their trunks, a barely discernible lump on the front seat that brought a chill.

63

In the other picture the woman lay sideways on the seat, her head under the wheel, hands extended to the door on the driver's side, her hair a thin spiky stubble on a blistered misshapen head. Her legs were drawn in toward her stomach, her face buried in the crack formed by the seat and the backrest. Her clothing had been reduced to thin brittle fibers welded to her flesh, and her exposed skin was black and raw and withered.

"Okay," I said huskily. "It's terrible. It makes me want to puke. But what does this have to do with Susie?" Tiny alarm signals were beginning to go off in my head, jagged fracture lines materializing around the edges of my control.

"Maybe nothin'," he said, then amended it, "probably nothin'. But you ain't looking, boy."

"What the hell is it, Homer? What am I supposed to be looking for?"

He sighed and picked up the picture of the car. "What do you see?"

"A burned-out car!"

"Which way is it pointing?"

"Pointing? What the hell . . ." It hit me like a slap in the face. "Jesus Christ! The damn thing is backwards."

"Right," he said with sardonic admiration. "I'll say one thing for you. You don't miss the obvious, not when it's pointed out to you."

"Then she didn't just run the car over the edge. But how the hell could it have gone down backwards without being hit and turned around or something? There were no marks of any kind, Homer. I was there within a few hours. There was no collision on that road above the car. I'd stake my life on that."

He nodded. "Now take another look at the woman."

I picked up the picture and looked at it again, focusing on the burned victim, blanking my mind to what that shape was, what it had once been.

"Okay, she's on the wrong side of the car. I noticed that before, but she could have been thrown over there, so that doesn't mean anything." I looked at him, saw his crooked mocking grin. "You say no?"

"Look a little closer. What's that shiny thing in the bend of her belly?"

"Hell, that's just her ..." And it hit me again, harder this time: little ripples of shock that zeroed in on my midriff. "Seat belt?" I looked at the photo again, vibrating a little in my shaking hand. "Jesus Christ, if she was belted in on the passenger side ... who was driving the damned car?"

"Precisely!" he boomed. "Give the little feller a cigar."

I dropped into the chair in front of his desk.

"You'd have picked up on that a lot quicker ten years ago," he said.

"I'm out of practice," I said absently, my mind racing. "Then what they have here is not necessarily an accident. What did they say in Fort Worth?"

His smile disappeared like a dandelion in a hailstorm. He leaned forward, elbows on his desk, and fingered the edges of the pictures.

"They already got it closed out." His eyes came up and met mine. "Accident."

"You're kidding!"

"Wish I was." He picked at something between his teeth with the nail on his little finger.

"But how can they, Homer? If we ... you could pick this up so fast why couldn't they? And they were on the scene to boot."

He shook his head. "These ain't their pictures. Theirs don't show anything like this." He tapped the pictures with a yellow pencil, then began worrying it between his sausage-sized fingers.

"Then whose are they?"

"Free-lance photographer named Frank Demas. Got himself a police band radio. He was cruising down Loop 820 when the call went out. He whipped right over there, got there right after the fire truck and squad car. One of the uniformed cops knew him and let him get a couple of shots as soon as the fire was out. You can still see some smoke there in the corner."

"What about the official pictures? They had the same subject."

"Not exactly," he said heavily. "Oh, it was the same girl all right ... but there was no sign of the seat belt in their pictures."

"Maybe it wasn't fastened. Maybe the fall threw it across her body."

He shook his head again. "Not likely. It's on a recoil mechanism. Besides, the photographer says he's sure it was fastened."

"How'd you find out about him?"

"I run down the uniforms who caught the squeal. One of them mentioned Demas being there."

"You've had a busy afternoon."

He nodded, his eyes troubled, his wide brow wrinkled, creating a deep line of Vs down the center of his forehead.

"What do you think is going on, Homer? Somebody's doing some damn sloppy police work. Either that or somebody's covering up something."

He shook his head slowly. "It's not the patrolmen. I'd bet on that. I talked to them for a while. Course they mainly handled traffic, that kind of thing. The tech squad worked the wreck itself." He leaned back and passed a hand over his eyes as if trying to dispel unpleasant visions.

"What are you going to do about it?"

He glowered at me, his eyebrows bunching. "Me? Not a damn thing. Not in my jurisdiction. My only interest in this was how it might relate to Susie. I'm beginning to think it don't, just like we figured at first. I got plenty troubles here at home without messing around in Fort Worth."

I glowered back at him. "The hell you say! Well, I don't have to worry about jurisdiction! And how the hell do you figure this might not relate to Susie? For somebody who's supposed to be so damn smart, you're not showing me much. Don't shit me, Homer. I know what your problem is. You

66

think something's coming down that might reflect on one of your fellow officers and you're shying away. And as far as Susie is concerned? Well, what you've got here, what you've found out, makes me almost certain it *does* have something to do with her instead of the other way around."

He leaned back in his chair again, his face red. "I don't follow you."

"The hell you don't! The paint on the fender, the car going down backwards, the girl buckled in on the wrong side . . . what does it take? Who was the driver? Why did he leave the scene? What was his connection with the girl? Why hasn't he come forward? There's more unanswered questions here than a damn quiz show." I stood up and paced up and down in front of his desk.

"What do you think happened?" His voice was deceptively mild, his eyes peering up at me over the spectacles. I knew the signs; he was mad as hell. To hell with him; so was I.

"I don't know exactly. I haven't got that far yet. But if there was a driver in the Corvette and Susie was involved in some kind of accident with them, what would have prevented that driver from taking Susie's car . . . and her along with it?"

"But you said yourself there was no collision on the road above the wreck."

"Okay, maybe not a collision. Maybe just a scrape, a side-swipe . . ."

"Maybe, maybe! You're doing a lot of guessing, boy. You want to tell me how the car got down the gully? Backwards? How come the girl was still in it? If Susie was there with the driver, how come they didn't go for help? How come . . . ?"

"Dammit! I said I didn't have it all worked out yet. But at least it's something to think about. A damn sight more than we had before."

I stood glaring down at his lowered head, bracing myself for the blowup, girding my loins as they say, determined to tell him to kiss my ass and walk out when it came.

67

But it didn't come; instead, he raised his head and gave me an obscenely mocking grin.

"All fired up, ain't you, boy? Well, that's good. That's what I been wanting to see. Now maybe you'll get off your dead ass and do something. Even if it's wrong."

Sucked in again. I stared down at him, wondering how many times it had happened before. I dropped back into the chair. "You bastard, you had it worked out like that all along."

He rolled thick rounded shoulders in a shrug. "It's a logical conclusion. We know some things for sure. Susie would have passed along there about that time. The car went over the edge of the ravine backwards, a curiosity in itself. We suspect the woman was buckled in the wrong seat, and we know there was paint from the same year and model car that Susie was driving: we suspect there was another person present, the driver of the other car. Now, if *all* those things are true, then it's only logical to assume the driver left the scene and took Susie with him ... to what purpose we can only guess. If only the things we know are true are really true, and the others aren't ... well, then we're back where we started. ... Susie's missing and Fort Worth has another accident statistic." He looked at me and smiled faintly. "You tracking?"

"I think so."

He folded his hands on the desk. "It's going to be mostly your baby. I can't go nosing around over there too much. I can help some, put out some feelers with the guys who worked the case, things like that. But right now I'd say we need to find out how many of our guesses are fact. What do you think?"

I nodded. "The ambulance drivers, paramedics, whatever they were. They ought to know about the seat belt. It was probably burned, but the locking device would still have been hooked. Maybe they noticed."

"Right. I didn't know to ask the patrolmen when I talked to them. Maybe I can touch base again without stirring up too much dust."

"It all hinges on that damn belt. If it was latched, then everything else falls in place. There *had* to be another person at the scene."

He nodded slowly. "Whether Susie was there . . . we can only guess at that, but it's a pretty good guess if the other thing shapes up. What happened and why they left . . . well, I won't speculate about that."

"You think there's some kind of cover-up going on?"

"I don't know. Maybe it's like you said, sloppy police work. I hope so."

"You know of any way we could get hold of the report?"

He shook his head gloomily. "Not without coming right out and asking for it. We do that and they're gonna want to know why."

"Why not tell them?"

"I'd rather not, not just yet. We don't know what's taking place. Might be better to hold off, see what happens first."

"You know anyone over there you can trust?"

He turned his eyes on me, already beginning to chill. "I know a lot of guys I can trust. I just don't want to put anybody on the spot until I see what's what."

"Okay, don't get hostile."

"Where you gonna start?"

"Only place I have. The dead girl, Charlotte Wilkins."

He nodded, complacent again. "There may be hope for you yet. Seems like you ain't near as quick as you were when you were a cop."

"Thanks."

"Don't mention it. Wouldn't hurt to touch bases with the paramedics as soon as possible. Sooner we know about that seat belt, quicker we're gonna know where we stand."

"I figured they work the swing shift. I thought I'd go by the dead girl's apartment this evening and catch the paramedics tomorrow. Maybe I can pick up something from her neighbors."

"You telling me or asking my opinion?" The caustic edge was back in his voice.

"I'm telling you," I said, nettled. "Why?"

"No reason. I was just wondering."

"I take it you approve, then," I said.

"What's to approve? You don't work for me anymore." His voice seemed to hang for a second. "You'd do well to remember that."

"What the hell's that supposed to mean, Homer?"

"You better leave that cannon of yours at home."

"I've got a license to carry it anywhere in the state of Texas."

He shrugged and lumbered to his feet. I took that as a sign of dismissal and walked to the door.

"See you later."

"Okay. Just remember one thing."

"What?"

"You may have a license to carry that thing, but that don't give you no license to use it." The desk light reflected against his glasses, turned them into gleaming silver discs.

I gave him an evil grin. "Feller don't need a license to shoot varmints, Homer. Never did."

/ 10 /

I drove west on Highway 183 toward the Oak Meadows Apartments, passing unhurriedly through Midway City and the rapidly growing cities of Bedford and Hurst. They had been small country towns two decades earlier, but the western migration of the seventies, the advent of the Dallas–Fort Worth Airport, the influx of recession-weary, job-hungry northerners had brought about unprecedented expansion in these strategically located municipalities. Unprecedented problems, too, I thought, if recent crime statistics indicated a trend.

Highway 183, at one time the primary artery between Dallas and Fort Worth, was relatively deserted, a welcome relief from the incessant, nerve-shattering cacophony of the Airport Freeway a few miles to the north. Essentially congestion-free except for shift-changing time at the Bell Helicopter plant, the wide thoroughfare afforded local residents and businessmen a sane, moderately safe passage from the vast DFW Airport on the eastern border of Midway City to the outer strands of the intricate spiderweb that was the Fort Worth freeway system.

But since everything in this life is a trade-off in one way or another, the old highway exacted its own toll for traffic-free, tranquil driving; traffic lights abounded. Two of them in front of the sprawling Bell Helicopter plant alone, and I sat smoking at the last of these watching an ancient Huey gunship paddle-wheel its way into the air and across the highway in front of me, the grays and browns and greens of its battle coat twanging at some almost forgotten chord, bringing a visceral tightening, an empathic recollection of other ships and other times, the stench of burning flesh, of gunpowder, of napalm, the terrorizingly acute perceptions that only intense fear can bring to the senses. And yet, despite the horror and shame of it, remembrance sometimes brought an insidious spasm of pride at having been there, at having survived, a sinking realization that the agonizing and immoral war against little brown men who wouldn't quit had been the high point of my existence, somehow the focal point of my manhood.

The light changed and I drove on, the concussive beat of the helicopter blades receding overhead, becoming fainter, a drumbeat, primitive accompaniment to some ancient and terrible ritual.

Finding the Oak Meadows Apartments was easy, but locating Apartment 1216 proved to be a bit more difficult. A large sprawling complex of two-storied white-brick structures separated in clusters of four buildings each, the entire development covered at least a hundred acres, with each cluster of four in haphazard juxtaposition with its neighbors as if placed there by the hand of some myopic giant in a moment of pique. Crooked streets studded with traffic bumps meandered between the buildings and, after ten minutes of aimless wandering, squeezing by illegally parked cars and abandoned toys, I returned to my point of entry and went into the manager's office for directions.

Apartment 1216 was on the second floor. For some reason I had expected it to be dark and silent, but there was light coming through the small draped window and I heard the faint sounds of music as I pushed the bell on the recessed door.

It was opened almost immediately by a young round-faced girl in a green brocade robe, a bath towel wrapped around obviously damp hair. Her freckled face looked freshly scrubbed, and she had large brown eyes that looked me up and down coolly.

"Mr. Ramos?" she asked.

"Roman," I said, staring at her in surprise.

"Oh, well, I'm terrible with names." She smiled a lavish dimpled smile. She held out her hand and, when I took it, drew me into the room. "I'm Alicia," she said, "and you're early. I must look a fright." She poked at damp tendrils of wheat-colored hair dangling down her cheek. She smiled again. "I guess I can stand it if you can."

"Not at all. You look fine." I watched her animated face, puzzled, wondering if Homer could possibly have called her.

She patted my cheek. "That's sweet." She led me to a gold-colored velvet sofa.

"Have a seat, Mr. Roman . . . or would you like for me to call you by your first name?"

"Yes, of course. That would be fine."

She cocked her head, an expectant look on her face. I stared back at her, bewildered by the entire course of events. Finally I realized what she was waiting for.

72

"Oh, it's Dan. Dan Roman. Just call me Dan."

"Okay, Dan." She dimpled up again. "What would you like to drink?"

"Nothing, thanks. I believe there's been some—"

"Aw, come on," she said, wrinkling her short, pert nose, highlighting the spray of freckles that extended like tiny petals into her cheeks. "I know a big old boy like you can handle just one little drink."

"Well, if you're sure it's not too much trouble?" I decided to ride it out for the full eight seconds.

"Of course not. What'll it be? I have scotch, bourbon, sherry . . ."

"Scotch will be fine."

"On the rocks?"

"Yes, thank you."

She swayed toward a small cart in one corner that served as a bar, slender and lissome, her heelless houseshoes slapping the carpet with tiny popping sounds at each step, one hand gripping the edges of the robe, pulling it tight across her rounded bottom.

"Well, Dan, has it made up its mind whether it's going to rain out there or not?"

I could hear the clink of glasses and ice cubes and the muted whir of an electric blender.

"There's some lightning out west of Fort Worth and the wind's picking up a bit. But it looks like it's going around to the north of us. Probably won't get a drop like the last two or three times." After I finished the weather report, I sat back and crossed my legs, feeling foolish and even more bewildered. I wanted a cigarette, but there were no ashtrays in evidence in the tastefully decorated room, and I hesitated, assailed by the modern-day smoker's niggling caution in the face of an intolerant society's growing disapproval that was constantly being fanned by an ever-increasing encroachment of big government into our lives, nibbling relentlessly at our God-given right to destroy ourselves any damn way we chose.

I sighed and admired the large airy room instead, the subtle blending of low-slung, pale gold furniture and beige, almost-white, carpeting that must have required professional cleaning at least once a month. Sandstone-colored draperies covered one entire wall and one small window, and through a small arched doorway I could see a gold-tinted refrigerator and a small portion of countertop of the same shade. Two doors were set into the wall opposite the kitchen, one closed, one open, and since there were no other exits, I concluded that each bedroom must have its own bathroom. Since I had already learned from the gabby apartment manager that the apartment contained two bedrooms, it wasn't one of my more spectacular feats of deduction.

A grouping of three multicolored masks that looked like African art adorned the wall to the right of the bar cart, and a vividly green plant hanging from the ceiling in one corner provided a splash of contrasting color. Small gilt-edged original paintings hung everywhere and a large Oriental rug protected the beige wool carpeting between facing velvet sofas.

There was a lushness about the room that seemed designed for comfort and relaxation, an ambience of feminine sensuality that was almost an aphrodisiac; a room for seduction, I thought idly, watching the well-turned figure across the room, crossing my legs the other way and wishing again for a cigarette.

She came back with the drinks: hers, a green concoction with crushed ice and a lemon slice on the rim; mine, three fingers of scotch and two ice cubes.

"Maybe not," she said, leaning over to hand me the drink. The robe had loosened and two plump little breasts peered out at me, soft-looking and freckled.

"I beg your pardon?"

"I said, maybe not. Maybe the rain won't go around." She removed the towel and began fluffing her hair. She paused. "It would only take a minute for me to brush my hair, fix myself up a little—" She broke off, her eyebrows raised inquiringly.

"No, no. You're fine. I'll only be a minute."

Her eyebrows went up again, rosebud lips quirked with amusement. "My," she said. She crossed her legs and the robe fell open to her hips; and I began to have a dark, terrible suspicion.

She gave her hair one last puff with the towel. She tossed the towel across the back of her chair and brought her drink to sit beside me on the couch. She took a small sip and let her hand drop to my thigh. The robe gaped carelessly.

She turned on her devastating smile. "Honey, why don't we get the nasty old business out of the way ... then we can relax and enjoy ourselves."

I looked into her eyes and returned her smile; the longer I looked, the wider my smile became; finally I was grinning.

Her smile wavered, returned, then went away completely. It was replaced by a tiny frown of annoyance.

"Don't tell me that dumb-ass Terry already took the money?" She puckered her lips and brushed an impatient hand through her hair. "Damn. The last time he did that I didn't get my money for a month." Her fingers tightened on my thigh irritably. Then she sighed, made a face, and patted my leg. "Well, it's not your fault, is it? I promise I won't take it out on you." She looked at me curiously. "Do you grin like that all the time?"

I laughed. "I'm sorry, Alicia, but I think we've got what you might call a breakdown in communications."

She snatched her hand away. "Communications? Oh, no! Don't tell me you're a cop!" She screwed her face up into a rueful grimace. "Oh, damn!"

"No, no!" I said, choking back an insane desire to giggle.

"Oh," she said, the grimace turning back into a smile, her hand returning to my leg. "Boy, honey, you sure had me going there for a minute."

"I'm not a trick either, Alicia."

She took her hand away again, lips parted, her eyes growing wide. "Well, lordy, what are you?"

"I'm sorry. I should have told you in the beginning, but ... well, my name is Dan Roman, all right. I'm a private detective."

"A private detective? Well . . . goodness, a private detective. I've never seen one of you before."

"Believe me, you haven't missed a lot."

She gave me an almost shy smile. "It's kinda funny. I thought you were a . . . my date."

"I thought you were certainly a friendly kid," I said, chuckling.

She joined in, ended with a giggle. "Just imagine, a private detective." Then she sobered abruptly. "What do you want with me?"

"Charlotte Wilkins. She was your roommate?"

"Charley?" She bobbed her head gloomily. "Yes, she was. Wasn't it terrible what happened to her?"

"Yes, it was. Was she a . . . was she a working girl like you?"

"Uh-huh. But she was a lot better at it than me. She made a lot more money. She went out with some really rich johns."

"Anyone in particular?"

She shook her head. Her hair was almost dry, fine and light, beginning to curl around her face. "No. I mean, I don't really know. She almost never worked here. She always went somewhere . . . home with them, or to a motel. I haven't known her very long."

"She ever talk about them, mention any of their names, what they did, anything like that?"

She started to shake her head, then pursed her lips and changed the gesture to a nod. "There was this one she talked about once. Kinda like . . . well, bragging a little, you know."

"Did she mention his name?"

"No, not really. I think she called him Jay . . . yes, that's it, Jay. I remember because I thought of the bird, you know."

"That's all?"

"Well, this one day she was talking about him. Talking about how he was going to be a big shot someday . . . you know, an important man. She said he was already wealthy, but that he would someday really be . . . something." She picked at a thread on her robe, dark eyes watching me gravely.

"She didn't say what?"

She shook her head. "No, that was all. Just that one day she talked about him. He took her out a lot, though. She usually told me when it was him she was dating."

"Anyone else?"

"Well, she mentioned a Tom once. I'm not too sure if he was a trick, though. I just seem to remember a Tom. He might have been her brother or something."

"She must have made a lot of money. That Corvette didn't come cheap."

She nodded eagerly. "Boy, did she! She made twice as much as me. I hope someday I can—" She broke off, grimacing. "I'll bet I sound awful greedy."

"Nothing wrong with wanting money. That's one thing everybody agrees on—except maybe the rich. They don't like to talk about it."

She gave me a rueful smile. "Well, I don't think I'll ever get rich."

"Never can tell. Maybe you'll find somebody like Charley's Jay. Who knows what can happen?"

"We make pretty good wives," she said, and lifted her eyebrows coquettishly.

"That's what I've always heard."

"Do you ever go out with working girls?"

"Not lately."

"You have a girl, I'll bet."

"I have a wife." There was a glowing vitality about her, a nimbus of wide-eyed innocence that struck a responsive chord somewhere deep within my masculine vanity. She had not yet acquired, or had somehow avoided, the brittle crusty exterior, the shrewdness, the innate contempt for the male species that was the hallmark of her occupation. A gleam of eagerness burned brightly in brown eyes not yet dulled and hardened by inner turmoil, exterior conflict. She seemed somehow untouched . . . illogically wholesome.

"If you want," she said, "we have time for a quickie. I'll

only charge you thirty-five . . . that's less than half." There was an odd kind of look on her face, half teasing, half serious, her eyes sparkling with merriment above an enigmatic smile.

I shook my head and drank some more of my scotch, refusing to let her see how much I was tempted, refusing to acknowledge to myself the creeping influx of desire.

"I'd better not," I said, not surprised that I felt a small pang of regret. "Some other time, maybe."

"Okay," she said equably. "I'll probably be here." She worked her face into a wry, pixie grin. "Most of the time I really like my work. I guess that's why I do what I'm doing." She watched for my reaction. "I'm really good, too," she added succinctly. "I don't cheat. I never pretend to come when I don't. I think that's important, don't you?"

"I guess so," I said. "I suppose every job has its imperatives."

"And another thing," she said firmly. "I don't do any of the sick things. I think that stuff is really gross."

"I can see where it would be."

"You ought to hear some of the things men want us to do."

I gunned the rest of my scotch and got to my feet. "Maybe I'll come by sometime and you can tell me about it. Right now, I think I'd better be going. Anyway, isn't it about time for your, ah, date?"

"Isn't it funny? His name is Ramos, or something like that. Almost like yours." She followed me to the door, appearing strangely reluctant to see me go. Maybe the only way she ever talked to men was on her back . . . or her knees, or wherever.

"One other thing, Alicia," I said at the door. "Do you know of any reason anyone might want to hurt Charley?"

Her eyes grew wide. "Hurt her? Goodness no. Why would . . . didn't Charley die in an accident?"

"As far as we know, she did."

"Well, there's always some johns who want to get mean sometime . . . is that what you mean?"

"No. I mean really hurt her. Kill her, maybe."

She shook her head slowly, her face perplexed, worried. "No. I sure don't know about anything like that."

"Well, don't worry about it. It was a thought somebody had. If you remember anything that might help, give me a call." I handed her my card.

She dredged up a smile. "Okay. You remember. If you decide you want a really good time, you know where I am." She sucked her lower lip into her mouth and gave me an amiable leer, the robe swinging wide before she caught it with a lazy, indifferent hand, young-old eyes gleaming with ancient knowledge.

"All right," I said, turning away. "I'll sure do that." I moved toward the stairs, resolutely, one step at a time. It wasn't easy.

"Don't forget now," she said in a soft, exaggerated Texas drawl. "Y'all come back to see me, huh?"

I glanced back at her and she measured me a full portion of her lovely smile, corn silk hair fluffed and dry, billowing about her face, the slender sensuous body posed artfully in the doorway.

The thunderheads had decided not to bypass the Fort Worth–Dallas corridor after all and large squishy raindrops splattered on my windshield, sliding in on the still-western wind that scouted for the formation of dense blue-black clouds blanketing the horizon.

I made it home before the deluge, but just barely, feeling discontented and self-righteous in turn, and more than a little ashamed of a crazy impulse to get back into my car, storm or no damn storm, drive back over there, and take her up on her offer.

/ 11 /

The next morning, I called the Stevans Ambulance Service and asked to speak to the supervisor. When she came on, I gave her the date and location of the Wilkins accident and requested the names and addresses of the attending paramedics.

Since ours has come to be an apprehensive society, and all its members are wary, she demanded to know who I was and why I wanted to know.

"Sergeant McAtee, Fort Worth Police Department, ma'am. A valuable gold money clip has been found at the scene and we can't seem to locate the owner. It occurred to me that perhaps one of the paramedics lost it."

Her cool little laugh was incredulous. "Not if it was very valuable, Sergeant, not on the kind of money we make."

"Yes, well, if you don't mind . . ."

"Probably belonged to the DOA."

"We thought of that, but . . ."

"These clowns around here certainly don't hang on to money long enough to keep it in a money clip."

"I'd like to check with them all the same."

A heartfelt sigh. "All right. It's your time and our tax money you're wasting. Hang on."

Everybody's a cynic, I thought morosely as I waited.

"Here you are, Sergeant McGee."

"McAtee."

"Whatever."

She read me the addresses and I copied them down laboriously, read them back to her slowly, taking a perverse delight in her impatient sighs and sounds.

"Thank you, ma'am."

"What kind of money clip was it, Sergeant?"

"The kind you put money in. Good-bye."

Theron L. Marsh lived in a modest tract home in North Fort Worth. An older home veneered with rough-textured red brick, it boasted a two-car garage and a lush green lawn as precisely clipped as the waist-high hedge along the front of the house. An ancient Ford pickup and a shiny new pocket-sized Plymouth sat side by side in the driveway. Despite the coolness of the day the front door was open, and I heard angry voices the moment I got out of the car.

". . . out there working my butt off on this nothing job. And what are you doing? I'll tell you what you're doing, putting out to some damned intern, that's what! How many times, Loretta? Just you damned tell me that." A rough male voice, strained and hoarse. He had evidently been at it for a while.

"And just what do you expect, Theron Marsh? You're always gone on that stupid job, and when you're home you're so tired you don't ever want to do anything. And when you do, you can't always get it up. Besides, it wasn't any big thing."

"No big thing? No big thing? My wife out screwing some damned skinny kid just out of school and she says it's no big thing! No big thing! Damn, woman, I ought to bust your ass!"

"Will you keep your voice down? They can hear you all over the block."

"Who gives a damn? Everybody probably knows you're nothing but a damn tramp anyway. How many of the men around here you been putting out for? Tell me that, you bitch!"

"Wouldn't you like to know!"

"You goddamned tramp!"

I stopped at the corner of the garage, debating the advisability of driving around the block, maybe two blocks. From the sound of it they were just getting wound up, a lot more to go.

And there was still reconciliation to come, a little slap and tickle in the bedroom, maybe, to cool the head of steam, the passions they were building.

I lit a cigarette and turned back toward my car. But it was too late: behind me came the sound of the screen door slamming and footsteps on the concrete walk.

"Hey! Hey, you! What're you doing?"

I stopped halfway down the drive. He was short and stocky, as broad as the front end of a truck. Thin carroty hair, an incipient paunch, and a face the color of old copper. His lips were locked in a thin white line, nostrils flaring.

"What're you doing on my driveway, fellow?"

I walked a couple of steps toward him. "Mr. Marsh?"

He drew up short a few feet away. "Yeah. Who're you?"

"My name is Dan Roman, Mr. Marsh. I'm a private detective. Your office gave me your address. I wonder if I could ask you a question about the woman who burned in the Corvette a few days ago. Up on Lucas White Road. You and—"

"Yeah, I remember. What kind of questions?" He took a deep rasping breath.

"Just one, Mr. Marsh. You helped take her out of the car. Did you happen to notice whether the seat belt was fastened or not . . . the lap belt?"

"That seat belt was burned to a crisp, like everything else inside the car."

I nodded. "But do you recall if the locking mechanism was engaged?"

"Yeah," he said. "It was. It fell off on the floorboards when we moved her. The belt was locked all right. I remember thinking maybe she might have got out . . . sometimes people forget they're fastened in, they're too terrified to think, I guess."

His skin had lost some of its ruddy color, the tautness gone from his face. "From the way she was lying, looked like she was trying to open the other door. Hers wouldn't open. Sprung a little. We had to use a pry bar on it."

"Did it look like it might have been hit ... by another car, say?"

He shook his head. "I didn't see any dents, or anything like that. Probably just got sprung when the car hit the rocks. It wasn't too hard to get open."

"How about the driver?"

He shook his head. "I didn't see anybody else. I just figured he was in one of the cop cars. Damn lucky, whoever he was."

"Yeah," I said. "Damn lucky."

He took out a package of Carltons and offered me one. I accepted it and he held the flame of his lighter to the end.

"You working for the insurance company?"

I nodded; it was simpler that way.

"Do you have any idea how the car got turned around? Why it went down backwards?" I asked.

He moved over and leaned against the pickup. He gazed at me reflectively. "I don't know. You know, I hadn't really thought about that until you just mentioned it. That sucker was backwards, wasn't it?"

"The police didn't seem to notice it either."

"Well, that was a pretty deep gully. Maybe it hit a rock or something and turned as it was going down."

"No. There was just one set of tracks. Straight as a tight line to those rocks."

He nodded, his lips pursed. "That's why you were wondering about the dents?"

I nodded.

"You ain't seen the car yet?"

I shook my head. "Not yet."

"Thought you was with the insurance company?" He was watching me steadily.

"Life," I said tersely. "Somebody else has the car."

"I see," he said, no longer interested. His eyes strayed toward the house.

I held out my hand. "Well, thanks, Mr. Marsh. I appreciate your help."

"Glad to do it." He pumped my hand a couple of times and turned away. He stumped back up the walk toward the door, shoulders squaring, head lifting, eager for the fray.

Grover K. Edmonds rubbed one thumb across the surface of the board he had been hand-planing. He was tall and well built, black as coal dust, heavy-muscled, and capable-looking.

"Marsh was on that side, Mr. Roman, but I did see the seat belt mechanism fall to the floor. I couldn't swear it was locked, but I can say this, though. The right side, the part that comes from the floor. It was extended all right. I remember seeing it across her hip. Burned to a crisp, but you could see the outline. So, my guess would be it was fastened all right." He placed the board on his worktable.

"What difference does it make? You'd still have to pay off, wouldn't you? No matter what? Or is there some kind of seat belt clause you guys are slipping in on us now?"

"No, it's nothing like that. We just like to have things neat and tidy. No loose ends, you know what I mean?"

"Yeah," he said good-naturedly. "Damn insurance companies always looking for a way out."

"That's a fact. They're shifty."

He cocked his head. "Thought you was one of them?"

"I might have to work for them, but I don't have to love them."

He smiled and folded his arms. "Sad damn world. I hate my boss's guts, too."

"Being a paramedic a pretty good job?"

He shook his head gravely. "I like the work okay. But the pay stinks, the hours are lousy, and there's no fringe benefits, no security."

I lit a cigarette and moved toward the door. "There's no security anywhere today."

*　*　*

Homer Sellers peered up at me over the edge of his glasses. "You look like a mangy fox creeping up on a rabbit." He pronounced the words heavily, with elaborate sarcasm.

I sat down in front of his desk and lit a cigarette. "We were right, buddy. I got a positive confirmation on that seat belt. And the second paramedic said it was in the right position to be in use." I was unable to keep the excitement out of my voice.

"Simmer down, little feller. I never doubted that for a minute."

"Then why did I run all over hell's half acre trying to confirm it?"

He shrugged. "Give you something constructive to do. Get you out of my hair, so I could get a little work done, a little real detective work."

"Like what?"

His eyes met mine squarely. "Like they've closed out the case. Got the Wilkins woman listed as the driver. In spite of the fact they know it ain't so as well as we do."

"How'd you find that out?"

"Bought that Detective Mahoney half a dozen beers, is how. Run into him accidentally at Pete's Bar—after I followed the sucker for two hours."

"How are they explaining the fact that she was belted in the passenger seat?"

"They're not. The report don't mention it."

"How about their photos?"

He shrugged. "I didn't see them, but I imagine they substantiate the report."

"Jesus. Then it is some kind of cover-up?"

"Looks like it."

"How can they account for the seat belt being burned in the first place when it should have been in a coiled position if it wasn't in use?"

"Don't have to. Who's gonna raise the question? Like Mahoney says, she was just a hooker, after all."

"They know that, then?"

"They do now. They probably had her identified before they left the scene. After all, it was her car and she's been busted before." He leaned back in his swivel chair and removed his glasses. He pinched the bridge of his nose. He looked as old and weary as I felt.

He put his glasses back on and looked at me. "There's one other thing. I took a little run out to see the car itself. The paint on the fender?"

"Yeah, what about it? Did you see it?"

"Nope. It was gone. Burned off. Blowtorch, most likely."

"I don't believe it!"

"Believe it. Two strips down the edge of the fender. Maybe a foot long. Rest of the fender's in pretty fair condition, considering."

"Okay," I said softly. "That damn sure cinches it. A deliberate wash job. There's no way that could be accidental."

"Yeah," Homer said wearily. "Up till then I was willing to give them the benefit of the doubt. Not after that, and not after talking to Mahoney. We talked about it some and it wasn't what he said as much as what he didn't. A few nudges and a sly wink or two. Just a couple of old vets who know the score."

I paced back and forth in front of his desk. "All right. Let them close their damn case. All that means is we're going to have to find the driver of that car ourselves."

Homer's head followed me like a front-row tennis fan. "Yeah, that's what we got to do all right. Any suggestions?"

"Yes. Her neighbors. It's a place to start."

"I thought you'd already done that."

"No. She had a roommate. Another hooker. But she couldn't tell me anything. I'll just have to go back over there and canvass the whole damn apartment complex if I have to."

"How many apartments?"

"Maybe twenty-five or so in her cluster. Probably three or four hundred in the whole damn complex."

86

He smiled faintly. "Pretty big job for one man."

"Whatever it takes, Homer."

"I can give you a hand a few hours in the evening."

"I don't know, old man. You look pretty beat."

He gave me a dirty look. "Oak Meadows Apartments. What was her apartment number?"

"I believe it was 1216. Last cluster of four at the very back. Second floor. Oh, by the way, if you talk to her roommate, take it easy, will you? Don't go flashing your badge around. She's a nice kid. Scares easy."

He looked at me suspiciously. "That why you didn't get around to checking the neighbors last night?"

"As a matter of fact, it was. But it wasn't entirely wasted time. She did tell me about one of Charley's—that's the Wilkins girl—boyfriends. Some joker named Jay. Supposed to be loaded, headed for bigger things. She mentioned another man named Tom, wasn't sure but what he might be her brother. That's something else. Her family. We need to find out where they live."

"Dallas. Highland Park. Big bucks, according to Mahoney. John T. Markette. Funny thing to me, if he's so rich, why's his daughter a whore?"

"It's the sexual revolution, Homer. Where've you been? A woman can do anything she wants to do. She's master of her fate. Free choice."

He glowered at me over his glasses, a burly scowling anachronism. He still believed in things: chivalry, honesty, honor, the eventual triumph of good over evil.

"You get Markette's phone number, too?"

"In the book," he growled.

I stood up and moved toward the door. "I'm going to grab a bite and run back out to Oak Meadows. You want to come along?"

He shook his head, fingering the edges of a pile of papers on his desk. "I got some stuff I have to clear up here. I'll come on over there later."

"I'll take the second floor. You can start on the bottom. Okay?"

I opened the door and hesitated. "Still think I need a bath, old man?"

He eyed me solemnly, critically. "Can't smell you, but you could stand a shave." He took off his glasses and dropped them on his desk, massaged his eyes with a thumb and forefinger. Then he put the glasses back on and picked up the stack of papers.

"There ain't no shortcuts in this life, Dan," he said solemnly. "No detours. You gotta go through it, right down the middle if you can."

He looked down at the papers. I watched him for a while and when he didn't look up, I laughed softly and went out the door.

/ 12 /

He was waiting for me when I got home, sitting inside a red Datsun parked in my driveway, long yellow hair disguising his gender until I pulled up even with him.

We got out simultaneously. He nodded at me across the top of his car, a tall, thin boy in a brown polo shirt and tan slacks. He was handsome: clean, chiseled features and a flawless complexion a lot of women would have bartered their souls to possess.

"Mr. Roman?"

"Yes, I'm Dan Roman." I walked around to the front of his car and waited. He advanced and held out a long-fingered hand. His grip was firm, his palm damp.

"My name is Thomas Markette, Mr. Roman. Charlotte Wilkins was my sister."

I've never been very good with words in the aftermath of personal tragedy, so I just nodded and waited, already hating him a little for his extraordinary good looks.

"Al told me you came by the apartment last night."

"Al? Alicia?"

"Yes. Alicia Turner, my sister's roommate." He seemed ill at ease. "She gave me your address."

I nodded again. It was his ball, let him run with it.

"I—uh, she said you were asking some . . . funny questions."

"No, I don't think so. They weren't meant to be funny."

His face reddened. "I don't mean . . . humorous. I mean, well, odd questions, then."

"Such as?"

"Alicia got the impression you seemed to think there was something wrong about Charley's accident."

"Why don't we go inside, Mr. Markette?"

He nodded and followed me silently up the walk. Inside, I ushered him into the den. "Have a seat. Could I get you something to drink?"

"No, thank you." He sat down on one end of the couch and I went to the bar and poured scotch into a glass, added a couple of ice cubes for appearance' sake.

"I'm glad you came by." I dropped into the leather recliner across from him. "I was planning on looking you up—not you particularly, but Charlotte's family."

"Then there was something wrong?"

"There's always something wrong with violent death, accidental or not."

He made an impatient gesture, a languid wave of a slender hand, a graceful toss of his head. "You're being evasive, Mr. Roman."

I nodded and tasted the scotch. "Have you known Alicia long, Mr. Markette?" I asked coldly, ignoring his comment, regaining control of the conversation.

"No. I never met her before this morning. Why?"

"You called her Al. That indicates a certain familiarity."

He made the impatient gesture again. "That's what my sister called her. What's your point, Mr. Roman?"

"No point, I was just curious. You didn't visit your sister at the apartment, then?"

He stared at me for a moment, then smiled wryly. "Are you trying to find out if I'm aware that my sister was a whore?"

"Yes, I suppose I was." Not only good-looking, but halfway smart, too.

"No. I never went to my sister's apartment. She preferred it that way."

"Did you see her often?"

"Often enough. Is there some point to this, Mr. Roman?"

"Yes, there is, Mr. Markette."

"If you don't mind, I'd prefer you called me Tom or Thomas. Mr. Markette is my father's name." He paused, his face composed, deadly serious. "I'd just as soon not be reminded of him."

"Okay, Tom, I answer to Dan myself."

"May I remind you that you haven't answered my question."

I smiled faintly. "May I remind you, Tom, that I don't have to answer your question if I don't want to. Remember, you came to see me."

He smiled suddenly, an attractive display of white, even teeth. "You're right, of course. I'm sorry if I seemed arrogant. It runs in the family."

"I will answer your question. But there are some things I need to know from you first. Deal?"

He nodded, the smile losing some of its brilliance, becoming crooked, enigmatic. "My life is an open book, as they say." He leaned back and crossed his legs and looked at me expectantly. "Whenever you're ready." His eyes were dark and expressive, with lashes so long they looked artificial. I had a feeling they created a lot of fluttering in female stomachs.

"You don't seem overly . . . upset by your sister's death."

His gaze was steady. "She's being buried tomorrow. I'll save my grief for then." He watched while I lit a cigarette, then added, "I'm not the ashes-and-sackcloth type. Sorrow is a very private thing with me."

I nodded. "All right, I can accept that. You said you saw your sister often. Did she ever mention any of her special . . . johns?"

"You mean her customers?" The enigmatic smile returned. "Yes, I guess you could say she did."

"Names?"

He shook his head. "No. No names. Everything else, but no personal descriptions or names." He paused. "Other than whether the man was tall, short, fat, thin . . . like that."

It was my turn to hesitate. "Your sister didn't mind you knowing what she did for a living?"

He made a sound that could have been a laugh. "She wasn't doing it for a living. My sister was a millionairess in her own right."

The shock must have shown in my face. His expression didn't change but his eyes seemed suddenly filled with sardonic humor. "Does that surprise you?"

"Yeah, some."

He nodded matter-of-factly. "I know it's hard to understand. Not for me. I understand her motivations, you see. But I can also understand why it would seem incomprehensible to . . . quote, normal people, unquote." The last words were heavy with irony.

I felt a sudden flash of irritation. "I'm not concerned with what your sister did or why she did it. The only thing that concerns me is whether there was someone else in that car with her. Someone driving the damn thing. Someone who left the scene and took something of mine with him. I'm going to find that someone and there's a very good possibility that I'm going to do some very nasty things to him . . . or her."

He bobbed his head, the humor gone out of his face. "Susan Roman," he said.

I crossed the distance between us without conscious thought. I had my hands twisted in his shirt, shaking him, before I became fully aware of what was happening.

"What do you know about her?" His face was only inches away from mine, the dark eyes big and wide, bright with sudden fear, features contorted, frozen.

"Hey!" His hands plucked feebly at mine. "Hey, take it easy! It was in all the papers." He made small defensive motions with his hands. "Take it easy! I don't know anything except what I read."

"How did you connect her with the accident?" I was taking in air in heaving gulps, my body trembling a little as the adrenaline drained away.

"You did, man. They said she disappeared in that area. When you just said . . . they said she was your wife . . ."

I dropped him on the sofa and turned away. The glass was on its side on the carpet, a dark stain a few feet away. I took out my handkerchief and pressed it against the spot. Behind me, he cleared his throat nervously.

"I'm sorry," I said.

"Hey, it's okay, I understand."

"No you don't."

I picked up the glass and poured some more scotch. I returned to my chair and drank half of the drink. He cleared his throat again.

"Are you certain that's what happened?"

"I'm certain."

"Well . . . what about the police? What do they think? There was no mention in the newspapers about a connection. Are they keeping it quiet?"

"The police don't know anything about it. The police don't give a shit."

"I don't understand."

I looked at him with a thin mirthless smile. "I don't either, but I'm going to find out."

We were silent for a while; he crossed his legs again, then

moments later crossed them the other way. He tugged absently at the thin shirt where I had stretched it out of shape.

"Did your sister ever mention anyone named Jay to you? One of her special customers, maybe?"

His head came up quickly. He shook it. "No, I don't think so. She was pretty careful about names."

"Why?"

He shrugged thin shoulders. "I don't know why. There was one she talked about more than the others. But she didn't call him by that name." He hesitated, the crooked smile appearing briefly. "She called him Father."

"Father?"

He nodded, his dark eyes mocking. "She said he reminded her of our father."

I gazed at him curiously. "Isn't that a little odd?"

He crossed his legs again, clasped his hands around his knee, and pursed his lips meditatively. "Yes, I suppose it seems so to you. But not to us, Dan. We're an odd family . . . to say the least."

"That may be so. But comparing a trick to her father seems a trifle more than quaint, even for a prostitute."

He leaned forward and steepled his long fingers, elbows on his knees. He seemed to be making up his mind about something.

He leaned back again and sighed. "She was referring to her customer's ambitions, his drives, avarice, ruthlessness . . ." He hesitated. "But most of all, I think, to his moral degeneracy, his predilection for dirty sex . . . the dirtier the better."

He licked his lips and swung his crossed leg in short, jerky movements. "My father is all those things . . . and more."

I started to tell him it was his sister I was interested in, not his father, but I watched the agitation in his face and remained silent.

"You can't amass millions of dollars without being ambitious, ruthless, greedy. And he certainly did that. He's one of the wealthiest men in Texas."

"What kind of business?"

"Businesses. None now. He's retired. And he's bored and restless. He's been a heavy contributor to the Republican party. Not for nothing, of course. He expects an appointment in Washington for his generosity. He's hinted at a cabinet-level job. What he would like, of course, is secretary of the Treasury. He'd be very good at that. He's a good economist and money is his god." He stopped and his sardonic smile returned. "One of his gods. He has one other and he pursues it with the same vigor he gave to his business."

Our eyes locked. "My father likes his sex dirty . . . and so did my sister. So do I, for that matter."

He waited a moment, his dark eyes searching my face; but when he decided I wasn't going to comment, he went on. "Three worms on the same hook: my father, my sister, and I. But at least Charley and I had the excuse of being indoctrinated into it at a tender age. My father didn't. If you bend the sapling, the tree grows crooked. That's what happened to Charley and me. He bent both of us . . . so much and so long that neither of us ever recovered from it."

I shifted uneasily and cleared my throat. "It isn't necessary that you tell me this."

He smiled his crooked appealing smile. "I told you a while ago that my life was an open book. My father might have been born again, but I have yet to experience that glorious transformation." The smile degenerated into a sneer. "Born again! Pious and humble beside my mother in church on Sunday. The goddamned hypocrite! He was still going to my sister up to the day she died."

"Are you saying . . . what I think you're saying?"

"Exactly. He started in with her when she was eight or nine years old. Me? I was lucky. I was twelve when he brought me into the act. Old enough to know better. But I had the sickness, too. To my sister and me, our father was God. He could do no wrong."

Along with a feeling of embarrassment, I felt a tiny thread

of curiosity, a worm of uneasy fascination working on me, prodding me into egging him on.

"How about your mother? Couldn't she see what was going on?"

"My mother is a cipher, a nonentity. She lived so deeply in his shadow she couldn't see the sun. I'm certain she knew it was happening, but she took refuge in her prayer beads. He was her God, too. Not much less, I think, than the one she spent so much time on her knees to. He was careful, but I still think she knew. I've wondered a lot what kind of sex life they could have had together. It's almost impossible to imagine. I'm quite sure she would never have allowed any of the things he so lovingly and painstakingly taught his son and daughter."

Despite my resolution not to encourage him, I asked the obvious question. "Why didn't you refuse? At some point in time you must have realized what you were doing was . . . unhealthy, to say the least."

He shook his head. "It didn't work that way. My last shrink told me sexual perversion is the greatest narcotic of them all, the most difficult to shake. I can believe it. Besides, as Freud would say, we were hereditarily tainted." He stopped and looked at me soberly. "My sister became a prostitute out of guilt, I think. Or possibly a lack of self-esteem. She didn't do it for the money, certainly. My father is obscenely wealthy. He gave each of us a million dollars on our twenty-first birthday." He stared down at his hands. "Or maybe not. Maybe because she knew she could never find a man who would tolerate the kind of sex she needed. She tried it once. An older man named Jonas Wilkins. It lasted less than six months."

I hacked at phlegm in my throat a couple of times. "I'm not a priest or a doctor. Why tell me all this?"

He shrugged, the brown eyes mocking again. "Maybe because you're a good listener. Besides, my shrink says it's good for me to talk about it. An emotional catharsis, I believe he calls it. I'm sorry if it has upset you."

I shook my head, the flash of irritation returning. "It doesn't upset me. I didn't know your sister and I don't know your father. I don't know you either and, nothing personal, but I'd just as soon keep it that way."

He nodded, his smile steady. "Fair enough. However, I think you may want to meet my father." He rose to his feet and straightened his shirt.

"Why?"

"I can't know for sure, of course, but it's entirely possible he was with my sister the night of the accident."

My chest tightened and something flexed in the pit of my stomach. "Why do you say that?"

He moved his shoulders eloquently, spread his hands. "A guess. I do know he wasn't home. I stopped by to visit Mother, and he hadn't been home when I left at nine o'clock or so. And I do know he had been seeing Charley a lot lately. It's a possibility."

"Why are you telling me? Do you hate him that much?"

He moved toward the door. "I'm not even sure I hate him, Dan. But I loved Charley and if he went off and left her to die or caused it in any way, then I want him to pay for it." He paused, his face tightening. "I would gladly kill him myself."

"Would he . . . is he capable of harming . . . someone else?"

His narrow face sobered completely for the first time. "My father is capable of anything."

"You understand my only interest in the accident is whether it relates to my wife's disappearance. I have no interest in your sister or your father beyond that possibility."

"I understand that," he said lightly. "But to find out you have to know if my father was there or not. That's what I want to know. I'll hire you, if you like."

I shook my head. "Not necessary," I said. "This one is on the house."

Milo got me out of bed at noon; or rather, the telephone got me out of bed and Milo was on the other end of it.

"You sound just like me when I'm hung over."

"Not enough sleep lately."

"Hey, did I wake you up?"

"No problem, Milo. Time I was up and around."

"How's it going? You had any luck?"

"Not enough to brag about."

"That's rough. Like I told you, I been nosing around some. I don't know, might be something, might be nothing, but I got a name for you. A connection with the gal who got burned in that wreck."

"What kind of connection?"

"It's thirdhand, man. My old lady's sister got a friend does day work for a guy lives up there in White Lake Hills. She swears she saw the dead girl up there at his house a couple of times when his wife was out of town. Pure-D accident both times. Both times the man didn't know she was gonna be there. Looked to her like he was doing a little cocking while his woman was out of town."

"What's his name?"

"Just a minute. You got something to write with? Okay. James Joseph Hammond. I ain't got no address. But she says he's some big shit. You ever hear of him?"

"Milo, don't you ever watch TV?"

"Not much. Why?"

"He's been on at least twice a night since about May. He's running for something, attorney general . . . I think."

He laughed. "You ain't watching too close."

"There's something the papers didn't mention about that girl. She was a hooker."

"Do tell? That kinda accounts for her being up on the hill, don't it? Might not mean as much as I thought. I was thinking maybe she was his second woman or something."

"Never can tell. According to her roommate she had a lot of high-class clients. As a matter of fact, she was high class herself if money has anything to do with class, which I've heard rumors it has."

He chuckled. "I might argue with you about that. That asshole Conrad has all the money in the world and class was just something he slept through and flunked out of."

"Have you had any leads on a job?"

"Don't say that word so loud. My woman hear you, she's gonna get ideas in her head. I got her convinced I'm on one of them extended vacations."

"I feel responsible for you being fired."

"No way, I'd about had all the ass kissing I could handle for a while. My days were numbered. Anyhow, I can make more hustling pool than at a regular job. I'd probably do it for a living if the woman would stay off my case. She don't think that's a fittin' job for a growed man wid a collich edjication."

I laughed. "Hang in there, Milo."

"You bet, man. I'll keep my ear to the ground, see if I can come up with something else." He hesitated. "It don't look good, does it?"

"No, it doesn't. Every day . . ." I let it trail off.

"Don't give up."

"I'll never give up, Milo. It's just that I'm running out of options. Until we can come up with her car, there's not much more we can do. Unless something comes out of the missing persons' network . . ." I let it drift, aware that my feelings of futility had crept into my voice.

"I'll be in touch."

"Come see me, Milo."

"I'd invite you down here, man, but you'd never get through the South Dallas Ku Klux Klan."

He was chuckling when he hung up.

/ 13 /

"Thank you for seeing me, Mr. Markette. I apologize again for intruding at a time like this, but my business with you is pressing."

"So I gathered from your telephone conversation, Mr. Roman." John Markette was taller than his son, heavier, fleshed out from too many years of too much good food and sedentary living. Nevertheless, the resemblance was amazing. The hair color was different, the older man's shorter, steel-gray, coiffed in the latest fashion. The facial structure was almost identical right down to a small cleft in the square resolute chin.

"Allow me to apologize in turn for greeting you here at the gate house. As you can imagine, the main house is in something of an uproar, what with relatives and friends dropping by to offer their condolences. My poor wife, I'm afraid, has more than her hands full. People mean well, but I think wakes and postburial condolence gatherings are somewhat barbaric, antiquated practices." His eyes were even darker than his son's and his skin had a smooth, pampered look that spoke of sunlamps and skillful fingers. "I must say the tone of your conversation has aroused my curiosity, to say the least. But first, may I offer you something to drink?"

"No thanks. It's a little early for me." I regretted the small lie almost at once. He walked across the large room, selected a cut-glass decanter, and poured a generous dollop into a glass.

"You don't mind if I have something?" he said.

"No, of course not."

He came back and made himself comfortable on a brown-

and-beige-striped love seat across from me. He sipped the drink, his dark eyes frankly appraising over the rim of the glass, bold, penetrating, with a quality of assurance his son had not possessed.

"Now, Mr. Roman, what can I do for you?" There was a pleasant curve to his lips, glistening slightly from the liquid.

I decided a frontal assault would be the only thing this man would understand, the only approach that would have a chance of piercing the obvious shell of self-control, calm self-assurance.

"Were you with your daughter when she died, Mr. Markette?"

His head cocked slightly to one side and one eyebrow lifted quizzically. That was all.

"I don't think I understand."

"It wasn't a difficult question, sir. Were you in the car with your daughter at the time of the accident?" I could feel frustration building already. Whatever reaction I had expected hadn't occurred. My frontal assault hadn't so much as reached the moat.

The pleasant curve of his lips shifted, became a faint ironic smile. "Do I appear to have been in a fire, Mr. Roman?"

I shook my head doggedly. "You know what I mean. Were you in the car *before* the accident?"

"No, of course not. Why do you ask?"

I ignored his question. "But you were seeing your daughter quite often, were you not?"

"Certainly. As often as I could find the time."

"Isn't that a little odd?"

His look was a masterpiece of incredulity. "I don't find it odd at all, sir. Quite the contrary. She is . . . was my only daughter. And I loved her very much."

It wasn't an easy thing to say, and I found myself wishing I had accepted his offer of a drink. I felt a tiny shiver of apprehension—but I said it anyway.

"Wouldn't it be more appropriate to say you loved her *too* much?"

His eyes flickered, a deep flash of something that surfaced

and disappeared; a nerve twitched at the corner of his mouth. The smile changed without appearing to move, became derisive, taunting. He drank from his glass of scotch. He touched the corners of his mouth delicately with thumb and forefinger and sighed.

"Ordinarily, sir, I would have you thrown off the premises . . . rather forcibly, I might add. But since I happen to know you have been talking to my son, I'll subdue my natural instincts and consider that fact and the exigencies of your present circumstances."

"What about my present circumstances? What the hell do you know about them?" My eyes raked his placid face, searching. But I might as well have been studying a topographical map of Siberia.

"My son told me, of course. Your missing wife is what I am referring to."

"I don't believe you," I said harshly.

He shrugged and finished his scotch. He placed the empty glass on the table at his elbow.

"I'm afraid my son makes a very poor conspirator. He has a tendency toward self-flagellation that makes it difficult for him to be secretive for long. He is also extremely neurotic, as well as totally obsessed with the more fanciful aspects of sex." He fingered the end of his nose. "He also has delusions," he added thoughtfully, and smiled.

"I wasn't referring to your son's sexual hang-ups. He believes you were with your daughter at the time of her death."

His expression was more curious than angry. "You are a detective, Mr. Roman. Where is your supporting evidence?"

"I don't have any. Not yet. But now that I know where to look, I'll find it. You can believe that."

He shook his head. "You're wasting your time. There's nothing to find. If pressed, I can prove my whereabouts on that tragic evening, but I have no intention of explaining myself to you." There was no rancor in his voice, but there was an air of finality.

"You couldn't explain yourself to me if you tried," I said savagely. "Incest and child molesting—how do you explain that to a normal human being?"

His lips thinned, tiny white lines at each corner of his mouth; his golden tan had become faintly mottled, a red spot appeared high on each cheekbone.

"I thought I explained to you about my son."

"Okay, talk to me about your daughter. Tell me why she became a whore. Tell me why you, a pious, upstanding member of the community, would accept that, would visit her all the time knowing she was a prostitute by choice and not by necessity. Tell me about that, Mr. Markette."

He shook his head slowly, his face the color and texture of Indian clay. "You can't live their lives for them," he whispered. "You can only teach them."

"Yeah," I jeered, re-coiling the loop for another throw. "I heard what you taught them. In living detail. Your son may be neurotic as hell, but he paints a graphic picture."

"Stop it!" He was on the edge of the seat, hands fisted on his knees, his face ashen, eyes imploring. "You are deliberately misconstruing . . . you can't understand . . . what I did, I did out of love. . . ."

I threw back my head and laughed. "You bet. I do it out of love all the time."

He lowered his head and wagged it wearily. "Children . . . They must be taught—they must know what the world is like. I only did what I thought was . . . right."

Somewhere deep inside me something quivered and anger splashed in my brain like an acid rain, obliterating caution, congealing reason.

"You sanctimonious—" I broke it off and slipped the .38 from under my arm. I reached across and held it a foot from his bowed head, thumbing back the hammer when he didn't move, the sound sharp and clear and ominous in the silence.

"Look at me," I said softly. "Look at my face."

He raised his head slowly, looked into the bore of the gun,

and seemed to shrink within himself, the handsome face ragged with unreasonable fear.

"Where is she?" I breathed. "Tell me now . . . or you're a dead man."

"I—I don't know." The words were barely audible. "I swear to God, I don't know!"

"Were you there? At the accident? I'll check you out, bastard, and if you lie . . . so help me, I'll kill you."

"No! No . . . I was with . . . a . . . woman. I can prove . . . if I must." His lips were slack, trembling, his cheeks ballooning oddly, as if he were whistling.

"You must, shitbag! Who is she?"

He had to wet his lips before he could talk. "Al . . . Alicia, Charlotte's . . . roommate."

I stared at him, shock tightening the muscles in my face, not wanting to believe him, but believing suddenly, realizing how it would have been . . . the two of them together. She was, after all, a whore.

"You and Alicia?" More difficult to say than to believe.

I thought I was going to have to prod him with the gun, but finally he looked away and nodded.

I put the gun away and stood over him. His elbows rested on his knees, his face cupped in his hands. The carefully styled hair had somehow become mussed, and I noticed a button missing from the vest of his three-piece worsted suit.

I had regained my equilibrium, or most of it, but the sight of him still filled me with a hot pulsing contempt.

"You're sick, Markette. Whether you realize it or not. And I think you do. How did you feel after the sex? With all your money, all the power that goes with it, I wouldn't trade places with you for one minute . . . not even a second. The greatest pity is you can't be punished for it . . . except maybe by yourself."

I stared at the top of his bowed head while I lit a cigarette. I threw the empty pack on the table. I reached out with my foot and touched his calf with the toe of my boot.

"How about it, Markette, you want to borrow my gun?"

Then, half sick with disgust and frustration, I walked out and left him there. My head was throbbing, my insides thrumming gently, a dark pall closing over my mind like a warm heavy liquid. Signals. Old familiar harbingers of violence were the only things left here, and I wasn't ready for that. Not yet.

/ 14 /

She responded finally to the pounding on her door, had to open it to see who it was because I held my thumb over the peephole. She was disheveled, the robe held together in front by a freckled fist. Her eyes were sleep-swollen, her hair wound into a bun on the back of her head. I brushed past her.

"Come in," she said from behind me.

"You lied to me about Charley's father," I said grimly.

She yawned. "No, I didn't. I just didn't tell you about him. Why should I? What possible difference does it make?"

I walked to the open bedroom doorway, stood looking at the rumpled bed, still warm no doubt from the heat of her body.

"Is this where you did it . . . the three of you?"

She looked at me curiously, the freckles like splashes of brown paint on glass. "What's your problem?" Her small mouth curved mockingly. "You never heard of two women and one man before?"

"Not often," I said tightly, a small hot hand squeezing my throat. "Not when two of them are father and daughter."

"Oh, that." She wrinkled her face in a jeering grimace. "So what's new? My old man started in on me when I was ten."

"Was he here the night she was killed?" I interrupted harshly.

Her eyebrows lifted and the beginnings of a smile tilted the corners of her mouth. "Yes. He stayed almost all night. For an old man, he can be a real bull when he wants to be." The curve to her lips built into a sardonic grin. "He was very inventive, and he could keep it up longer than anyone I ever saw. He'd cover it with whipped cream and then—"

"Cut it out."

She paused in the act of shaking loose a cigarette from a pack. I could feel her eyes as I walked over and held my lighter. She watched me through the flame and smoke, steadied my hand with both of hers. I pulled quickly away.

"He let me eat it," she said, blowing a puff of smoke that broke across my chin.

"Dammit, I told you—!"

"Dammit, don't tell me!" she flared, her eyes sparking fire. "Nobody tells me! That's why I'm a whore. No damned man to tell me what to do. Not ever! You have to understand that, Dan Roman." She stopped, her expression softening, oddly serene, submissive. "Before we do what you came here to do," she added quietly.

"Do! Do? What the hell are you talking about?" I was shouting by the time I reached the second word. "I came here to—"

She stopped my mouth with her hand, the one holding the robe, and nothing short of instant blindness could have kept my eyes from what was revealed by the parting cloth. Without appearing to move, she came closer, her bare front inches away.

"You came here to make love to me," she breathed. "It was in your face the other night, but it was too soon. You had to get used to the idea of wanting me. Not just lusting for me, but wanting me. That's the difference between making out and making love."

"You're not even pretty," I said harshly, barely aware that I was speaking.

She swayed again, pressed against me, her arms going around

my neck. She closed her eyes and smiled. "I know," she murmured.

"And you're a whore," I said roughly, knowing it wasn't going to work, feeling her hand slide down my side, across to touch me with the tentative delicacy of a virgin bride.

"Yes," she breathed against my mouth. "I'm your whore. I also knew that the other night." Her lips brushed mine, lingered, pressed lightly, then moved away across my cheek to my neck. "If you want me." Her hand moved expertly and I felt a cool wash of air across my chest. She pressed her bare abdomen against me. "Don't you want me?" It was a plaintive, supplicating whimper that fired my blood, sent desire racing through me like a small hot wind.

"No," I said faintly, an ignoble lie that both of us ignored.

/ 15 /

She watched me dress with sleepy heavy-lidded eyes. "Do you have to go so soon? You could stay and have a cup of coffee and talk and then I wouldn't feel like you just dropped in for a quick piece." She flipped over on her back, arms and legs widespread, an incredibly open, vulnerable position. I suddenly felt old and weary, more than a little vulnerable myself.

"I'd like to stay, but I've got to have a chat with Mr. James Joseph Hammond."

"Who's Hammond?" she asked disinterestedly, still undecided whether to pout.

"One of Charley's better-class clients, or so I have reason to believe."

"How do you know?"

I slipped on my boots. "Someone told me."

She sat upright in the center of the bed. "Hah! I'll tell you if he is or not." She rolled off the bed and swept past me into the living room. She rummaged in the center drawer of a white writing desk shoved into a corner. She clicked her tongue against her teeth in exasperation, then made a tiny sound of triumph and held up a small white leatherbound book. She tossed it at me. "That's what Charley called her hit list." She smiled. "I didn't give it to her brother when he came by for her things. I didn't think he'd be interested."

It was small, no larger than a pack of cigarettes, half as thick. I leafed through it slowly, feeling a faint ripple of shock as I recognized some of the names.

"Look under the H's," Alicia advised. "There's only twenty in there. Twenty active ones, that is. The ones with the X's are inactive for one reason or another. Some of them are dead." She fished my cigarettes out of my shirt pocket and shook one free. "Can you imagine? Only twenty johns."

"Light me one, too." I sat down on the couch and worked my way through the entire book. A lot of the pages were empty; thirty-five had names and fifteen of those were criss-crossed with a huge X. A few had addresses listed, complete to the zip code. Some had names and telephone numbers, and the balance names only. Five I recognized. Two senators, a congressman, a state senator, and a Fort Worth city council-man. James Hammond was in there also. Several others were vaguely familiar, but I couldn't pin them down except for a faint impression of political affiliation.

I closed the book and removed the cigarette from the corner of my mouth. "She seemed to like politicians."

She nodded and idly scratched one breast with a fingernail, completely unself-conscious in her nudity. "I think her father was a big shot politician at one time, the way she talked."

"Did you know how wealthy she was?"

"Yes. She told me . . . or more like let it slip one time when we were talking."

"Did you ever wonder why she lived like this with all that money?"

She gave me a wintry smile. "You mean slumming?"

"No. I didn't mean that at all. I mean here in this small apartment . . . with men coming in and . . . all."

"You make it sound like a South Dallas whorehouse," she said stiffly. "They have to have an appointment, you know."

I studied her taut face, the tiny white lines around her small mouth. "I think you're deliberately misconstruing everything I'm saying. You know very well what I mean."

She returned my gaze for a moment, then her face relaxed. She smiled wanly. "I guess I am, Danny. You make me kind of . . . touchy about it." She turned her gaze down along her body, seemed to become aware of her nakedness for the first time. A spot of pink appeared high on each cheekbone. She sat down abruptly.

"I know why she lived here," she said quietly. "She liked to talk about it . . . you know, the things she did with men. Some of them . . . well, I certainly wouldn't do a lot of the things she did."

"Such as?"

She shook her head, the color deepening. "Just nasty things. Things that made me feel funny . . . dirty. Animal things, a lot of them."

"Then why did you listen?"

She shrugged. "I liked her. She had some weird hang-ups, sure, but who am I to judge?"

"But you won't tell me what they were?"

She looked at me curiously. "I didn't think you'd like that really dirty stuff."

"I don't particularly. But everything I can find out about her helps."

Her lips tightened. "Well, I'm not going to tell you," she said, with an air of finality. Then she smiled to soften the refusal, a teasing light in her eyes. "It might give you some naughty ideas."

I stood up. "Okay. Subject closed."

She was on her feet in a flash, moving in on me, small freckled hands reaching. "Are you sure you can't stay?" She lowered her voice to a husky meaningful whisper.

"Stop it," I said sharply. "You're forgetting something. I have a wife. A woman I love."

"But . . . you may not . . . find her."

"I'll find her," I said harshly, suddenly cold all over. "I have to believe that." I stared down into her dark eyes. "Do you understand that?"

"Yes," she said simply. "I understand, Danny."

"Give me the ones without addresses or phone numbers," Homer said, snuffling into a damp handkerchief, blowing his nose with a thick, gurgling sound. "I think we can eliminate the senators and the congressmen."

"Why? They're men, too, Homer. I'm not eliminating anybody, at least not yet."

He gave me a derisive glance. "What are you going to do? Walk up and ask them when was the last time they shacked up with a whore named Charley?"

"Something like that. I never knew you to back away from power in the old days, Homer."

"Nor now," he grunted. "Not if I had reason to suspect them of a crime. It ain't that much of a crime to buy a piece of tail. Not if you don't get caught at it, it ain't."

"They're no different than the rest of the men on the list. In fact, they have more to lose than most."

"You do it, then," he said, annoyance showing in his voice and in the look he gave me. "You can be a stubborn jackass sometimes. You know that?"

"I had a good teacher."

He snorted. He finished writing down the names and handed me the little book. "I never found out a damn thing from her neighbors. Most of them never even remembered seeing her.

How about you? I saw your car in the lot the other night but I didn't see you."

"Not a thing," I said, ducking my head to light a cigarette, remembering with a mild shock that we had divided up the surrounding apartments for canvassing. I didn't have the guts to tell him I had never gotten any farther than Alicia, and felt a flash of resentment at a sudden absurd impulse to justify myself.

"Well, never expected much out of that," he said. "People nowadays don't even know their next-door neighbors."

"That's the damn truth," I said heartily. "Well, we've got something to work on now."

He raised his head and watched me steadily for a moment, his eyes glinting behind the spectacles. I had a sinking realization that he knew, that in his own peculiar fashion he was dredging up all sorts of sorry rationalizations to explain my behavior in a way he could accept and still remain my friend. I sometimes had the feeling that each year he lost a little more faith in me, found the specious reasoning a little harder to formulate, the contradictions and inconsistencies in my life a little harder to swallow.

But all he said was "Okay, let's get at it."

James Hammond was a tall, slender man in his middle forties. Meticulously groomed, he had a hearty handshake and a ready smile that didn't go with the thin-lipped, predatory face. His large curving nose and dark piercing eyes would have looked at home on the face of an Arab sheik. His hair was a tight mass of brown curls, his skin flawlessly tanned. There was an air of elegance about him that society editors would have probably called good breeding; I would have called it the cultivated awareness of a ruthless man who knew what he wanted from life and had made all the hard decisions a long time ago.

He faced me across the desk in the small office at the rear of his campaign headquarters, thin manicured fingers clasped loosely in front of him. He pursed his lips and stared at me thoughtfully. Finally, he leaned back in the swivel chair and raised one hand in a gesture of capitulation, his eyes like splintered chips of brown stone.

"Very well, Mr. Roman. I won't deny that I knew Charlotte Wilkins. I won't deny that I saw her on occasion." He paused. "I could, you know. We were very discreet. With her dead there's no possible way you could prove otherwise." He smiled faintly. "I'd give a lot to know how you came by the information."

"It doesn't matter how. And I couldn't care less how many times you saw her or for what purpose. All I want to know, Mr. Hammond, is were you in the car with her when she had the accident?"

"No, of course not," he said sharply, his eyes holding mine steadily, unwavering.

"Where were you at that time . . . and can you prove it?"

His eyebrows lifted and his lips curved on the verge of a smile. "You're rather direct, aren't you?"

"I don't have time to pussyfoot around, Mr. Hammond. Would you like to answer my question?"

"She died on a Monday, I believe. What time of day?"

"Seven in the evening. Around there."

He leaned forward and smiled again, a relieved smile. "There's no problem, then. I can prove beyond a doubt that I was here . . . in this office. Each Monday evening we have a staff meeting. Six o'clock to usually around eight or eight-thirty. My business manager, my campaign manager, my finance officer, and myself."

"I'll check with them if you don't mind."

"Not at all. In fact, Ted Blum, I believe, is outside now. Shall I call him?"

"Is he in your employ?"

He shook his head. "He's my finance manager for the campaign. Strictly volunteer. I must say he is a friend of mine, though."

111

"Call him in, please."

He got up and walked to the door, paused. "I'd appreciate it if you didn't mention the girl."

"I won't. All I want is to confirm your statement. You can handle the questions as long as that's clear."

He nodded and opened the door. "Marty, would you ask Ted to step in here a moment?"

He left the door open and went back to his chair. He slid a pad across the desk and picked up a pen. "I'll give you the names and phone numbers of the other two."

He wrote rapidly, then ripped off the sheet and handed it to me as a short, stocky man came in the door. He was perfectly bald and had a round, harried face; his stubby hands were dirty and there were black smudges on the front of his white shirt. He nodded at me and looked inquiringly at Hammond.

"You want me, Jim?"

"Yes. You remember last week's staff meeting? It was on Monday as usual, wasn't it?"

"Yeah, why?"

He ignored the question. "Let's see, besides you and me and George, who else was there?"

The short man raised thick eyebrows. "Bob Murphy. He's always . . ."

Hammond grimaced. "Of course." He chuckled ruefully. "I guess I need a break. I'm getting fuzzy around the edges."

The short man looked at me triumphantly. "That's what I been trying to tell him. He goes like a house afire all the time." He grinned. "When he wins he's gonna have to take a vacation before he can start working."

"Thanks, Ted. How are the directs coming along?"

"On the button. Be in the last mail pickup tonight. That all you wanted?"

"Yes, thank you."

The bald man nodded at me and scampered out the door.

"Good man," Hammond commented. "Well, Mr. Roman, are you satisfied?"

112

"I will be. After I check with the others."

He flashed his politician's smile and rose to his feet. "Fair enough. Be disappointed if you didn't. I appreciate thoroughness in a man." He came around the desk and extended his hand. A good solid grip, not enough to be ostentatious, but enough to give an impression of strength and determination. "Attorney general's office can always use competent investigators. If you're interested, drop around and see me after the election."

"Confidence," I said dryly. "I appreciate that in a man."

He laughed. "Touché. I think perhaps you and I might get along, Mr. Roman."

"Wouldn't be surprised," I said.

Vernon Canby turned out to be a doctor: a gynecologist. I cooled my heels in his crowded reception room for an hour before I got tired of the whispers and giggles and borrowed a piece of paper and an envelope from his receptionist. I wrote "Charlotte Wilkins" on the paper and sealed the envelope and asked her to see that he got it at once. That bought me a haughty glare and more titters, but it got me into the inner sanctum within the next five minutes.

Another short, bustling man, balding, rough skin with old pockmarks. He had a short pug nose, upturned like the muzzle of a bulldog. An ugly man. Maybe his job was the only way he could get close to a woman.

He ignored my hand, glared at the piece of paper in his own. "What's this? Who's Charlotte Wilkins? I'm a very busy man. I have no time for foolishness. Who are you?"

"My name is Dan Roman. You know who Charlotte Wilkins is. Otherwise I wouldn't be in here. Let's not shit each other, Doctor, shall we?"

"I don't like vulgarity in my office, sir. I don't think I like you. I think perhaps you had better—"

"I don't give a damn what you like. I only want to know one thing from you. Where were you when Charlotte Wilkins died in her car?"

"I was here!" he shouted. "Here in my—" He broke off, red flooding his face, his eyes beginning to glaze. "I was right here," he went on weakly. "I—I can prove that."

"You're going to have to."

He licked his thick lips. "Are you a policeman?"

"Does that worry you?"

"No! No, I have nothing to hide."

"Good. Are you a married man, Doctor?"

"Why?" It was an agonized gasp.

I shrugged. "No reason. I was wondering why a married man went to a prostitute."

He stared at me as if I had just got off the boat. "Why . . . why everyone does."

"Not everyone," I said, wondering if he could be right. "What were you doing in your office at seven o'clock at night?"

He blinked up at me. "Always," he said excitedly, "we always work late on Monday. I take Wednesdays off. We work until eight on Mondays to make up."

"I'll check that with your receptionist. I suppose you have an appointment book."

"Of course, of course! You think we don't keep records? Look, I can show you." He took off for the door.

I stopped him. "Never mind. I'll check on the way out."

He fidgeted nervously. "You won't say anything . . . about the woman." He gave me an ingratiating smile. There was a faint glint of perspiration on his forehead despite the artificially cooled air.

"I'm not out to make trouble for you, Doctor. All I'm trying to do is find Susan." I watched his face closely, found nothing there but perplexity mixed with a kind of docile anxiety.

"I don't understand," he said hesitantly. "Susan?"

"Never mind, Dr. Canby. I apologize for taking up your time." I turned toward the door.

"Not a bit," he said effusively. "Not at all. Glad to be of help."

I paused with my hand on the knob. "By the way, where did you go for your little sessions with Charley?"

His face paled; he licked his lips, then smiled uncertainly, man-to-man. "Here," he whispered. "I have a . . . an examining table in the other room."

I gazed at him thoughtfully, the image of the pudgy little man groaning between the stirrups bringing a grin to my face. "Yeah, I'll bet that's real handy."

/ 16 /

Solemn campaign promises to the contrary, elected officials rarely maintain the sort of open-door policy we grubby little constituents would like, and inveterate cynic that I am, I had few illusions about my chances of being put through to Senator Blakely if I gave my real reason for calling.

So I lied. I became Sylvester P. Wilberforce, only grandson of "the Wilberforces," genteel Houston aristocracy of old Texas, oil, cattle, and silver speculation second only to the Hunt boys in scope and dimension. Five minutes of bluster sprinkled with "bleeding-heart liberals" and "jackass Democrats," and a not-too-subtle hint at a forthcoming campaign donation of substantial proportion worked wonders with the stony heart of his frigid-voiced secretary.

"Just one moment, Mr. Wilberforce," she interjected smoothly when I paused to gather in breath. "I'll see if the senator is out of his meeting."

I lit a cigarette and gave myself two-to-one odds that he would be, grinning a little as her lilting voice came back almost immediately.

"Thank you for waiting, sir. The senator is on the line."

"Yes, Mr. Wilberforce, what can I do for you?" Senator John Rupert Blakely's jovial voice was familiar, and I could picture in my mind's eye the craggy, handsome face with the square jaw and heavy, overhanging eyebrows.

"First of all, Senator, I'd like to apologize for deceiving your secretary."

There was a momentary silence, the sound of asthmatic breathing, then his voice, not quite so jovial.

"I don't understand. She mentioned something about a contribution . . ." His voice trailed off suggestively.

"There's no contribution, Senator. My name is Dan Roman. I tried to get through to you before without success. I thought money might be the open sesame. It seems I was right."

"What is your business, Mr. Roman? If this is some kind of joke, I don't think it's funny." All traces of humor were gone; his voice was brusque, annoyed, on the edge of anger.

"No joke, Senator. I'm calling about the recent death of a lady named Charley."

There was another silence: longer this time. Then the sound of expelled breath.

"What does that have to do with me?"

"That's what I'm asking you, Senator."

"Are you a police officer?"

"No. Should I be?"

"Don't be impertinent."

"I beg your pardon, sir. I didn't realize I was. Would you mind telling me where you were when the lady died?"

"What right have you to ask me anything? I think this whole affair is ridiculous. I'm going to terminate this conversation at once."

"All right, suit yourself."

"Why are you calling me about this . . . this Charley person?"

"Do you really want me to say over the phone, Senator?"

"I was at a fund-raising dinner in Dallas. I was the principal speaker."

116

"What time was that, sir?"

"What do you mean what time was it? It was that evening, that's what time it was."

"What time of evening?"

"I spoke at eight-thirty."

"What time did you get to the dinner, sir?"

"Oh, I don't know. An hour before . . . perhaps forty-five minutes. I didn't keep a precise timetable, you know."

"Who accompanied you to the dinner?"

"I want to know by what authority you are asking all these questions."

"My own."

"Well, that's not good enough. I don't even know who you are."

"Dan Roman, sir. I'm a private investigator. I'm looking into the circumstances of her death."

"Circumstances? She burned to death in an automobile accident. It was in the papers. What circumstances?"

"There were some discrepancies. . . ."

"Dammit, why call me?"

"I think you know, Senator."

"But it has absolutely nothing to do with me."

"That's what I'm trying to determine, sir. If you wouldn't mind telling me who accompanied you to the fund-raising dinner. That could clear the whole matter up as far as you're concerned."

"I—I drove in from my ranch. I was alone."

"What time did you leave the ranch?"

"Dammit, I don't know for sure . . . maybe five or five-thirty."

"Where is your ranch, Senator?"

"Corsicana. East of Corsicana a few miles."

"About an hour's drive, would you say?"

"At fifty-five? No. More than that. Anyhow, I'm not exactly sure when I left."

"Where was the dinner held?"

"At the Hyatt—now look here, I think this has gone far enough. I absolutely refuse to answer any more questions."

"Did you go straight to the hotel, Senator?"

"No, not straight. I stopped and had a couple of drinks."

"Where?"

"I don't remember. Some bar."

"Was the bar in Fort Worth?"

"Fort Worth? What the hell would I be doing in Fort Worth?" His voice was becoming strained, rasping.

"That's what I'm asking you, Senator."

"This time I mean it. I'm not answering another damn question. And I want to warn you. If you start spreading any rumors, anything, this close to the election . . ."

"Senator, I'm not interested in the election. I couldn't care less. But sooner or later, sir, you're going to have to answer these questions truthfully. Either to me or someone else. With me, there are no reporters nosing around."

"How do I know who the hell I'm talking to? You may be some damn Democrat for all I know."

"As a matter of fact I am, Senator. When I work at it. But you have my word that what you say won't go any further—if your answers are the right ones and truthful."

The silence was even longer this time, the breathing heavier. I could hear him when he swallowed.

"All right," he said finally. "I'm putting my future in your hands." He stopped and I heard the rasp of a lighter. He coughed. "I stopped off to see . . . a friend."

"What friend, sir?"

"I can't tell you that. I won't tell you that. It would be political suicide. You'll just have to accept my word. It was a lady friend."

"Not the lady in question?"

"No! Absolutely not."

"All right, Senator. We'll let it ride for now. There may come a time in the very near future when you'll have to tell me who. It may become unavoidable. It may very well be that you already know why it will become unavoidable. If that's the case, you can save yourself and everyone concerned a lot of grief by letting her go. If she hasn't been harmed . . . well, I'll have to make that decision when I get to it."

"Let who go, dammit? What in the name of God are you talking about?"

"I'll be in touch, Senator. Have a nice day."

"Hey! Wait! What . . .?"

I hung up before he finished.

I checked out one more name before calling it a day. Norman T. Stocker, architect, was in the hospital with a broken back. A six-foot fall across a stack of building blocks and he faced the prospect of six months to a year in traction. He had been in there for three weeks. I crossed him off the list.

I chased a bologna-and-cheese sandwich with a beer and drove over to the Midway police station. Homer was in a meeting with a group of his homicide detectives and I sat on the corner of Mitzi's desk and watched her cleaning up in anticipation of the six o'clock bell.

"When I was a cop," I said fatuously, "we didn't come and go to no startin' and stoppin' bells. We stayed till the job was done . . . and then some."

She giggled. "I was here, remember? Things have changed, Danny. We're organized and mechanized now. Everything by the numbers. May as well be working in a five-and-dime store. It's not nearly as exciting as it used to be. I very rarely get to see the bad guys now. They bring them in downstairs, book them, and have them in a cell before we know what's going on up here."

"How do you like this new building? Pretty fancy."

She made a face. "I don't like it. We may have been too crowded over there, but at least you felt like a part of something. Here, everything is too . . . too antiseptic, and we're isolated from everybody."

"Progress, Mitzi, you can't fight it. How's papa bear been treating you lately?"

She grimaced again. "Like he's got a thorn in his paw. He's working too hard, as usual." She gave me a worried glance. "You haven't found out anything about Susie?"

I shook my head. "Not a trace, so far. That's one of the reasons he's been putting in so many hours."

The buzzer sounded and she closed her desk drawers and locked them. She picked up her purse. "They should be through in there by now." She poked idly at her hair. "I'd stay and keep you company, Danny, but I've got an appointment at the beauty salon." She gave me a doleful smile. "Lord knows I need it."

"I'll be fine, Mitzi. Take care."

"Come and see us, Danny." She wiggled her fingers at me and marched sturdily toward the entrance doors; small, compact, and even at fifty-odd years of age she still managed to maintain an air of innocence in a world filled with cynicism and distrust.

The meeting broke up a few minutes later. The men filed out solemnly. I nodded at several familiar faces and chatted for a second or two with one I knew well.

"Still giving his pep talks, Red?"

Red Dawson crimped his mouth in a sour smile. "More like a reaming, Dan. How you been?" He was a tall, dour man, fast approaching retirement age.

"Fair to middling. How about you?"

He grimaced. "Had to downshift a few years ago. Getting too old to run in high all the time."

I laughed. "Ain't we all?"

Homer was hunched over his desk reading. He grunted to acknowledge my presence and I sat down and lit a cigarette and waited for him to finish.

After a minute, he closed the folder and leaned back. He took off his glasses and massaged his eyes. "Need to get another examination. Everything's a little blurred."

"You've been saying that for a year."

"Yeah. Guess I'll get it done when I can't read anymore." He wiped the lenses and replaced the glasses on his eyes. "Any luck?"

"Depends on how you look at it. I've eliminated two on the list and another probable. I've come up with one good possibility, I think." I hesitated. "It's one of your senators."

He looked back at me stolidly. "Who?"

"John Rupert Blakely."

"What makes you think so?"

I shrugged. "He can't . . . or won't . . . account for his time. Plus I've got a gut feeling about him. He just doesn't sound right."

"Gut feeling, huh?" He grinned.

"Well, he seems like a likely candidate. He's worried as hell about being connected with the Wilkins woman, yet he up and tells me he was seeing another woman that night. Then he comes on with some sincere shit about putting his career in my hands. I always thought he looked shifty-eyed."

Homer shook his head. "He'll be a hard nut to crack, buddy. How about the probable?"

"James Hammond. He more or less verified where he was that evening, but I still have some more checking to do. How about you? You had time to do anything?"

"I've eliminated four for one reason or another. I've got one who looks a little ripe. Feller named Jerry Canelli. Says he was home with his wife. I haven't verified it yet." He paused. "I've been dreading it as a matter of fact."

"Why?"

"I know her. Used to be a clerk over in records. Nice little girl. But she ain't dumb, and how am I going to ask her about her husband without some kind of story?"

"Want me to do it?"

"Naw," he said glumly. "I'll think of something. I probably wouldn't bother except he's got a record over in Dallas. Two drug busts when he was younger. One charge of soliciting for prostitution."

"Sounds like a small-time hustler. He doesn't fit the pattern. According to Alicia, the big twenty were all supposed to be high-class citizens. Although I'd be inclined to argue about that."

His eyes gleamed at me. "Who's Alicia?"

"She's . . . Charley's roommate. I thought you knew that." I could feel heat rising in my cheeks. I wondered if it showed.

"Oh, yeah, the other hooker." His voice was bland, his expression innocuous, but I had known him too many years to be fooled.

"All right, Homer. Something's on your mind."

"Sure. Susie's on my mind. That's all."

"What do you mean by that? You think she's not on mine every damn minute?"

He leaned back and crossed his legs. "Well, boy, now that you brought it up, no, I don't." He smiled thinly. "Not every minute."

"You saying I've been slacking up, not looking for her as hard as I might?"

"No, I ain't saying that at all. I know you've been doing everything possible to find her. But that don't mean you ain't been dipping your wick either."

"Are you talking about Alicia?" I asked coldly.

"Yep, that's who I'm talking about, all right." There was a touch of meanness in his voice. He was a moral man in an immoral age.

"Don't push it, Homer," I warned. "That's none of your damned business."

"Maybe I'll just call some buddies of mine over in Cowtown and have her ass busted."

"Don't do it, man," I said, feeling a little sick. He was just ornery enough to do it. "We've been friends a long time. Don't jack around with that." I took a deep breath. "I'm serious."

Sixty long seconds crawled by while he looked at me. Finally he shook his shaggy head. "I believe you mean it," he said wonderingly. "A hooker! Boy, she's a damn hooker! You could be screwing up your life for a whore." He made a sound of disgust. "I knew you had the scruples of a buck rabbit, but I never doubted your smarts before. What about Susie? What are you going to do when you get her back? You gonna keep your little blond hustler on the side? Boy, I oughta whip your dumb ass. Dammit, don't you know . . ."

He was building a rare head of steam. I knew from experience that his control was about to go. I knew that if I didn't get out of there, everything between us was also going to go.

I got up and walked out without a word.

They were waiting for me when I got home; one came from the thick round Italian cypress at the corner of my house and the other from behind the hedges across the front. My head was down, searching through my keys. I must have heard something, maybe the rustle of their feet on the grass, or a dry twig snapping, but suddenly I was aware of them, and my hand was streaking inside my denim jacket for the gun, coming up empty. I cursed as I remembered exchanging it for the flat .32 nestled in my belt at the pit of my back.

There was no time for another try. They were on me: one with a knife, the blade gleaming brightly in the light of Hector's gaslight. The other one had a gun.

I was cut off from the house. I backed warily across the grass, brought up against Hector's pickup in his driveway. I risked a quick glance toward his house. The windows were dark and silent. I was on the verge of trying a yell anyway when the big one with the gun stepped in close and hit me in the stomach with his left fist.

It should have ended right there; I was doubled over, interested in nothing except the fire in my stomach, my chin at waist level, a perfect position for a solid roundhouse right to the jaw. But the big one took time out to turn and snarl at the other one.

"Put that goddamned knife away! We ain't supposed to kill him, you asshole! Put him away for a couple of weeks . . . now, do it."

The other one, younger, shorter, broader, shrugged and slipped the knife into his pocket. He took a step forward and swung his right foot backwards.

I raised up and kicked him in the face. I felt something tear under my boot heel, and then I wasn't feeling much of anything except a searing, leaping pain in the side of my head. Something jerked my head back and a hard bony fist began to pound. The big one was holding my hair in his left hand and smashing me with his right, a steady, measured beat, almost monotonous after it stopped hurting and the black cloud began to descend.

Finally he must have realized the only thing keeping me up was his grip, and he released me. I went down like a sack of dirt. I felt the rough concrete against my cheek and whimpered a little as I tried to raise my head and bumped my ear on Hector's pickup.

The young one was on his knees a few feet away, cursing, holding a handkerchief against his nose.

"The son of a bitch ripped it off!" His voice sounded syrupy and far away.

"Naw, it's all right. Just looks bad with all the blood. It'll stop in a minute."

"I'm going to gut the dirty bastard!"

I began inching sideways under the pickup.

"No, you ain't," the big one said. "We got our orders. Break him up some if you want, but I ain't facing no murder rap for what we're getting. Come on, let's bust him up and get the hell out of here."

I was halfway under the truck, fervently blessing Hector for leaving it there and Detroit for making it higher than a car. I rolled over on my back and found a handhold, jerked myself sideways. Something jabbed me in the small of my back, jolting my memory of the gun. I was trying to force a hand between me and the concrete when I heard them again.

"Hey, the son of a bitch crawled under the pickup!"

"Go around on the other side. Force him over this way. Use your knife if you have to, but we've got to get him out of there quick!"

My fingers were on the butt of the little gun, but it was pinned to the concrete by my hips and I couldn't raise my body any higher: the transmission was in the way.

I kicked out frantically with my right foot, caught against something solid and shoved. I slid backwards a few inches, slammed my stomach upward again, touched the smooth handle of the automatic with my fingertips just as the young one stretched out his arm and sliced at me.

I felt a stinging pain in my left biceps and an almost instant wetness along my arm. The man grunted and did it again, stabbing this time, pushing the blade into the muscle. I felt the point grind against bone. I screamed and dragged the gun from beneath me, then shoved it across my body as far as I could reach.

He saw it a fraction of a second before I pulled the trigger; he had time to grunt again, widen his eyes, maybe time to know he was going to die.

The hollow-point bullet hit him above the bridge of his nose. There was a splash of blood and a frantic scrambling movement, but no further sound. Or maybe the vacuum of concussion had deafened me. I could hear enough to detect the sound of a car motor out on the street as the big man sped away, leaving his partner dead or dying, his legs jerking spasmodically, blood coming from between his eyes.

I reached for the edge of the truck with my one good arm, painfully dragged myself from under the truck. I climbed shakily to my feet and promptly fell flat on my face, so I rolled over onto my back and raised the automatic. I fired three times, a heartbeat between the shots. It was a distress signal Hector Johnson had half-seriously suggested a long time ago.

I fought off the darkness until I saw his porch light come on, heard the slap of his houseshoes on the concrete walk. Then I gratefully lowered my head to his neatly manicured lawn and faded to black.

/17/

"Well, you done it again, boy." Homer's broad face swam in and out of my darkness, highlighted by pinwheeling flashes of light.

I sat on the edge of the emergency room table grimly determined not to faint. My left arm was bulky with bandages and my face was beginning to hurt. The effects of the shot the paramedic had given me were beginning to wear off, and the young doctor was standing at the medicine cabinet preparing another.

"What the hell would you have done? Turned the other arm?"

"I'd have shot his head off just like you done. But I'm a cop and you're not. I can get away with it and you can't." He sniffed and reached for his handkerchief.

"You going to arrest me, Homer?"

"You're already under arrest, boy. I just hadn't told you yet."

"Well, you damn well better put the cuffs on me, then, because I'm gonna get the hell up and walk out of here . . . in just a minute."

He snorted. "You couldn't crawl out of here, much less walk."

The doctor appeared beside me with the hypodermic. "Don't you think you should lie down?"

"I'm not afraid of a needle." I winced at the tiny stinging puncture.

"Can you focus your eyes?" He fished a light out of his pocket and put me through a drill of eye movements. "We didn't find any evidence of concussion, but the side of your face and head took a pretty good shellacking."

"No fooling?"

"Don't pay him no mind, Doc. He's a wiseass most of the time." Homer took a deep breath and blew into the handkerchief, drawing a quickly smothered look of dismay from the young doctor, who grimaced, then gave me a quick smile and left the room.

We stared at each other silently for a while. Too long. I broke eye contact and scooted back across the table, leaning against the wall. After I located my crushed cigarettes and found one that wasn't torn, I lit up and looked back at him again.

"We hit a nerve, Homer. Somewhere . . . one of us. Offhand, I'd say it was me."

"They say anything?" He wiped absently at the edges of his nostrils, then sighed and put the handkerchief away.

"Enough to let me know they weren't out to kill me. Just to take me out of commission for a couple of weeks. That's what the big one said when the young one flashed his knife the first time."

"How come you killed him, then?"

"It all changed for the one I shot when I kicked him in the nose and crawled under Hector's pickup. If my arm hadn't been in the way, he'd have shoved that blade into my chest just as easy. He was trying." I shivered at the thought. "You ever been cut, Homer?"

"Couple of times," he said casually. "I walked a beat in Fort Worth a few years before I came to Midway City. Lots of knives over there."

"My first time. I'd rather be shot any day."

The doctor came back into the room. "We have a room for

you, Mr. Roman. They want to know out front if you have insurance."

"I've got insurance but I'm not going into any room. I'm going home."

"Hell you say," Homer said. "Either here or the jailhouse, little buddy. Take your pick."

I glared at him. "Are you really serious about arresting me?"

"Dead serious. You know the drill as well as I do. I can't just turn you loose. I've done it before and got my ass in a crack. We can take you before J. P. Ellridge. He knows you and he'll probably release you on your own recognizance until you appear before the grand jury. I'll vouch for you, but that's as far as I go this time."

I felt the blood rushing to my face. "You're still pissed! You're pissed at me over the girl and—"

"No, I'm not. I'm just covering my butt, is all. Now, what's it going to be? Here for the night or the jail?"

I turned to the intern. "I got Prudential."

I left a little before midnight. Right after the night nurse came by and made me get into bed and turned off the TV and the light. I got up, dressed quietly, and walked out the door, down the corridor, and out of there. There was no guard, of course. I guessed Homer didn't think I was a desperate enough criminal for that. I was convinced he was doing the whole damn thing out of pure meanness, anyway. It was a clear-cut case of self-defense.

I stopped by my place to change out of my dirty, bloody clothes. While I was buttoning my shirt in the bedroom I pressed the play button on the Answerphone, trying to remember when I had last listened. There was a call from Homer, two business calls, and one other. It was a flat mechanical message in the type of metallic, toneless voice you hear from a computer: *"Mr. Roman. We have Susan Roman. She is in good health and will stay that way if you will desist in your efforts to find her. If you do not . . . we cannot*

*promise anything. Just be patient. A couple of weeks and
you'll have her back safe and sound."*

"Oh, my God," Alicia gasped. "What in the world happened
to you?"

Her arms came up around my shoulders and I relaxed into
them, pressing forward against her, thinking she was going to
help me inside. Instead, she herded me back out the door.

"Oh, Danny! I can't let you in!" Her eyes were stricken, her
face beginning to blanch. For the first time I noticed she was
in her robe, obviously nude underneath. "I—I have . . . someone . . . in there."

I managed a smile that cracked my face, and it must have
been something to see because her features contorted in misery and tears welled in her eyes.

"I'll wait," I said, all the juices inside me heading for the
hole in my stomach. "No sweat, babe, I'll wait in my car."

"Oh, no," she moaned, "you can't . . . I can't . . . oh, God,
Danny, he's already paid for . . . all night!" Her hands fluttered around my face entreatingly.

"Oh! Well, in that case, my fair lady, I'll just bid you adieu.
No harm done. Some other time, perhaps." I was proud of my
performance, despite my froglike voice and my stupid grin.

"Oh, no, no! Oh, God, Danny, why didn't you call?" She
clung to me, her voice rising in a wail, her clenched arms
bringing a stab of excruciating pain to my biceps.

"Hey! Hey, tiger, it's okay. Really. I only had a minute,
anyhow. I just stopped by to say hello." I hunched my shoulders and managed to work my injured arm out of her fierce
embrace.

"I'll send him away!" she said wildly. "I'll give him his
money back!" Her hands flew upward toward my face.

"You can't do that," I chided gently. "You're a business
lady, after all. The customer is always right, remember?" I
caught both her hands in my good one and hung on.

"I can't let you go like this," she whispered, her voice

cracking. "You're hurt, you need me ... the first time you need me and ..."

"Hey, it's all right. I'm okay, okay?" A man walking by the recessed doorway watched us curiously—until he saw my face. Then he jerked his eyes away and picked up his pace.

I thumbed the tear tracks off her cheeks and kissed her. "Call me tomorrow, all right?" I brushed her lips again, then moved away as her face began to blur and dissolve.

I felt fragmented, disjointed, everything just a little off center. I imagined I could feel her eyes on the back of my head all the way to my car, but when I arrived and looked back to wave, she had already gone.

I made it home okay. But just barely. I had to crawl the last few feet to the bed—but that was because I detoured through the den and grabbed a bottle of Jack Daniel's. I ran out of steam at the bedroom door, went to my knees, got down and crawled like a gut-shot wolf the rest of the way. I lay on my back and swigged from the bottle and felt sorry for myself. My arm was beginning to give me fits, and I wished I was back in the hospital. I wished Susie was home to take care of me—a sick man needs a woman's soothing, sympathetic touch. I wished I hadn't had to shoot the young man, and most of all I wished Alicia wasn't a whore.

And sometime in the wee hours of the morning, in the confusion of my delirium and uneasy sleep, I saw her face, felt her cool fingers on my burning body, heard the soft sounds of her voice murmuring, crooning, scolding, protested the persistent hands that stripped away my clothing, cried out with joy at her liquid coolness against my fevered flesh, almost wept at the softness, the warm security of her body.

And she was there when I awoke, swimming up out of darkness into a maze of pain, white fire on the side of my face, nails being driven into my arm, twisted and barbed for maximum effect.

"How are you, Danny?" she asked, her face glowing.

"I've been better," I croaked.

"Boy, you were really sick when I got here this morning." Her eyes twinkled. "You were pretty drunk, too."

"I remember being hot, then icy cold. Did I have fever?"

"Yes. I had to give you an alcohol rub to bring it down. Then after a while you began to shiver and I piled on the blankets and crawled in with you. I almost suffocated, but you began to get warm again." She felt my forehead. "You're pretty cool now, though. Do you want some water?"

She brought me a glass of water equipped with a bent straw. I emptied it and half of another. I sank back with a sigh.

"Are you having any pain?"

"My arm's pretty bad, but I'll live."

"I have some pain pills. The doctor said you could have one every three hours."

"Doctor? What doctor?"

Her face was faintly pink. "Just a . . . a friend of mine. I called him when you had the fever."

"He was here?"

She nodded. "He stopped this morning on his way to the hospital."

"A doctor who makes house calls? I'd like to meet him."

Her eyes were averted, her face growing pink again. "He changed your bandage and gave you a shot. You gave him a cussing. Don't you remember?"

I thought about it for a moment, but nothing came through the murky haze. "No, I don't. But I think I'll have a couple of those pills now."

She brought me a small white capsule and I took it with the rest of the water. I reached for my cigarettes on the nightstand and she caught my hand and held it in hers.

"You don't need to smoke right now."

"All right," I said meekly and closed my eyes. Almost immediately tentacles of darkness began to embrace my mind.

I opened my eyes. "How did you get in? I can't remember going to the door."

She smiled. "You left the door wide open, you dummy."

"Hmm," I said, and closed my eyes again. This time the tentacles closed in swiftly, a giant dark octopus that enveloped me, enveloped the world.

"It's not that I like what I'm doing, Danny," she said moodily, shading her eyes from the early November sun to watch the squirrels venturing boldly across the lawn in search of acorns. "But I guess I'm a little lazy, selfish, and probably a little too greedy. I want things like everybody else. Pretty clothes, a nice car, a nice place to live. And this is the only way I know I can have them."

"You could get married."

"Hah," she said scornfully. "I tried that. When I was sixteen. Looking back I know now that it was to get away from home mostly. I thought I was madly in love with him. He was tall and good-looking and he drove cars in races. I thought that was exciting and glamorous. But we were always traveling and there were always a lot of girls around. I soon found out that he had no intention of ever settling down. The only things he knew were driving cars and being a mechanic. He loved both as long as he had his own car. But he hit a long bad streak and lost his car. Things were terrible after that. He resented having to work on other people's cars. He drank a lot, slept with every racetrack tramp that came along. He ran off and left me in Louisville, Kentucky, without any money or anything. Hardly any clothes. I worked my way back to Fort Worth. You can guess how. After that it just seemed easier to go on doing it."

"I've heard worse horror stories," I said.

"I know. Maybe I just don't have any character."

"Maybe you like it more than you'll admit."

She gave me a quick, straight glance from under her hands, then turned back toward the yard, annoyance heightening the color in her cheeks.

"Maybe I do," she said tightly. "It's not all bad. Most of the men are nice. If they're not I don't let them come back again. I treat them fairly and honestly and I expect that from them at least. A lot of them are babies when it comes to sex. They really want to be mothered as much as anything. Sometimes it's hardly sex at all. They just want to look and touch, things like that. A lot more than you think is just a matter of kindness and understanding. If more wives were a little more understanding and took the time and trouble to try to understand their husbands' problems . . . well, there wouldn't be a need for many girls like me."

"Little earth mother," I said. "And a psychologist to boot. That's an unbeatable combination."

She turned quickly to look at me again, but she was smiling. "I think you're about well, Danny. You're trying to pick a fight with me. I guess it's time I was going home." Despite the lightness of her tone, the humor around her mouth, there was a look of pain in the dark eyes, and I was suddenly seething with self-contempt.

I struggled forward in the lounge, my good hand reaching for hers.

"Dammit! Don't let me do that! Don't let me get away with it. Don't be a doormat for me or anybody else . . . ever."

Her fingers touched my face tentatively, tenderly. "I don't mind it from you, Danny. I know why you do it." Her lips curved in a wintry smile. "Don't worry. I can take care of myself. I've got a temper! Boy! You just haven't seen it yet."

There was something about her little-girl-whistling-in-the-dark bravura that brought a stinging to my eyes, a thickness in my throat, and I let her pull my head to her breast to hide my own vulnerability. The wall I had erected around my emotions was beginning to crack, to crumble around the edges, and I was suddenly scared to death.

/ *18* /

I humbled myself and she agreed to stay through the day. But eventually I found myself alone again. Alone with slowly diminishing physical pain and rapidly increasing mental anguish. The swelling and inflammation in my face were receding nicely, only the scabs and bristly stitches over my left eye and below my ear serving as grim reminders. My left arm was surprisingly mobile, the muscle obviously healing well. It was only when I forgot and contracted my biceps that I wanted to scream.

I spent most of the night after Alicia left drinking and bemoaning my wasted past, my useless present, and my hopeless future. I missed Alicia, I missed Susie, and I hated myself for wanting both of them. I wondered vaguely about Homer, why I hadn't heard from him, and finally decided he had yanked my chestnuts out of the flames one more time. I had a momentary feeling of guilt, then belatedly realized he had planned on doing it all along. In his own convoluted fashion he had been trying to force me into taking at least a modicum of care of myself.

I debated going to see him, eventually accepting the telephone as a more prudent course of action. I dialed quickly, before I could lose my nerve.

"Hidy," I said.

"Hi," he said, as if nothing had happened, as if I hadn't been a fugitive for more than two days. "What's going on, boy? You up and around?"

"Not too well," I said, whining a little just in case he was sandbagging me.

"Nurse still there?"

"Nurse? What nurse?"

"The one who answered the phone them two times I called. Said her name was Alice."

"Alicia," I said automatically.

"Uh-huh." His voice was flat, noncommittal. "Sounded like a real pro, a real hustler."

"That's a cheap shot, Homer."

"I thought it was kinda funny. You know, a play on words."

"It doesn't require an explanation. I just called to tell you I received a message. They said they had Susie and if I would quit looking for her she'd be returned in a couple of weeks unharmed."

"No kidding? When?"

"I'm not sure," I lied. "It was on the answering machine. Alicia must have turned off the extension in the bedroom. I didn't know you had called."

"Male voice?"

"I couldn't tell. It was mechanically distorted. I'd say it was male, though."

"Well, how about that?"

"You know what it means, don't you, Homer?"

"Not right offhand, no."

"All right. We had already decided that whoever took her had to have a good reason. Either that or it was some nut. Well, the guy on the phone didn't sound like a nut."

"So?"

"So what's happening within the next two weeks that's important?"

There was a moment of silence. I was about to provide the answer when he blurted it out. "The election!"

"Right. So that means whoever has Susie is probably a candidate. He couldn't afford to be connected with the death of a known prostitute, accidental or otherwise. Susie witnessed the accident and he took her with him."

The line hummed while he thought about it. "Nice clean line of thought there, boy, but it's a little patchy."

"I don't see that."

"Well, dammit, what's he going to do with her after the election? He can't keep her his whole damn term. Unless—" He broke off, obviously unwilling to vocalize the unthinkable.

"If that's his intention, she's probably already dead, Homer." I said it calmly, despite the hole yawning in the pit of my stomach again.

"Naw," he went on, "nobody would do that just for an elected job for a few years."

"I hope you're right. A lot would depend on the job, wouldn't it? How about a seat in the Senate, or Congress? How important are they? How much can a man want something like that? The money involved, the prestige, the power? How much does that mean to a man, Homer? Can you make that kind of judgment? Can you balance that at one end of the scale against maybe a scandal, or even prosecution, at the other? We don't know what happened up there. Maybe the girl's death was a simple, unavoidable accident, maybe it wasn't. Maybe negligence was involved at the very least. Maybe something heavier than that. Only two people know for sure. Susie and the man himself. How do we know he's not just playing for time? Stalling to let the spoor get a little colder? Are you willing to take that chance, Homer? Well, I'm not."

The line hummed emptily again, then he sighed. "I reckon you're right, Dan. No way to know what's in a man's mind, what his priorities are in something like this. Men have . . . done worse for less. Okay, how many on your list would fit the bill?"

"Hammond and Blakely. Hammond looks all right as far as I've gone. Blakely, I told you about him. He can't account for his time, or won't, which amounts to the same thing. I have two more candidates. A councilman and a congressman."

"Incumbents?"

"No. I don't know about the councilman, but the other guy's race looks pretty good from what I hear."

"You don't really think a candidate for councilman would . . ."

"Priorities, Homer. I'm not ruling out anybody."

"All right. We'll check him out. I've been through my list. Everybody checks out okay. Gimme them two names."

"Cecil Armand is the city councilman candidate. All I have is a phone number. The guy running for Congress is Jesse S. Morris. He has a campaign office in Dallas."

"Okay. You get back on them other two and I'll work on these. You up to it?"

"I will be by tomorrow." I paused to light a cigarette. "The more I think about this, the more I'm convinced we're on track. The guys the other night, they mentioned putting me out of commission for a couple of weeks. And now the phone message. It's too much of a coincidence not to have something to do with the election."

"Maybe so. All we can do is give it another shot."

"Oh, there's one other thing. A man named Robert Murphy and a guy named George Winscott. They're on Hammond's campaign staff, supposedly with him at the time the Wilkins girl died. Could you run a make on them for me?"

"I'll see what I can do. I'll get back to you."

"Thanks, Homer."

I had been off the phone for half an hour before I realized that he hadn't mentioned either my arrest or the young man's killing.

I was going out the door the next morning when Thomas Markette's red Datsun zipped into my driveway and came to a stop beside my station wagon. He sat for a moment, then got out as I approached. His lean face was haggard, his eyes darkly shadowed.

"Good morning, Mr. Roman."

"Good morning."

He leaned against the fender of my station wagon. He folded

his long arms and made a feeble attempt at a smile, his eyes squinted as if looking into the sun.

"Mr. Roman. You recall our conversation the last time I saw you . . . the one about my father?"

"I remember."

"I—I'm not sure how to go about this, what to say . . . but I'd like to ask you to forget it. I was completely wrong about what I said . . . about my father being with Charley when she was killed."

"I know that."

"You do?" He blinked rapidly, relief showing on his face.

"Yes, I know where your father was that night."

"That's good." He bobbed his head emphatically. "That's good. I was upset, angry, and hurt. I wanted to blame him, I guess. I wanted to blame somebody." He hesitated and blinked again. "And the . . . other things I . . . I told you. I'd appreciate it if you didn't repeat them to anyone."

"I'm not a gossip."

"No, I'm sure not," he said hastily. "It's just my father . . . well, he knows what I told you and he was furious that I would discuss family matters with a stranger. And rightly so. I don't know what got into me. I never did that before. Not even to my shrink." He stopped, his pale face slowly growing pink. "I lied to you about that."

"Your family problems don't interest me, Tom. They never did. I told you that at the time."

He nodded eagerly. "Yes, you did. I remember. I just wouldn't listen, would I? I may have misled you about my father, Mr. Roman. He isn't a bad man . . . he just has . . . problems. And he's very sensitive about our family name. I—" He broke off and turned as a car left the winding street in front of my house and wheeled in behind his Datsun. A gleaming silver-blue Mercedes with heavily tinted windows, it drifted to a whisper-quiet stop, and we both stood silently watching as the door opened and John Markette climbed out. Impeccably dressed in a rust-colored suit that brought out the umber tones in his pampered skin, he moved up the driveway a few feet and stood quietly watching his son, his features curiously vacuous.

"Did you tell him, Thomas? Did you explain that you lied to him about me?"

"Yes." Thomas Markette unfolded his long arms and moved to lean against his own car, his deep-set eyes sardonic. "Yes, Daddy, I explained it to him."

John Markette looked at his son for a moment longer, then turned his smoldering gaze on me. "Just in case he didn't explain fully, Mr. Roman, I'll add that most of what my son told you was fantasy. The rest of it ... well, he and my daughter Charley ... they were too far along in their perversity by the time I discovered it to really do anything about it. The sickness had gone on too long. They didn't want to change ... to stop. It was like a ... well, a sickness. I sent Charley to an all-girls school and Thomas to a military academy. It mattered little. They resumed their degrading behavior as soon as they were together again. I managed somehow to keep it from their mother. She's a very delicate woman, both physically and mentally. . . ."

"Tried to kill herself twice," Thomas said, his eyes on a blackbird dive-bombing an oak tree across the street, an enigmatic smile lifting the corners of his mouth.

Markette turned to look at his son. "Mr. Roman isn't interested in our family history."

"Tell him about the time she tried to kill you," Thomas said, then jerked open the door of his car, his face suddenly pale and strained. "You didn't have to follow me here. I told you I would tell him." He switched on the motor, whipped the wheel as far as it would go to the right and gunned the little car. The rear wheels squealed, then skidded as he hit the grass in Hector Johnson's yard. He made a looping curve, the wheels spewing bits of turf, then leaped over the curbing and drove off down the street.

Markette turned back from watching his son. He smiled

ruefully and shook his head. "I'm sorry about that. My son, I'm afraid, is still a deeply disturbed young man. This thing with Charley dying hit him pretty hard . . . as it did all of us. I hope you understand at last that all the things he told you were just . . . just fantasies. My part in it, at least. I tried my best to put them both on the right—"

"All this isn't necessary," I interrupted impatiently. "I no longer have any interest in your family, Mr. Markette. I'm sorry to be rude, but I have some pressing business."

"Yes, yes, of course." He smiled apologetically and held out his hand, but I was already opening my car door. He lifted the hand in a wave instead and climbed into the Mercedes. I lit a cigarette and waited until he was gone before I backed out and headed the car toward Fort Worth and James Hammond's campaign office.

George Winscott was an incredibly ugly man. He had limp, black hair that lay dull and lifeless across the top of a head rapidly going bald. His nose was long and blunt-ended above a thick bristly mustache the color of soot, and his lips were thick and red.

I waited patiently in front of his desk, trying to figure out a way to avoid shaking his hand, while he finished a telephone conversation.

He hung up the phone, looked up at me, and smiled. He stood up and extended his hand across the desk. I held it long enough to discover it was cold and damp and as limp as his hair.

"George Winscott. You'd be Dan Roman." He looked at his watch and smiled. "Right on time, too."

"I try to be punctual," I said. "I realize you must be a very busy man."

"Oh, yes indeed. Time is of the essence, as they say." He barked a warm little laugh. "We are running out of time, as it were. Only six days until the big one, you know." He sat back down and folded his plump hands on a white desk blotter. "Now, Mr. Roman, what can I do for you?"

"I believe you know why I'm here, Mr. Winscott. I'm sure you must have spoken with Mr. Hammond within the last few days."

His eyes glinted. "Ah, yes, of course. You'd be the Mr. Roman who was inquiring about our staff meeting on Mondays." He paused and raised thick eyebrows. "That would be correct, would it not?"

"Yes, it would," I said.

"Well, you may rest assured that Mr. Hammond was present as usual, sir. Along with Bob and Ted and—"

"Dick and Jane," I said.

His eyebrows shot up again. "I beg your pardon?"

I smiled and ducked my head. "Just a crude attempt at humor, Mr. Winscott."

"Ah yes, I see. Well, if that would be all, Mr. Roman? You said it yourself, sir, we are incredibly busy at this time."

I rose to my feet and towered over him. "If I might be allowed to ask one more question, Mr. Winscott?"

"Yes, of course." Surprisingly, he had nice green eyes with long curling lashes. He blinked them at me.

"What are your duties with Mr. Hammond's organization, Mr. Winscott?"

"Why, I'm . . . I'm his campaign manager, of course."

"I'm aware of that. I mean what do you do exactly?"

He spread his hands on the white blotter. "Oh my, I couldn't begin to enumerate my duties. . . . Why, I do just about everything there is to do at one time or other." He laughed self-consciously. "I guess you could call me a jack-of-all-trades."

I leaned forward across the desk and smiled at him. "How about little boys? Is that one of your trades?"

The color left his face with incredible speed; his hands came together on the desk with an audible slap, fingers intertwining, the little white teeth gleaming at me through gaping lips.

"What?" he whispered. "I—I don't . . . I don't understand."

141

"I think you do," I said quietly. "Have you been back to Teterboro lately, Mr. Winscott?"

"Oh, God!" he gasped. "How—how did you know?"

"You've been arrested twice. Did you think it was a secret?"

"But way . . . way back there. How—"

I waved him silent. "Does Hammond know?"

"No! No, please . . . why . . ."

I leaned across the desk again. "Now tell me. Was there a staff meeting a week ago Monday night?"

His eyes slid away from mine, frantically searched the tiny room, then came sliding back like two flakes of metal to a magnet.

"Tell me. There wasn't, was there?"

He shook his head miserably. "No," he whispered. "That's just . . . something we use to get . . . to get away from our wives for a night out."

I straightened, realized I had been holding my breath. I found a cigarette and lit it.

"This night out. Do you go out together?"

"Yes . . . sometimes. Sometimes not."

"That Monday night. Together, or alone? Which was it?"

He ran his tongue across thick lips, wetting them, bringing out the blood-red color. "Alone."

"Where did Hammond go? Do you know?"

"No. Some woman . . . I don't know who."

"Where can I find him now?"

"Luncheon . . . I believe Ramada Inn."

"Where? Which one?"

He wagged his hanging head from side to side.

"I don't know," he said dully. "Maybe Marty can tell you."

"Who's Marty?"

"Redhead outside. Desk next to the door. She keeps his schedule straight." He looked up at me. "You're not going to . . . to tell him?"

I shook my head. "No, I won't tell him. I think you've got enough problems just being you."

* * *

The redhead Marty was tall, lanky, and had cool gray eyes. I had noticed that much on the way in. I walked past the long table where four people were busily stuffing envelopes with propaganda flyers. A dozen other women sat at desks around the room with telephone receivers clamped to their ears. The redhead was one of those. There was a thick computer tab run on her desk, and as I walked over she hung up the phone and placed a check mark beside a name. She looked up and smiled.

"Did you find George okay?"

"Sure did. Thanks. He told me you would know where Hammond was having lunch."

She nodded, the thick red hair dancing. "The Ramada Inn on Beach Street. Some of his major contributors." I caught her surreptitious glance at my faded jeans and worn windbreaker.

"Don't worry," I said. "I won't embarrass him. Could you get in touch with him, do you think?"

She frowned and started to shake her head, then stopped. "I could, I suppose, if it were really important."

"It's important. Just give him a message, please. Tell him I'll wait in front of his house until one o'clock. If he isn't there by then, I'll discuss his Monday-night staff meetings with his wife."

She stopped writing and looked up at me, the frown gone, her face a smooth white mask, the gray eyes cold.

"Did you get it all?"

"I got it," she said icily. Something flickered in the frosty depths before she lowered her eyes to the slip of paper. "What was your name again, please?"

"Dan Roman."

"Does Mr. Hammond know you?"

"Not as well as he's going to."

/ 19 /

It was a nice enough house. Brick veneer. Probably half again as big as my eighteen hundred square footer. Not overly ostentatious for a would-be public servant, but not exactly a slum dwelling, either. There were several native oak trees in the large front yard and others that had obviously been planted; pecan and maple and mulberry, ten to twelve years old, judging by the amount of growth. The house was located in a relatively new development in northeast Fort Worth, scattered along the slopes of low wooded hills, where no lot was less than two acres and the average was five. Tucked into the slope of a hill on a sharp curve in the winding street, the house was in a position that afforded almost complete privacy from inquisitive neighbors.

I drove past slowly, then eased to the curb at the beginning of the curve. It was then I saw the small blue Buick parked a hundred feet up the street. James Hammond was standing beside it beckoning.

I parked across from him and watched him cross the street. The wind had ruffled his hair and there was a scowl on the tanned handsome face. He walked swiftly, with long, sure strides and the air of a man who knew where he was going, and how.

"What is this?" he barked at me while he was still ten feet away.

I looked at my watch. "Fifteen minutes to spare. You must have broken a few speed laws. Not nervous, are you, Mr. Hammond?"

He stopped a few feet away, the scowl becoming a red-faced angry glare. "I thought we had settled this matter. What right do you have to come sneaking around interrogating my employees behind my back . . . making threats?"

"Employees? I thought they were campaign volunteers."

He made a furious, deprecatory gesture. "What the hell difference does it make? I want to know what you think you're doing. I'm not without influence in this town. Licenses can be revoked, you know."

I shrugged. "It doesn't matter. I don't work at it much, anyhow." I grinned at him. "I'm like you, Mr. Hammond, I'm independently wealthy. It's just a hobby . . . sorta like you running for the Senate."

His thin lips thinned even more. "What kind of game are you playing, Roman?" He was obviously making a supreme effort to control his voice.

"No game, Hammond," I said. "You lied to me. I'm doing you the favor of allowing you to tell me why before I go inside and search your house."

He stared at me, eyes wide with disbelief. "Search my house! Are you crazy? You'll do no such damn thing!"

I opened the door and got out of the car. "You watch me."

He backed away a few feet. "Man, you can't just . . . you can't go in my house. I won't allow it!"

I squared off in front of him, looked him up and down insolently. "Are you going to stop me?"

"The police! I'll get the police!"

"You do that." I took a step toward him. He backed away, pushing at me with his hands.

"Wait! This is crazy! What do you hope to gain by searching my house?"

"Maybe nothing. But then again maybe you have something in there that belongs to me."

"What? Man, I don't have anything of yours. What is it? What are you looking for?"

I shrugged. "You either know, or you don't. If you know, I

don't have to explain. If you don't, then it's none of your business. Either way, I'm going to find out." I stepped around him and started down the street. He ran to catch up with me, grabbed my good arm.

"Look, wait! What is it you want to know?" He was breathing in gasps, glancing fearfully toward his house, almost hidden behind a thick line of oaks. "Wait, let's talk!"

I looked down at his hand on my arm. He dropped it like a hot poker.

"The Monday-night scam you're running on your wife. Tell me about it."

His face blanched. "How . . . ?"

"Never mind that. Just tell me about *the* Monday night. You know which one I mean." I stepped back to stand beside my station wagon as a car came down the street. He followed me nervously, his features averted from the passing car. The arrogance was missing from his face, but the smooth tanned skin slowly regained color.

"All right, all right. I have nothing to hide. You just have to tell me it won't . . . go any further."

"I don't have to tell you anything," I corrected. "You're the one doing the talking."

He waved his hand jerkily. "Okay! Okay!" He licked his lips and cleared his throat. "The Monday nights . . . it's just . . . you know, a night out from a hard drill. A chance to unwind, to have a little fun without . . ." He fumbled for a finish.

"Without your wife."

"Yeah." He tried a feeble man-to-man smile that didn't come off. "Nothing big . . . just, you know, a few drinks, have a few laughs . . . and like that."

"A little pussy."

"Yeah, that too . . . sometimes. You know how it is." The air was cool, but there was a gleam of sweat on his forehead.

"No. I don't. But you can tell me."

He stared into my eyes, his face sincere. "Man, I wasn't with her that night. I—I wanted to be. I went to her place that night. I'll admit that. But she wasn't there. Her ... roommate said she was gone, that she wouldn't be back. I—"

"Why didn't you call first?"

"I was in the neighborhood, on my way back from a ... a friend's house in Dallas. I just decided on the spur of the moment."

"What time was that?"

"I'm not sure. Around seven, I think. Yes, it must have been seven at least."

"Charley's roommate, did she know who you were?"

He shook his head. "No. I always met Charley somewhere other than her apartment. It worked out better that way."

"Why did you decide to stop by that night?"

He squirmed a little, gave me another feeble grin. "I was ... you know, horny. The thing in Dallas hadn't panned out. She was ... well, I was, you know, hot. I just decided to stop by when I came down Loop 820, just on the chance she might be free."

"And since she wasn't there you came on home?"

"Well, no, not right that minute. Her roommate, you know, she's a hooker, too. I thought ... well, I said I was horny." His grin had straightened itself out, arrogant again, patronizing.

I had a sudden savage desire to rip off his face.

"Are you saying you screwed her roommate?"

His eyebrows lifted. "Why not? Not quite the same as Charley, but ..." He shrugged eloquently and let it die away.

I felt my face twisting into something like a grin. I took a step toward him. "I'll tell you why not, you son of a bitch! She was busy, that's why not! She had another man with her. You're lying, asshole!"

His hands flew up, made the pushing motions again as he backstepped. "Hey, wait! She wasn't going to ... but then I offered her fifty. No big deal, man. She just gave me a quickie right there in the living room."

Hot anger washed over me. I had an almost uncontrollable urge to hit him, smash the condescending leer off his face. He watched me, wide-eyed, his face beginning to blanch again. He backed away slowly, poised to run, eyes flicking from my face to my clenched fists.

"Hey! Hey, what is it? What's wrong with you? I'm telling you the truth!"

I sucked in a deep breath, felt a painful tremor shake its way through me. I let my muscles sag, my hands open.

"You'd better be," I said shakily, my voice trembling despite a concentrated effort to control it. "I'm going to check you out. If you're lying again . . ." I let it trail away and climbed into my car.

"You've got no right to talk to me like that." His voice was tentatively angry, but he was still watching me warily. "Calling me names, cursing me . . . I have a good notion to—"

I was pulling away. I slammed on the brakes; the motor coughed and died. I shoved the door open and glared at him.

"What? Go ahead—you have a good notion to do *what*?"

His lips crimped into a thin line, a white knife slash across his narrow handsome face. He opened his mouth to say something, then clamped it shut and whirled toward his car.

I waited while he turned the Buick around and gunned it down the street away from his home. Then I started the motor again, and drove slowly away, feeling angry, jealous, and very much alone.

She faced me across the width of her living room, her hair tousled, angry red welts on her cheek where she had slept on it. Her eyes were wide and frightened.

"Dammit! Why didn't you tell me that before? That Hammond was here that night? Do you have any idea how much time I've wasted on him?"

"I'm sorry, Danny! I didn't know who he was even. Just that he was one of Charley's johns. After I told him she wasn't here, he wanted to . . . do me, but I couldn't because . . ."

"Yeah, yeah, I know! Because you had Charley's old man in your bed."

She looked at me without speaking, her chin tilted defiantly.

"So then you just got down on your knees and gave him a . . ." I couldn't make myself say it. I dropped heavily onto the sofa and fumbled for a cigarette.

Her voice, when it came, was low and stifled, almost inaudible.

"That's one of the things I do, Danny."

"Jesus," I said softly, staring dully at the floor, the walls, the ceiling, anywhere but at her. I puffed on the cigarette, realizing belatedly that I hadn't lit it.

"I'm sorry if it bothers you. I—I thought you had accepted what I do." There were tears in her voice, but it didn't matter.

I shook my head wearily. "I can never accept what you do. I'm not even sure anymore if I can tolerate it. Dammit—I don't even know why I care."

She came up behind me, dropped her hands lightly on my shoulders. She took a deep sighing breath. "I'm sorry, Danny, but I guess that's your problem. I can't change what's happened, and it's too late to stop being what I am. I don't know how I could if I wanted to. Not if I want to go on eating."

"You could get a job like everybody else."

"Doing what? Waiting tables? Making less in a week than I make in one night? It's so easy to say, Danny, so easy to judge. I don't know how to do anything else. I've had enough of struggling, poverty, eating junk food, buying my clothes at discount houses, wondering if maybe next month I'll be able to afford a new pair of shoes, or go to a movie, eat out at a nice restaurant, wondering if my old car will make it through the week, the sick, miserable feeling of knowing you can't ever afford anything better—"

"All right," I said, cutting into the rising hysteria in her voice.

Her hands pounded my shoulders. "You just don't know, dammit!"

149

I reached up and caught her fists, ignoring the stabbing pain in my left arm. I pulled her forward until I felt her breath on my ear. "Just calm down."

"It scares me, Danny," she whispered. "It frightens me to death. I just can't go back to being poor . . . no matter what."

I left her with her memories. I couldn't afford to share them. I had too many of my own.

/ 20 /

"Nothing at my end. The councilman and the congressman come out clean." Homer swished the dregs of his scotch around in his glass, then emptied them into his mouth.

"Then we're back to Blakely."

"How about Hammond?"

I shook my head. "He wasn't there."

He rose and went to the bar. He sloshed scotch into his glass and held it up to the light. "You got good taste in booze, anyhow," he said musingly, looking at me as if that had some direct bearing on our conversation. He went back to his chair and sat down heavily.

"You know what we gotta do, don't you?"

I raised my head and looked at him.

"We gotta do what we shoulda done in the first place." He took a drink of scotch and made a face. "We gotta call in the FBI."

I laughed, a sharp mirthless sound. "What the hell could they do that we haven't done?"

"I dunno, but they're trained for things like this."

"Like what? They don't want ransom. Are you even sure they'd take it on?"

"You got that message on the tape. That proves she's been kidnapped."

"Not really. That could be some damned crank. Some jerk who read about it in the papers."

"She's been gone too long, Dan. Don't worry, I can get them on the case."

"I don't know, Homer. We get a bunch of jokers running around making cop noises, this guy's liable to panic."

"Yeah, he might turn her loose." His voice was light, with carefully metered sarcasm.

"He might kill her, too."

He held the glass of scotch in both hands, swirled it gently, his eyes avoiding mine. "You gotta consider that, Dan. He might have done that already."

"Don't you think I have?" I said harshly. "I have nightmares about it." I got up and paced restlessly around the room, stopped at the patio door and stared out into the darkness. "What if we're wrong, Homer? This thing about the election, maybe it's just a pipe dream. Maybe it doesn't have anything to do with it at all. Maybe some nut, some damned psycho, got her. Some sick son of a bitch like that—"

"Whoa, boy. Ain't gonna do no good maybeing. I think it's time we got some help, some professional help, with this."

I whirled on him. "What the hell are we? You're a cop and I'm a professional manhunter. We're not exactly amateurs, you know. What the hell can they do besides get things stirred up?"

"They got manpower," he said stubbornly. "They got resources, equipment, technical know-how. That tape you got. They can maybe take that and come up with something. Voiceprints, things like that. They can run it through a computer. No telling what they might get out of it. They've got lists of these nuts you were talking about."

"Yeah, yeah. They're a bunch of Captain Marvels." I went back to my seat and lit a cigarette.

The rocker squeaked protestingly as he shifted his bulk and crossed his legs. "Then what do you plan on doing?"

"Check out Blakely. If that washes out . . . then we'll just have to wait, I guess. I don't know where else to look." I stubbed out the cigarette and went to the bar. I found a wine goblet and filled it half full of vodka, dropped in a couple of ice cubes.

I could feel his disapproving eyes on the back of my head. I went back and sat down, gave him a fleeting glance, and tilted the glass to my mouth, feeling absurdly like a teenager committing his first act of defiance.

"That ain't gonna help."

"Ain't gonna hurt. I don't get a hangover from vodka."

"That's not what I meant, and you know it."

"Stay off my case, old man. I didn't harp at you when you had two double shots of scotch."

"Three," he said. He got up and shuffled to the bar. "Difference is, boy, I know when to stop."

"Yeah, when you fall on your fat ass."

"Huh. That'll be the day." He sat down and sampled the scotch, then looked at me and chuckled wheezingly. "You remember that time up at Grapevine Lake? I whipped them four fellers for cussing and talking nasty in front of Barbara and Ida?"

"Where do you think I was? Asleep under a tree somewhere?"

"Oh, you was there. I don't remember you doing much of anything, though."

I snorted. "They would have carved you up in strips and packed you in brine if I hadn't been there, old man."

He chuckled a little, his head down, lost in reverie, the drink cupped in both big stubby hands, resting on top of his paunch. He took a drink and sighed. "Them was two fine women, boy. Too damn bad they had to up and die on us."

I thought about Barbara, my first wife, a gentle, loving woman. Her slow death from cancer had killed a part of me, too. A part of me that just disappeared.

"Yeah," I said, and lifted my glass in a toast. "Two fine women."

I was thirty yards and two cars behind the small yellow Plymouth when it made the right turn onto Jefferson Boulevard and headed toward Oak Cliff. Two days of stakeout, two miserable days of cold coffee and plastic sandwiches, aching bones and cramped muscles. But finally he had broken free of the pack. The good senator was all alone in the Plymouth, more or less disguised in old faded Levi's, scuffed run-over boots, the distinctive silver hair packed carefully under the crown of a sweat-stained cowboy hat. A pair of oversized green sunglasses completed the disguise. I would have missed him coming out of the campaign headquarters parking lot had it not been for his furtiveness and the fact that I was watching for something just like that.

He drove leisurely, carefully, with the air of a man who knew where he was going and was enjoying the trip.

It was a lower-middle-class neighborhood that he led me to; small brick houses, neat and tidy for the most part, and racially integrated, judging from the colorful mixture of people on the sidewalks. I was half a block behind him when he turned into a driveway, and I speeded up in time to see him drive into the open door of a garage attached to a small red-brick house. I watched the electronically controlled door drift downward, then speeded up again and turned around at the corner. I pulled into the driveway and parked near the front porch, then got out, climbed the steps and pushed the bell.

The woman who answered the door was the color of milk chocolate, with long black hair, finely chiseled features, and a small voluptuous body wrapped snugly in a mint-green nylon robe. I suddenly realized what Blakely had meant about political suicide.

She stood watching me quietly, eyebrows arched above dark intelligent eyes. "Yes?"

"I'd like to see the senator, ma'am."

153

Her lips struggled to build an incredulous smile and failed. "I'm afraid you have the wrong address."

"Tell the senator my name is Dan Roman. I think it's time we talked."

Her frown worked much better than the smile. "I don't know what you're talking about, sir, but—"

"Let him in, Rose." The harsh voice came from somewhere behind her, and she stepped back without hesitation, her face abruptly expressionless.

Senator Blakely was standing in the center of the room, the hat and sunglasses missing, the silver mane of hair tousled. His fair skin was congested with blood, his face bunched with anger. He was taller than he appeared on TV, thinner, with long arms and knobby hands.

He moved his hand in a swift furious gesture. "Are you satisfied now? You just couldn't take my word for it, could you?"

"No, sir, I couldn't. Is this the woman you were talking about?"

"She's the one." He shot a sideways glance at the woman standing quietly by the door. "How many do you think I have, for pete's sake?" His eyes came back to mine, locked, and there was a warning in their depths—or pleading, I wasn't sure which.

"Two weeks ago last Monday night? Was he here?"

She smiled faintly. "He comes every Monday night," she said, her voice soft and melodious. She looked at him and the smile widened. "When he's in town, that is."

"What time did he come?"

"About this time. Six, or a little after."

She returned my gaze calmly, a tiny impression of the smile still lingering around her lips, her expression hostile, but not obtrusively so.

I nodded. "All right. I'm sorry to have intruded. Thank you, ma'am, Senator."

He held the door for me, his color returning to normal, his face arranged to scowl or smile, depending on my answer to his question.

"This ends it, then?"

"Yes. Your part in it."

He stuck out his hand to shake, a habit so deeply ingrained it was pure reflex. Politician to the bitter end, he gave me a wide smile and a pat on the arm.

Three long hazy days later—or maybe it was four—I sat watching the election returns, drying out. Not from desire, but out of necessity. I had run out of booze and everything was closed for the election. I sat drinking the last of a lonely six-pack, watching the newscasters predict Senator Blakely a sure winner, and Hammond too close to call. I sat shivering and burning in turn, watching the numbers displayed in dielectric wonder, convinced that somewhere in this maze of redundancy there lurked a clue to Susie's fate. By midnight I was disenchanted and almost sober, shaking and weak, filled to overflowing with a terrible blazing thirst. When I could stand it no longer, I dressed shakily and went out to my car.

I drove slowly and carefully, stopping for all the lights, making all the correct signals, and an eternity later I sat looking up at the light in Alicia's window wondering what I would find: an inconsequential consideration in view of the raging fire in my stomach.

After a while she opened the door, her face flushed, damp, lips swollen, the lovely dishevelment I knew so well. Taking no chances, I brushed past her and headed for the bar cart, thrusting my hands in my jacket pockets to keep them still.

"Danny!" she hissed fiercely, "what are you doing? You can't come in here . . ."

I waved my hand airily. "Don't let me interrupt. Just go about your business."

She stamped her foot. "Damn you! I won't have . . ."

I had stopped listening; I was drinking from the bottle, the glass chattering against my teeth, choking the fiery liquid down my throat to quench the flames below. Once more, and I paused to wipe my mouth with the back of my hand and saw him at the door to her bedroom. He nodded and smiled uncertainly, his expression wavering between anxiety and embarrassment. He was fully dressed, complete with vest and tie.

"Hello, Thomas. Come and share our benefactress's largess with me."

"Hello, Mr. Roman."

"I—I found some more of Charley's things. . . . Mr. Markette came by to pick them up." She edged around the corner of the sofa, freckles in stark relief.

I fixed her with a stern, pitying gaze. "Do not lie to me, my dear. You and young Thomas have been dallying in yon bedroom. Not that I blame him, mind you; you are eminently dalliable. Is that not so, Thomas?"

He glanced at her, then back at me, and grinned sheepishly. "She's telling you the truth, sir. I did come to pick up some of Charley's things." He walked toward me.

"Ah," I said, "but you lingered to taste the fruit. Come, come, we are all adults here. The lady is a whore and you were simply availing yourself of her services. Not so?"

He nodded. "Yes, that's true." He accepted the glass of bourbon and looked into the Styrofoam bucket for ice cubes.

I wrinkled my lips in what I hoped was a sardonic grin and looked at Alicia. "See, my dear, it really doesn't matter."

She turned without a word and marched toward the bedroom, both hands gripping the robe, the ends of the sash trailing behind her like an aviator's scarf.

He looked at me over the rim of his glass, dark eyes quizzical. He touched his lips to the whiskey and lowered the glass. "You're kind of hard on her," he said, his voice carefully neutral.

I shrugged and took the bottle with me to the couch. "She's a whore. She's tough."

He sat on the edge of the chair across from me. "I—I've been wondering how . . . how things were with you."

"Fine. Peachy keen, as a matter of fact. And how are things with the Markette household?"

156

He smiled faintly. "All right. Dad's man got elected again, so that means he'll be going to Washington soon. He's a very happy man tonight. Particularly since Mother came home yesterday."

"Oh," I said politely. "I didn't know she had been away." I wished he would shut his damned mouth and go away.

"Yes," he said, his face composed. "She's been in the hospital since the day of Charley's funeral. She collapsed at the cemetery." He shook his head. "She's never been strong. Charley's death was too much." He paused, touched the whiskey to his lips again. "What I meant was, has there been any news . . . ?"

"No," I said, "there hasn't. Look, I appreciate your interest, or whatever the hell it is, but if you don't mind, I'm not in the mood for small talk tonight."

He set the glass on the end table and nodded, his face suddenly pale and taut. "Yes, of course, Mr. Roman. Sorry to trouble you." He got up and walked out the door.

"You forgot Charley's things, Thomas," I said to the empty room.

After a while, when it became abundantly clear that she wasn't coming to me, I drank the rest of the whiskey in the bottle, belched, sighed, and went into the bedroom to her.

She was in a fetal curve in the center of the bed, the thick, luxurious hair covering the side of her face. Her hands were clasped, tucked under her chin, her eyes were closed.

I sat heavily on the side of the bed, balanced myself on one arm and leaned over her. After a while I gently stroked the curve of her hip, my hand on the nylon material of the robe creating a faint whispering sound.

"I'm sorry, kid. I'm a sorry bastard sometimes."

There was no response, no sound or movement, except the faint flicker of an eyelid.

I waited for a while and tried again.

"That's all I know to say, Alicia. Anything else would be just so much bullshit."

157

"You don't love me," she said petulantly, her voice swollen with self-pity. "I don't think you even like me."

I pushed the hair back from her face with a clumsy finger. "I never said I loved you. Not once." I made my voice as low and gentle as I could. "I like you. I like you very much. Maybe that's all there is in me."

"You stay away for days, then you come to see me only when you want to f— make love."

"No. I didn't come to make love tonight. I came because . . . I was lonely. Scared and lonely, I guess." God don't mind the little white lies.

"I'll bet." Her eyes were suddenly open, fixed intently on my face.

I leaned over and kissed her behind the ear. "It's the truth. I stayed away as long as I could. It was a long hard battle . . . and I lost. Or maybe I won, I don't know anymore."

Her eyes were in deep dark shadow. "You couldn't stay away?"

"I'm here," I said simply.

Her hands unclasped and she touched my cheek with a tentative finger. "And you're not mad . . . about Thomas?"

"I'm not glad, but we settled that. . . . It's the way you make your living."

She gripped my hand tightly between hers and kissed my palm. "Come to bed," she whispered, her face glowing like an October sunrise. "Make love to me!"

I shook my head sorrowfully. "I better not. I just came to . . . to see you. We'll talk awhile and then I'll go."

She shook her head wildly. "No! I'm sorry about what I said. Please, Danny. For me. Please!"

She helped me undress and I slipped into bed feeling lower than a snake's belly, but I consoled myself with the gratifying knowledge that it was such a small sacrifice to bring her so much happiness.

/ 21 /

I could never be sure if it was because I wasn't my usual
cautious self or whether it was because I was nursing a hangover from Alicia's bourbon that kept me from making out the
man in the light blue Ford sooner. It was only after I came out
of the supermarket with a couple of six-packs and a carton of
Carltons that the fact I had seen him at least three times
since leaving Alicia's wormed its way into my consciousness.

A small man, from what I could see of him, parked three
cars down the row, busily reading a newspaper with one eye
while the other peeked around the edge at me. Either new at
the game, inordinately clumsy, or he didn't give a damn if I
made him or not. I tried to decide which as I walked in his
direction.

I stood beside his car for a moment, staring in at him, at the
dark pants scurfy with cigarette ashes, the half-gallon ther-
mos with the cap off on the seat beside him, the candy
wrappers and hamburger napkins on the floor. Even before he
raised startled, red-rimmed eyes I knew why he was so clumsy.
He had spent a sleepless night outside the Oak Meadows
Apartments and he was probably so damned tired he no longer
gave a shit.

I clucked sympathetically. "Hard night?"

He almost grinned, stopped it in time, curved it into a
frown. "I beg your pardon."

I grinned down at him. "It's a bitch, ain't it?"

"I'm afraid I don't follow you, fellow." He looked friendly
enough, but he had hard eyes.

I laughed this time. "No. Not very well, you don't. But what I meant was, it's a bitch sitting chilly on some joker you know is in a warm bed with a lady and you're out there all alone freezing your balls off."

He looked up at me coolly. "Outside of the fact that you're rather vulgar, I still don't follow you, fellow."

I pushed my face close to his round, bland one. "You damn right you don't, Mac! Not anymore. You follow me off this lot and I'm gonna ram this son of a bitch"— I turned sideways and slammed my boot heel against the door—"like that, only harder."

I could feel his eyes as I stalked away, and my back muscles quivered a little.

He wasn't there when I looked in my rearview mirror a half block away, and was still nowhere in sight when I drove into my driveway, parked, and went into the house.

But he was there later that afternoon when I answered the doorbell. With him was another one, taller, heavier, face just as bland, but clear-eyed and smiling, with neatly clipped brown hair and a tight, buttoned-down look that gave me a hunch even before he opened his mouth.

"Mr. Roman. I'm Inspector MacKay and this is Agent Don Candle. We're with the Federal Bureau of Investigation. We'd like to talk to you a moment if you don't mind."

"I mind like hell," I said sourly, "but do I have a choice?"

He looked at me with a faintly pained expression. "Of course, Mr. Roman, but you must understand, sir, that we have your best interests at heart. Yours and your wife's." He smiled a warm, reassuring smile, formed an ingratiating expression that made me wonder how long it had taken to perfect in front of a mirror.

"Homer Sellers and his big mouth. He just had to do it."

"If you are referring to Captain Sellers, yes, we received the referral from him."

"Referral? You sound like an insurance salesman."

The smile became a trifle strained. "Could we come inside, Mr. Roman?"

"Sure. Why not?" I stepped aside and they filed past me. I gave Candle a small mean grin. "You need to get somebody to relight your wick, man. You look all burned out." He bobbed his head without changing expression.

I let them find their own seats, then jumped in before MacKay had a chance to take charge of the conversation. He looked like a take-charge guy.

"First thing. I want to know why Shorty here has been following me."

MacKay leaned back and sighed. He tapped the silver pen against the small leather notebook. "Captain Sellers warned us you might be . . . uncooperative, Mr. Roman, and I can understand the pressures you are undergoing. But I must warn you, sir, that this has now been referred to us as a kidnapping and we have assumed responsibility for the safe return of Mrs. Roman if at all possible." He stopped and looked at me steadily. "I strongly suggest that you cooperate, sir, for your own benefit as well as your wife's."

"Amen," I said, wondering what the hell I was doing, deliberately antagonizing a man whose motivations were undoubtedly of the highest caliber despite the prissy way he talked; the only excuses I could come up with were that my nerves were thrumming like banjo wires, depression hovered in my mind like a dank heavy mist, and my heart was a cold, hard stone somewhere inside my chest. Of course, there was also the fact that I had just been unfaithful to my wife. The wife that I was supposed to be so desperate to find. And I suspected that both of these guys knew that. And would hold it against me.

MacKay's face had changed perceptibly, lips thinning across small white teeth that were square across the front, prominent eyeteeth giving him an absurdly lupine look. "How well did you and Susan get along?"

I shrugged. "As well as some, better than most."

"The differences in your ages a problem?"

"Not to her."

"To you, then?" He smiled a cold smile, obviously meant to be deliberately offensive. "Any pressures on your libido, jealousy, resentment of her contacts with younger men?"

"I know what you mean, but you're not only misreading the score, you don't even have the right game," I said coldly.

"Very well, would you like to tell us what happened?"

"Sellers didn't fill you in?"

"We'd like to hear it from you. Fresh viewpoint. Besides, he only knows what you told him."

I told them. As accurately as I remembered. From the first phone call to Ray Tolliver at the TV station right up to the present, omitting only the things I considered irrelevant to the issue. I talked until my throat was dry, then opened a beer and talked some more. MacKay listened stolidly, interrupting occasionally to ask a question, the short one writing in a large notebook with a fluid ease that bespoke some sophisticated form of shorthand. When I finished, MacKay nodded, his unlined face noncommittal although his words were grudgingly approbative.

"You've done a good job, Mr. Roman. As far as it goes, and considering how little you've had to work with. However, I feel I could accuse you of a certain naïveté without being unduly censorious."

I cocked my eyebrows at him and touched fire to a fresh cigarette. "Say what?"

"What do you know about Mr. Harkness?"

"Harkness? You got me. I've never heard of him."

"Milo Harkness, Conrad's bodyguard."

I shook my head. "I don't know anything beyond the fact that he seemed like a right guy and that Conrad fired him."

He shook his head and smiled faintly. "No, I'm afraid that isn't the case, Mr. Roman."

I pondered that for a moment, then sat up a little straighter. "Are you saying Conrad *didn't* fire him?" A cool breeze drifted along the back of my neck and down my spine.

162

"That seems to be the case. According to the young lady who cooks and keeps house for Conrad, Harkness was back within the fold three days after you were there."

"That bastard." I stared into MacKay's quiet, cold eyes. "You think the whole thing could have been staged for my benefit?"

"I doubt it," he said dryly. "But they could have been playing it by ear. Up until the time it got out of hand and you started waving your gun."

"Are you saying they have her?"

He shook his head quickly. "No. No, I'm not saying that at all." He paused. "But are you sure you searched the entire premises? The garage apartment, for instance?"

I wagged my head slowly. "No, no garage apartment. And the house . . . I went through it hurriedly because—" I broke off and cursed softly—"because Milo rushed me through it, whining about losing his job if Conrad came back and caught me there." I squeezed the beer can, watching the foaming liquid spurt out the hole and cascade over my hand. "The son of a bitch took me in. I discounted Conrad mainly because of Milo. He said Susie left there around seven o'clock, said he opened the gate for her himself." I drank what was left in the can and threw it at the fireplace. "He's a smooth one," I added softly.

MacKay nodded. "He should be. He's lived by his wits all his life. He's been busted three times for confidence scams, no convictions, one assault that got him a year in county jail." He took the silver pen out of his jacket pocket and began worrying it with slender, supple fingers.

I looked at him. "I take it your men have been out there if they talked to the cook. I also take it they didn't find anything."

"No. Conrad's gone. Left a few days ago on a tour of the Southwest." He smiled wryly. "There seems to be some confusion about their exact itinerary. We're sorting it out with their booking agency in California, but it may take some time."

"You think it's possible she may . . . they may have her with them?"

"The girl told us there were three or four women with the group besides a couple of blond kids. She couldn't make Susan from her photo, but our man said she looked at it a second time." He shrugged eloquently. "So? How reliable is she?"

A sharp spike of pain was building between my eyes. I squeezed the bridge of my nose and spoke without looking at him.

"You know what Conrad wanted her for. A damned ego trip, man. She busted his chops and he couldn't take it. He even sent a muscle-bound kid to rack my ass because I wounded his dignity. That's what I thought at the time. Maybe I was wrong. Do you think he's crazy enough to take her with him by force?"

His answer was soft, succinct. "You did—once."

"Yeah," I said. "Yeah, I guess I did. I guess I still do." I suddenly felt disoriented, unable to comprehend what was happening, or what had happened.

His voice broke into my thoughts, his words low-keyed, even, but thunderous in their import.

"You—we have to consider, Mr. Roman, the possibility that she went with him of her own free will." He stood up and clipped the silver pen into an inside coat pocket.

"That's bullshit," I said. "How about the telephone call?"

He shrugged. "What better way to keep you off their backs until they were safely on the road?" He moved toward the front door with Agent Candle dogging his heels.

"You're wrong. Susie knows all she'd have to do is tell me she wanted to go with him. I wouldn't try to stop her. A marriage license is not a leash."

He opened the door and stood watching me, smiling faintly. "I'll be in touch," he said, and left.

/ 22 /

Despite a generous infusion of good Irish whiskey before I went to bed, I spent a restless night, starting awake at the slightest sound, or no sound at all, to stare at the glow of Hector Johnson's night-light filtering through the draperies on the window beside my bed. As a result I was groggy and belligerent when Inspector MacKay called me the next morning.

"We caught up with them in Kansas City, Mr. Roman. She wasn't with them."

I found no relief in his words; the load simply shifted.

"You're sure?" My voice was more abrasive than I had intended.

"Give us credit for knowing our jobs, Mr. Roman."

"Was that black bastard with them?"

"Yes."

"What are you going to do now?"

"We're already doing it. Covering much the same ground you've been over."

"You understand the risk? While a private cop and a local policeman might not worry him too much, you government types with your computers and your invincible mystique may send him into a panic."

"We're being very discreet, Mr. Roman. We want her back alive as much as you do."

"I doubt that, Mr. MacKay. Now you're the one who's being naïve."

He was silent for a long moment. "The girl who was burned

165

in the accident. We can find no connection between her and Susan."

I couldn't keep the disgust out of my voice. "There was no connection, dammit! Other than on the side of that hill. This whole damn thing hinges on that one fact. If you discount that encounter, a chance encounter, you might as well take your balls and bats and go home. Because there's no other place to look, no other place to start from if you've written off Conrad."

There was quiet, polite stubbornness in his reply. "We've examined the car. There's nothing, absolutely nothing, to indicate it was other than an unfortunate accident."

"What about the paint burned off the fender? The seat belt out of its reel and burned? Not counting the picture Homer gave you showing the locked mechanism in her lap."

"We examined the picture. It's inconclusive. There's no way to tell positively that the mechanism was engaged. It certainly isn't now. It's on the floor of the car in two pieces. But they would have had to unfasten it to get her out."

"Dammit! Someone covered up a sloppy job of police work. They burned the paint off the fender and disengaged the seat belt and dropped it on the floor. Either that, or it's a deliberate cover-up of some kind. Man, if you're not past that point, you're nowhere! If you can't accept that, there's nowhere for you to go!"

"We are pursuing the investigation," he said stiffly, "in accordance with established procedures. There is a certain protocol—"

"Protocol, my ass! What you're saying is you're pussyfootin' around a bunch of mucky-muck politicians and assholes with a lot of money and power. Yeah. Take you guys away from the activists, the terrorists, and put you up against the big politicians and you're scared shitless just like everybody else. What's the matter, MacKay, you got kids in school, a big mortgage, a promotion coming up?"

"Perhaps," he said coldly, "we should return to my original

line of questioning. Just where were you, Mr. Roman, when your wife disappeared?"

"Go to hell," I said, and slammed the receiver in his ear.

"I thought I warned you, Roman!" The voice was hollow, metallic, disembodied, incredibly chilling.

I sat on the edge of the bed, trying to shake the sleep-fog out of my brain, stuporous, half believing I was still asleep.

"And now you have brought in the FBI." It was slow, measured, mechanical, registering neither anger nor malice, but menacing of itself.

"No! No, I didn't! I swear to you I had nothing to do with it!"

"I don't believe you," the voice intoned. "I can no longer promise her safety. If they come again I will have to dispose of her." Hollow, dispassionate, impersonal.

"No, please!" My voice was hoarse, rasping, searing my throat. "I'll stop them! I promise. . . . Just please, please, don't hurt her."

"You leave me no alternative if you do not stop them."

"I will! I'll . . . somehow, I promise! Just please don't—"

"She is well." The voice was gone, the dial tone burring in my head like a dirge, and something indefinable prowled the room like a palpable flux, dark and menacing and deadly.

It was 10:00 A.M. before I could find MacKay, another hour before he met me at the giant sundial in Euless near the community library. I was waiting, pacing, on my third cigarette, when I saw him pull into the parking lot, climb out of the car, and walk toward me. Alone. I had insisted on that.

He stopped a few feet away, lit a cigarette of his own. He slipped the lighter into his coat pocket and waited, his cold eyes dispassionate.

"You have to stop," I said.

"Is that what you got me all the way out here for?"

"That's it. He called me last night . . . actually this morning. A few hours ago. He wants you to stop. There it is. There's no other choice."

His lip curled. "It's not your choice to make."

"She's mine," I said. "Who better?"

He shook his head. "No. She's not yours. A marriage license is not a title of ownership."

"She's mine, and I say you stop. Now."

His lips curled again, became a mocking smile. "Calm down, Mr. Roman."

I curled my lip back at him. "I hereby withdraw all claim of abduction. She's visiting her grandmother."

"Her grandmother where?"

I grinned at him. "I can't remember."

"Filing a false kidnapping report is a federal offense. Is that still your contention?"

I turned and pointed. "There's the police station over there. Shall we go pick up Captain Homer Sellers? He's the one who filed, not me."

"Let's cut out the bullshit, Roman. What did he say?"

"He said he would dispose of her if you didn't stop."

"Did you believe him?"

"Yes. I don't have a choice."

"If he's kept her this long, he's not going to kill her now."

"You'd stake your life on that?"

He shrugged neatly tailored shoulders. "I might not go that far."

"That's exactly where you are."

He flicked a glance at me, his nostrils flaring. "Are you threatening me?"

"Exactly. You stop now, MacKay. Call them in, all of them. You do that, and when she's home, I'll call you up and apologize, I'll thank you for it. You don't and she doesn't come home alive . . . I'll kill you. It's as simple as that."

"You just committed a felony, you know that? Threatening a federal officer is against the law. The penalty for that is prison."

I smiled genially. "Putting the life of my wife in jeopardy is against my law—Roman's law. The penalty for that is death."

He started to laugh, took another look at my face and decided not to. "I believe you're crazy enough to try it."

"Count on it."

He shrugged and lit another cigarette, stalling for time. I could almost see the wheels turning. He needed a way to get out without losing face. I gave it to him.

"I know you're on my side. I know you're just doing your job and evidently you're doing it well . . . too well maybe, or the guy wouldn't be running scared. I'm asking you to let it go, give Susie at least that chance to live."

He shrugged again, relief evident in his face. "Okay, like you said, she's your wife. I guess you're entitled to call the shots—up to a point." He crushed the cigarette carefully beneath his heel. "All right. For now. I'll just forget what you said here today. I understand the pressure you're under." He smiled frostily and turned on his heel.

"One thing, Inspector MacKay. Do you have a reading on who your men have approached on this?"

He made no attempt to hide his annoyance. "We've contacted all of them to one degree or another. The names you gave us. Why?"

"He said if you 'came again' he would kill her."

The annoyed frown faded into a faint thoughtful smile. "I see. He must be one of them after all. Otherwise he wouldn't be concerned. Right, Mr. Roman?"

"Exactly, Inspector MacKay."

He lifted his hand in a mocking half-salute and walked off down the ramp.

23

"You've pulled some dumb stunts in your time, boy, but I think this one takes the prize." Homer stared up at me, radiating outrage, his blue eyes bright gleaming smears beyond the distortion of the bifocals.

"It worked. That's the proof of the pudding, as my ma used to say."

"But threatening to kill an FBI man! I can't believe even you'd do that, boy. Not in broad daylight." He raked a beefy hand through his shaggy hair.

"That's the best way. Nobody would believe it. Except maybe him."

"You need to learn a little humility, boy. That mouth of yours is gonna get you in a peck of trouble someday." He banged a hand on his desk and adjusted his glasses in the same motion.

"I know," I said contritely. "Maybe someday you could give me some lessons in humble, you're so damn good at it."

He guffawed suddenly. "Yeah, ain't it the truth."

"Besides, this mishmash was all your fault. I told you to stay away from those big-city types. Our man is probably just one of the good old boys who got in over his head when he did something on the spur of the moment out of panic. You or I shook him up a little and he thinks he made a passing grade, but he'd be scared shitless of these button-down types with their silver pencils and their computers and their cold penetrating eyes. I've been subjected to more steely-eyed piercing looks in the last couple of days than in my whole life." I paused to catch my breath.

He yawned. "No shit?"

"Okay, okay. You're a hardass cynic and that's all right, too. I'm not saying they don't do a passable job when it's manpower that's needed or sophisticated electronic equipment or maybe money to set up a drug bust or scam some crooked politician into getting himself on the six o'clock news. But they're specialists, and maybe when there's ransom money to be paid, or electronic surveillance, or wire bugging to be done, well, maybe then they shine. But this isn't one of those things. This is just plain old foot-slogging, door-knocking, question-asking police work and I've seen a hell of a lot of underpaid cops who are better at it than they are."

He was nodding his head at that when I got up and leaned on his desk and shook my finger in his face. "And if that son of a bitch hasn't turned her loose by the end of this week I'm going to start at the top of that damn list and do it all over again—only this time I'm taking off the fucking gloves!"

I hibernated the next two days, filled with a nameless, amorphous dread. Soap operas and talk shows, newscasts without number. Newscasters without Susie's beautiful face and clear voice.

Late in the second afternoon, with a gusty glowering day slipping unnoticed and unmourned into evening, she came tapping at my door; like Poe's raven, the timid rapping fraught with meaning, portentous. I stumbled to the door with racing blood and pounding heart, blinded by visions of dark haunting eyes and sweet red lips, of honey-colored skin and raven hair, of warm compassion and a forgiving heart. I fought the chains and locks and cursed silently in my fumbling haste; I threw open the door and recoiled with an involuntary moan.

"Hi, honey," Alicia said timidly, uncertainly, taking a small half step backwards as she saw my face.

She was smartly dressed, a white coat with a fur collar framing an almost freckle-free face, rosy cheeks and darkly tinted eyes, pale red lips and honey hair piled high on her dainty head.

A vision all right, a vision of loveliness—but the wrong one.

I made up words and a welcoming smile, leaned over and kissed her to avoid her relentless, sorrowful eyes. She slipped out of the coat to reveal a tailored pale yellow suit that hugged her rounded shape with studied insouciance, highlighted the new golden sheen of her hair. She wet her lips and self-consciously posed for me.

"Hmm, nice," I said, realizing with something like shock that this was only the second time I had seen her out of the brocaded robe—out of her working clothes, so to speak. "More than nice," I added to make up for my graceless greeting. "Exquisite."

"Now don't tease," she protested, pleased nevertheless, the pale rose in her cheeks blooming, earnestly searching my face for approval.

"I'm not teasing," I said solemnly. "You are beautiful."

She laughed a small breathless laugh. "Lordy, I should be. I spent the whole day nearly in a beauty salon."

"All they can do is enhance," I said gallantly. "The ingredients must be there." I sat her down and fitted her hand with a vodka martini, suddenly uneasy, wondering what I would do if there should come another tapping at the door.

"It occurred to me," she said shyly, "that you had never seen me any way but almost naked." She giggled. "That old robe. I wanted you to see me like a normal person."

"A pleasant paradoxical reversal of custom," I said. "Usually one contrives diligently to divest the fair maiden of her raiment, not the other way around."

She laughed, dark eyes flashing. "I'm not exactly sure what you said, but I hope it's nice." She sipped her drink elegantly, peeping at me over the rim, flirting with arched eyebrows and knowing eyes. I suddenly felt exceedingly shabby, with my two-day growth of beard, bloodshot sunken eyes, and dirty wrinkled garments. But it's a well-known fact that a woman's capacity for acceptance of sloth and self-indulgence is seemingly unbounded, and she looked at me with warm adoring eyes. Such unconstrained, uncritical devotion was somehow frightening.

"How've you been, Danny?" she asked, from her end of a silence I couldn't seem to break.

"Busy, busy. And yourself?"

"Oh, not much." She hesitated. "I had some visitors. You'll never guess who."

"Two men; neat, clean-cut types in three-piece suits with shiny shoes and silver pencils."

"Oh, you knew."

"Just an educated guess. What did they want?"

"They wanted to know about Charley, who her johns were, like that." She looked away, a faint blush of color coming into her cheeks.

"Did either one of them come back later? Alone perhaps?"

She lowered her eyes. "Yes, the smaller one. He wanted a . . . a freebie."

"Did you give it to him?"

She nodded without raising her head or speaking.

"You should have kicked him in the balls."

She shrugged. "He was the law, Danny. I couldn't afford to make him angry."

"If the dirty little creep tries it again, you let me know."

She nodded doubtfully, then smiled. "All right, Danny, but it really doesn't matter."

"It damn well does," I flared. "It's thievery. No different than demanding a free suit of clothes from a haberdasher. You're in business same as anybody else."

"I thought you might come by last night." There was no accusation in her voice, but she ameliorated it hurriedly just the same. "But I guess you were busy."

"No, I wasn't busy. I was drunk, Alicia. I didn't think you needed that. Me sober is bad enough, but me drunk I wouldn't wish on the Ayatollah Khomeini."

173

She laughed. "You're just a big pussycat. I know how to handle you."

I scraped a hand across my jaw. "I could do with a bath and a shave."

"I can help with the bath, but you'll have to do your own shaving." She smiled impishly. "I might cut something off."

"I couldn't stand to lose any."

"Oh, I don't know." She fluttered her eyelashes at me roguishly, then stood on tiptoe and brushed her lips lightly across mine.

I fitted my hands around her waist, moved them upward into her armpits, my thumbs against the lower slopes of her breasts, working upward until they touched the bare flesh.

"Golly gee," I said, "you women sure are smooth and soft."

She chuckled throatily and pressed against me.

I had already felt the warning stir and I should have known better. I broke away and headed toward the shower, paused to sample parted, inviting lips again, lingered for one more taste as the stirring became a surge, a torrent of desire that robbed my legs of strength. She aided my fumbling fingers and an interminable time later our clothing was gone. I touched my lips to the soft undersides of her breasts, felt her shiver, and drew back.

"I'll go shave," I whispered, but she shook her head fiercely, gripped me with determined fingers, and sank slowly to the thick shag rug.

When it finally became obvious to her that I wasn't going to invite her to spend the night, she accepted it with whimsical grace.

"You're just a big fat chicken," she murmured. "You're scared to death she may come home and find me here."

"You're right," I admitted. "But I'm even more afraid she won't come."

"You haven't had any more phone calls?"

"No." I stared morosely at her face, illuminated by a beam

of light filtering through a crack in the bedroom draperies. I leaned across her to squash out my cigarette and she raised her head and kissed my chin.

"Do you always do it twice with her, too?"

"No," I said, the ever-ready cynic inside me almost adding that she wasn't all that used to it, but I stopped him just in time.

"Does that mean she doesn't do it as well as me?" She was a determined little cuss.

I touched her breast. "Nobody does it better."

She giggled. "That's a song title, silly."

"That's what you are. A song, a melody, a symphony of sensuality."

"I like the sound of that." She twisted her head to look at my face. "Even if you don't mean it."

"I do mean it, Alicia," I said quietly, feeling a sudden rush of empathy at her insecurity, her constant compelling need for reassurance. But there was an irrational thread of impatience there, also. Her emotional needs were beginning to twang at my nerves.

I could have told her that love made the difference, that love raised it above the animal level of pure physical pleasure, brought to it that indefinable ingredient that meant total and complete fulfillment.

But maybe she knew, maybe that was what compelled her to pull and pick at me as if I were the scab on an old sore. I could have told her, but I was just a big fat chicken.

She lingered at the door, holding my hand, eyes heavy-lidded and languorous, lips still puffy, freckles now shining on the freshly scrubbed face, her expression as close to smugness as it could manage. She shivered at the blast of air from the door and hunkered into the collar of her new coat, reluctant to leave.

"Oooooh, it's cold out there," she said reproachfully. "You're mean, making me go out in this. There's a blue norther on the way, they said. If I catch the flu, it'll be your fault."

"I'll come over and nurse you. So it wouldn't be a total loss."

"Uh-huh!" She closed one eye and gave me a pixie half grin. "We could tell her I'm your new maid."

"We could tell her you're my mother, too. She'd believe it about as fast."

"Oh, shoot! You're the hardest-headed man I've ever seen."

"I'm just practical. If she came home and found us together, she might shoot you. Then I'd lose both of you."

She gave me a startled glance. "Oh, you're teasing! She wouldn't do anything like that."

"She might," I said. "She's mostly Italian, you know. Sicilian. Fidelity's a big thing with them. In Sicily if a woman catches her husband screwing around she catches him asleep and—" I broke off and shuddered delicately—"cuts them off."

"You lie a lot, too," she said, her eyes glinting. She tilted her face to be kissed. "All right, I'll go. I sure wouldn't want you to lose your manhood."

"It's not my manhood I'm worried about," I said aloud a few moments later, watching her whip the small maroon car out of my driveway and drive off down the street wiggling her fingers at me through the half-opened window. "It's my sanity."

/ **24** /

By Monday morning I could stand the inactivity no longer. Ignoring my hangover, I pondered my options for a while, disconsolate with their sparsity, then finally sighed and called Homer Sellers's office.

"He's not here, Danny. I don't expect him back until this afternoon. Any messages?" I could hear Mitzi's typewriter clattering and I could picture her gray-streaked head canted to one side as she held the phone against her shoulder.

"No—yes. Tell him I'm going back out to Mickey Conrad's to look around."

"He's still on tour, Danny. Anyway, the FBI gave him a clean bill—"

"They're human, Mitzi. Then can make mistakes as well as I can." I wasn't surprised that she knew about Conrad or the FBI. Very little went on around Homer that she didn't know. Sometimes I wondered if maybe she didn't have his office bugged. "I have to start again somewhere, may as well be there."

"Why don't you wait for Homer, Danny? I know he'd go with you."

"Probably. But that would be another half a day wasted. I've wasted too much time as it is."

"You take care, then, Danny."

"Tell him I'll call him this evening"

"I hope so."

I parked at the gate and sat for a while smoking and looking at the house. Nothing moved. I looked for the garage apartment that MacKay had mentioned, but the driveway curved around to the back of the house. That, at least, gave me some small excuse for my carelessness. Some, but not enough. Not enough to make even a small dent in the shroud of depression that weighed on me like a heavy mantle of cold dank fog. I finished the cigarette and got out and flipped the butt through the metal gate. Convinced that I was wasting my time, I walked over and tried the door to the small guardhouse.

It opened. I went in. I pressed the button, held it down, listened to the hum and sizzle of the speaker. There was an abrupt click and the sizzling stopped.

"Yes. Who is it?" It was a soft voice, mellow, an accent that didn't have its origin in Texas.

"My name is Dan Roman. Are you Mickey Conrad's cook?"

177

"Yes."

"You are a friend of Milo's?"

There was a pause. "Yes, I know Milo. What is it?"

"You remember a couple of weeks ago, one night, Milo was with you. He came to the gate to let me in. We looked into his room. You were the one there?"

"Yes, I remember you, Mr. Roman. What is it?"

"I'd like to come in and talk to you."

"I'm sorry, sir, Mr. Conrad doesn't allow visitors while he's away."

"I'm not visiting Conrad. I'd like to talk to you."

Another pause. "Your wife left at seven, sir. Just the way Milo told you. I can't tell you anything else."

"Then you know why I'm here?"

"I think so, yes."

"You know that she's been missing since she supposedly left here that evening."

"Yes, sir. I know that. I'm sorry."

"And yet you won't talk to me?"

"We're talking, Mr. Roman. I couldn't tell you any more face-to-face."

"Did you see her while she was here that afternoon?"

"Yes. I served them tea."

"How did she look? Was he . . . I mean did he—?"

"She looked fine, sir. They were going over some type of script, I believe."

"And you know for a fact that she left at seven?"

"I only know that Milo told me that."

"Why would Milo lie about losing his job? I understand he came back to work in a few days."

"Yes. I don't know why. You'd have to ask Milo."

"You understand that you could get in trouble, become an accomplice to kidnapping, if you deliberately withheld information or lied to me?"

Her laugh was short, caustic. "So the men from the FBI told me, Mr. Roman."

178

"Who lives above the garage?"

"I do, sir."

"Could she have been held somewhere on the premises without your knowledge?"

"I don't think so, sir. She would have to eat." She sounded amused.

"Why are you staying there with Conrad out of town?"

"I don't have anywhere else to go. I live here."

"I could come back with police officers and a search warrant."

"All right, sir. If you do that I'll let you in."

Enough was enough; I acknowledged defeat. "All right, miss, thank you for your time and trouble."

"You're very welcome, sir."

"I'm going to kill him now, Homer. He's broken his word to me. He's kept her beyond the allotted time. I did what he said. I trusted him to keep his word, but he isn't going to turn her loose and if he kills her before I can find him, he's going to hurt before he dies. But whether he turns her loose now or not, I'm going to kill him."

Homer shifted uneasily. "That's just the whiskey talking, boy. I know that, but it's crazy talk all the same. Just talking like that you're breaking the law."

"Law? Law? What the hell has the law done for me? Or Susie? We're way past law time, courts, justice ... all that bullshit. It's a personal thing now, maybe has been from the beginning only I was too dumb to know it. He's put himself way above the law, so why should the law apply? What he's doing is to me and mine and I've got my own damned law."

He heaved himself to his feet and crossed to the bar. He set the glass down with a bang and turned to face me.

"I ain't listening to any more of this bullshit!" he said coldly. "I've known you to say and do some dumb things, but you go turning on the law, you're turning on me."

I shrugged. "If that's the way you want to take it. It's got nothing to do with you personally and you know it. Over the years you've done a hell of a lot for me. But that wasn't because you were the law. It was because we were friends."

His eyes bored at me, incredibly hard to face. "Maybe we ain't such good friends anymore."

I sighed. "Maybe we're not, Homer. But that would be a damn shame."

"Maybe so." He moved to the door, his face unrelenting. "Friendship is a two-way street. Ours is kinda one way."

"Okay, okay," I yelled, suddenly shaken. I had never seen him like this before and it was curiously frightening. "What do you want from me?"

"I don't want anything from you." His words were as cold and unforgiving as his face. "How can I? I don't even know who you are anymore. You ain't the cop I useta work with and you ain't the man I useta know. That man never got his guts out of a bottle and wouldn't have gone whimpering to the bed of a whore, wallowing in muck—"

"Watch it, Homer! She may be a whore, but she—"

He waved me silent with a short savage movement of his hand. "I ain't got nothing against an honest whore. But you got a woman . . . a woman you say you love, who wasn't gone a week before you was laying up with the first woman you saw." He shook his head in disgust. "And you go ranting and raving around here putting down everything I stand for, talking about killing like it meant nothing. I don't know you anymore, Danny boy, and I ain't sure I want to."

He closed the door and I stood staring at it dully, trying to remember if he had ever called me Danny boy before, wondering with a sick empty feeling at the contemptuous finality in his voice when he said it. He had based his whole life on doing the right thing and it was clear that I had finally done one too many wrong things for him to overlook. He lived by his code and I had violated it. It was as simple as that.

It took me a full day and half a night to find him and set it up the way I wanted. Luck had a lot to do with it, luck and the gut that hung over his belt that he liked to fill with brew before the end of his shift.

Detective Jack Mahoney. I stood shivering in the shadow of a pickup camper and watched him come through the rear exit of the bar. He was weaving slightly, walking stiff-legged and stiff-backed to counterbalance the weight of his swollen stomach. He went by me humming a rock tune off-key and fumbling with the keys to his car.

I hit him when he reached the dirty gray Pontiac, kicked him behind the knee and slammed his head against the door panel as he went down.

He lay spread-eagled on the pavement, my hand pushing his face into the rough asphalt before he made a sound.

"Wha—what're you think . . . hey, I'm a police officer." He rolled his right eye upward in an attempt to see my face. I shoved the gun barrel against it.

"Shut up, fatso," I hissed in his ear. I thumbed back the hammer on the gun, gave him a second for it to register in his stunned brain.

"Hey! Man! I ain't got much money."

I put my mouth close to his ear. "I don't want your money, you gutless bastard. I want an answer to a question. You get one chance. You got that? One! If I don't like your answer, I let this hammer drop."

"Hey, man, wha—hey, you can't . . ."

I rapped his head with the barrel. "I haven't asked it yet, stupid."

He groaned, lapsed into silence.

"The Wilkins woman . . . the one who burned? Who paid you to clean it up, make it look like an accident?" I rolled the barrel across his eye again. "Remember, you only get one answer."

"Hey," he said weakly. "Hey."

I rapped his head again. "That's not an answer! You want to try it again?"

"Hey, I didn't . . . he wasn't . . . I don't know who it was."

I leaned on his head, ground his face into the filthy black-top. He groaned quietly, sucked in a deep breath.

"I swear ... man. I—I never saw him before ... young punk, blond, short ... stocky build ... round fat face ... maybe two hundred ..."

I felt a sinking slide inside as I realized he was describing the man I had killed in Hector Johnson's driveway.

"You're lying," I said savagely. "You wouldn't take money from a man you didn't know. Even you're not that stupid."

"I—I got ... phone call ... first."

"Who?"

"Don't know, man. Higher up ... brass ... somebody, didn't know his voice."

"How did you know it was police brass?"

"He ... mentioned some ... things happened in the past. I didn't ... have no choice!"

"You've got one now," I said softly, pressing the gun against his eye. "You can tell me the truth or you'll be looking up your nose with this eyeball."

He tried to shake his head, moaned again as I slammed it downward.

"You—you'll have ... to do it, then. I swear it's ... truth!"

I pressed my knee into the small of his back, dug around him for the gun while I thought about it. I found the clip-on holster and ripped it free. Trembling with frustration and rage, I threw the rig into the high weeds at the end of the lot.

"Remember, Mahoney, I know who you are. You don't know me. If I find out you're lying to me, I'll be on you like a tick bird on a buffalo's ass."

His head moved minutely under my restraining hand. "No ... I swear. It's the truth."

"Your gun's somewhere out there in the weeds, Mahoney. I'd wait a few minutes before I went for it if I were you."

I shoved his head against the asphalt once more to give him something to think about, then slipped away from him into the shadows. I weaved through the parked cars to where I had left the station wagon on the street. There was still no sound or movement in the parking lot when I drove away.

I followed Jacksboro Highway from the bar to Loop 820, riding the high curving loop to the left. Once onto the wide thoroughfare, I set the automatic cruise control on sixty and let the heavy wagon take me north toward home. I was filled with a quiet numbing despair, the quiet hum of the big engine and the faint susurrus of the tires almost soporific. A natural reaction in the aftermath of the tension-filled incident in the bar parking lot? Or was I losing momentum? Losing my resolution because everything I touched turned to ashes that trickled through my fingers and left the bitter taste of acid in my mouth?

Almost three weeks and I was no closer to finding her. Anger, frustration, guilt, fear—how long could my emotions bear the load? How long before something blew? Before my circuits overloaded and all the wires came loose, short-circuited, sent a wrong message to an itching trigger finger based on emotional backlash instead of logic, and I blew somebody else away. More and more MacKay's words were returning at odd moments to my consciousness, quietly persistent.

"You have to consider, Mr. Roman, the possibility that she went of her own free will."

Maybe he was right. Maybe it was my pride that wouldn't let me accept what could be the obvious answer. Maybe she couldn't face it after all, marriage to a man sixteen years her senior, no prize at that. A man too old and too tired for the wearying vicissitudes of youth, too blasé and cynical for the frivolous games of young romantic love. A man who drank too much and needed too much reassurance, a man who could offer only a modicum of financial security and precious little else.

Maybe that's the answer, I thought gloomily, sadly. Bury the images of haunting eyes and midnight tresses, laughing lips and sensuous body as memories of another day, another place, keep them for the dark sleepless nights when the booze and the practiced sex don't work, trade them for freckled breasts and a pouting, voracious mouth, soft arms, and slavish devotion.

And at that moment of indecision I came to the intersection of Airport Freeway and the looping curve that led southward to the Oak Meadows Apartments. The old wagon was holding steady on an eastward course, nose into the wind and heading for home, but I reined her sharply, smothering with the aching pain of loneliness and losing, and headed south to Alicia.

/ 25 /

I could see his face over her shoulder: fat, florid, swollen with anticipation, just beginning to take on the shape and color of fear as he saw me and rose swiftly from the sofa to his feet.

I pushed past her, walked stiffly across the room to the bar cart, ignoring him. I poured a drink and turned to his apprehensive face and her flushed angry one.

"Give him his money back; get his ass out of here."

"I will not! You big bastard! You . . ." She choked up, on the verge of angry tears.

"Hey, what the hell is this?" He was scared a sickly white, but his pride demanded at least a show of truculence.

"I'll tell you what it is. If you're not out of here in five seconds, I'll throw you out." I said it pleasantly, even grinned at him, but he took me seriously.

"Hey, now, wait a minute." He was already edging toward the door. "I'll have you know I have an appointment here."

"You had an appointment," I explained patiently. "I just

canceled it. The lady just went out of business. If you have money coming, say so." I smiled at him gently.

He shook his head raggedly. "No, but I—but I ..." He looked helplessly at Alicia.

But she was watching me, her hands over her mouth, eyes big and shining, filled with comprehending wonder or black murder—I wasn't sure which.

The man had regained some of his composure, taking heart from my sudden loss of aggression, and the fact that he had probably realized he was younger and bigger than I.

"Now, look here, buddy, I've been coming to see this little lady a long time. She's my favorite ..."

"She's my favorite, too, Mac. Go home and play with yourself, find somebody else, but just say good-bye and go." I walked toward him.

He stood his ground another two seconds, then wheeled and tried to swagger as he went out the door, the drink forgotten in his hand.

I gunned the rest of my drink and looked at her, feeling the raw liquor burn a path all the way to my stomach.

She was still poised, frozen in time and space, her fingers pressed against her mouth, her eyes expanded to their outer limits, suspiciously bright and moist.

"I don't know," I said grimly, "if you understood what just happened here. If you didn't, then I'll tell you. He was the last, the last damned one. You hear me? Anybody touches you again I'll break their goddamned fingers. You understand?"

She nodded dumbly, a swatch of golden hair breaking loose and falling unheeded across her brow, the freckles blending nicely with the sudden flood of color into her face.

"And take your damn fingers off your mouth. I can't tell if you're smiling or crying, or what."

She was smiling: the small triumphant smile women never have to practice, never have to learn because they're born with it. She just stood there smiling and nodding, more hair falling loose, small clear drops of something that glistened trailing down across her cheeks and running into the corners of her mouth.

"Well, say something, dammit!"

"Oh, God! Oh, God, Danny," was all she could manage before she threw herself at me.

I thumbed at the tears every chance she gave me, in between the kissing and hugging and her fingers stroking my face like it was fine silk. And after a while, after she had become satiated with my kisses, she leaned back and stared fixedly into my eyes.

"What about her, Danny?"

"She's gone, Alicia. She's gone of her own accord, and maybe that's for the best, or if someone does have her, it's been too long. He's not going to let her go."

She watched my face for a moment longer. "But what if? What if she does come back someday?"

"I can't answer that, babe." I kissed the last tear from the corner of her eye. "Are you looking for guarantees? If you are, we're licked before we start."

"No. I don't mean that. I mean, would you still . . . still keep me after?" A desperate plea for reassurance that tugged gently at my insides.

"We could maybe work out . . . something."

"I have some money," she said solemnly. "You could have that. Don't laugh. It's quite a bit, you know."

I hugged her. "That won't be necessary. But I'll give you a little clue about what *is* necessary. . . ."

She smiled delightedly and squirmed in my lap. "I'd have to be pretty dumb not to notice." She squeezed my neck fiercely. "Oh, I'm so happy." She sighed. "Are you happy?"

"Yes," I said, lying, feeling doubly guilty—guilt over a belated sense of betrayal of Susie, and guilt for using Alicia to soothe my despair.

Later we lay side by side in the semidarkness and I smoked while she told me her sad tale. A not-uncommon story for a

186

prostitute. The only surprise would have been if she hadn't become one.

A hundred-acre hardscrabble farm in Tennessee, a father who eventually went to work for the railroad, home only on weekends, usually drunk, in later years always amorous.

Her mother had had seven children by the time she was thirty, all girls, and she closed her legs to her husband when the doctor told her another one would kill her. Then five years later Alicia was born, the result of the violent rape of her mother by her father. And sure enough, the doctor had been right; her mother had died a month later from childbirth complications.

Her sisters raised her, the oldest seventeen at the time of her mother's death. By the time she was seven, four of the girls were gone, driven away by the sexual demands of the father. And if anybody noticed, nobody cared. At least not enough to do anything about it. She was ten when the last of the seven sisters left.

Alicia eventually ran away with a racetrack mechanic, a bedroom hero who assumed she obtained her pleasure simultaneously with his and never thought to ask. Two years and one abortion later he left her stranded and she embarked on her career as a prostitute.

Her voice steady and dry, she talked into the dim glow filtering through the windows, moving against me as if she was softly seeking reassurance and security. She stopped finally and sighed.

"Pretty bad, huh?"

"I've heard worse, but I reckon I've heard better, too."

"Can you imagine all of us letting him do it to us?"

"Yes. He was your father, the figure of authority. I don't imagine it was too hard if he started in early enough the way he did with you." I thought fleetingly of the Markette clan.

"I know," she said, "but there was something . . . He never held a knife at my throat and made me do it, or anything like that. In fact, I don't remember ever being actually afraid of him. But when he'd tell me to do it . . . I'd get this funny feeling . . . like, oh, I don't know how to say it . . . like I couldn't help myself, you know. Kind of hypnotized like." She dropped her head on my chest, the fine light hair tickling my nose. "After a while . . . I didn't even . . . mind. I just didn't think about it. I pretended that I wasn't there. It was . . . like I became invisible. I never really understood how I felt about him. I never shed a tear when he died, so I don't suppose I loved him." Her voice was muffled and dry, filled with a kind of quiet agony.

"Maybe you're just not selfish enough to grieve."

"What?"

"Grief is about ninety percent self-pity, the other ten is more than likely guilt."

She raised her head, her eyes glowing faintly in the subdued light. "Is that what you feel . . . about her?"

"Probably," I said. "If it were possible to analyze my feelings accurately and honestly. There's an aching emptiness, a sense of loss, but there's a feeling of being cheated also, of being wrongfully deprived of what is mine. Possessiveness . . . it's about as close to selfishness as you can get."

"I never thought about it like that," she said.

"I didn't either," I said, "until just now."

She chuckled again. "You're a fraud. I thought you had probably spent a lot of time thinking that through."

"Just one of those flashes of insight we geniuses get."

Her fingers left a trail of goose bumps across my stomach. After a while she lifted her head and propped her chin on my left biceps.

"Maybe I can help a little with the emptiness."

I curled my arm around her neck, rolled her against me, the smooth softness of her flesh a physical pleasure, her eager acquiescence a chauvinist's delight.

"You have. More than you know."

We were both almost asleep, drifting easily in the narrow void between dreams and reality, when the telephone rang.

188

Alicia snapped upright, hands coming together at her breast. "Oh, Lord, I forgot to turn off the phone." She scooted out of the bed and padded into the living room.

I stretched and yawned and went into the bathroom. When I entered the living room a few minutes later she was still talking animatedly, perched on the arm of the couch, arching her eyebrows and grimacing resignedly at me over the pink receiver. ". . . to take a long, long vacation . . . maybe forever." She swung one foot as she listened, the freckles on her breasts like old faded spots of rust.

I slapped her on the fanny on my way to the refrigerator. I found a can of beer and came back into the living room.

". . . don't think so, Thomas. By the way, how is your mother?"

I turned on the Channel 4 news, sound low, found a seat, and watched the animated faces, the modulated, precise voices an indistinct murmur.

". . . would be naughty, Thomas. There's no reason in the world you can't. Just make up your mind once and for all and find a nice girl. If she's the right one, I don't think you'll have any trouble at all."

I lit a cigarette and took a drink of beer, then turned to look at her; she grimaced again and winked at me, her leg swinging with the precise beat of a metronome.

I stood up and crossed over to her. I took the receiver out of her hand and dropped it into the cradle. I went back and sat down and drank some beer. I never once looked at her face.

She slipped off the arm of the couch onto the cushion. We silently watched the anchorman's face fade from the screen and the beginning of a ridiculous painkiller commercial filled with repetitious inanities.

"That was mean, Danny. I was just helping him. That poor boy . . ."

"Poor, my ass. Let him get a shrink."

"I'm sorry if it aggravated you. He's having a lot of trouble knowing which way he wants to go. He's having an identity crisis, he said. He feels insecure because his father is so rich and successful and he can't seem to make a go of anything. And now with his father going to Washington it's even worse. And his mother. She collapsed at Charley's funeral and they had to take her straight to a sanitarium for—"

"He told me," I said irritably. I finished the beer and went back into the bedroom and began to get dressed. I was sitting on the edge of the bed pulling on my boots when she came in, the edges of the nylon robe gripped in one fist, the belt trailing.

"You're mad at me," she said, pouting prettily from the doorway.

"No, I'm not mad." I stamped my foot into the boot, then smiled at her.

"Come here."

She came obediently to stand in front of me, head ducked, lower lip protruding in mock repentance. I tucked in the robe and tied the sash. "There. You don't have to be ready to go at a moment's notice anymore."

She laughed and wrapped her arms around my head. "I do for you," she said, dropping her voice to a low husky drawl.

"Don't worry, you'll get plenty of warning from me." I gripped her hipbones in my hands and held her back far enough to see her face.

"You do understand," I said slowly. "I won't share you with anyone, Alicia. Not even verbally. Not even mentally if I can help it. I'm jealous and possessive. I just want you to understand the kind of commitment you're making."

She nodded soberly. "I understand, honey. It's what I want, too."

I stood up and she threw herself against me and squeezed my waist. "Do you have to go?"

"Yep. Gotta go tonight, but I'll see you tomorrow. Okay?"

She nodded reluctantly and walked me to the door, my arm clamped against her breast.

I kissed her good-bye and cupped her glowing face between

my hands. "And if weirdo Thomas calls again, you hang up on him, you hear? I don't care how many rich fathers or sick mothers he has, you're not his sexual therapist anymore. If he—" I stopped suddenly, staring at the pattern of freckles across her nose.

A flash of something . . . a quick blur of sounds and pictures across the screen of my conscious mind, a teasing will-o'-the-wisp, instantly gone, but leaving behind a nagging fading image.

"Danny? What is it?" She was watching me worriedly, wide-eyed.

"I don't know," I said slowly. "Something I almost thought of, I guess. Something . . ."

It was there again: a face, smooth, pampered, tanned, words with no meaning, subliminal impressions, fleeting, tantalizing, gone again . . . like a long-forgotten dream resurrecting on the tip of my mind.

I shook my head. "That was weird. Something flashed across my mind . . . like watching a movie in triple time, or something."

She laughed. "Boy, I think you do need some rest."

I kissed her again, said good-bye, and walked to my car, the residue of the incident lingering like shadowy filaments in some creeping spider's sticky web.

I drove home slowly, inexplicably troubled for no reason I could define. I sat motionless for a while in the driveway, deliberately trying to erase the blackboard in my head, opening my mind to whatever would come. But nothing came and finally the cold drove me inside.

I opened a beer and sat down with Johnny Carson and his guest, some starlet with mobile features, dark and lively, smooth honey-colored skin, and sculptured lips. So much like . . .

I shook my head like a dog coming out of water. No good. She was gone and I had to accept that, live with it as best I could, live with my guilt for surrendering hope, for Alicia.

191

I listened to the woman sing, seeing her fade as my mind wandered. I lay back in the recliner and tried to force coherence into thoughts that flitted from one pinnacle to another like a drunken butterfly, chips and slivers jumbled in stultifying resonance; fragments, snatches of conversation, segments of images, bits and pieces whipping in from the nether regions of my mind.

Mickey Conrad: arrogant, sneering . . . Thomas Markette: slender, weak, vacillating . . . John Markette: handsome, urbane, tanned, pampered . . . James Hammond: tall, thin, predatory, a hearty handshake and a ready smile that didn't reach his cold hard eyes . . . Senator Blakely: craggy, powerful, a hint of cruelty at the corners of his mouth . . . George Winscott: incredibly ugly, radiating obscenity like heat from a burning building . . . Milo Harkness: good-old-boy grin, eyes as opaque as the carapace of a black beetle . . .

Suddenly I was sitting upright: two voices, two bits of information, two ragged blips of conversation were coming together like the last two pieces of a crossword puzzle that didn't fit. . . .

Yeah! YEAH!

They didn't fit, dammit!

The son of a bitch had lied to me, had been lying from the beginning. A useless lie, unnecessary; but guilt and fear exert Draconian pressures, force compulsive answers to questions that haven't been asked, impulsive rationale to theorems that exist only in the convoluted thoughts of the liar.

I sucked in my breath, my head spinning, rocked back and forth like an addict in withdrawal.

I let it run through my mind again, worked it out, how it could have been, must have been, felt my hands clench into fists.

I sat transfixed a moment longer, wallowing in the sweet taste of enlightenment, the hot, sharp taste of vengeance to come.

Then I shook myself again, stalked across the room to where I kept my guns. My mind was finally clear, and seething with a cold and deadly purpose.

"Yeah." Homer's voice was heavy, rough with irritation and sluggish with sleep.

"Sorry to break into your beauty sleep, old buddy."

I waited a moment for my voice to register.

"Yeah, what's on your mind?" His voice was cool, his tone indifferent.

Slowly and distinctly, so he would understand it the first time, I told him. "I know who has Susie, Homer. I wanted you to know . . . just in case something goes wrong."

"Who?" he barked, the indifference gone, his voice an octave higher.

"I'm not going to tell you. I don't want any interference. I'm going after her. . . ."

"Dammit, boy!" he yelled. "Cut out the bullshit! Who died and made you God? If you know something, you damn well better tell me and cut out this melodramatic shit!"

"Not melodrama, Homer. Insurance. He's mine, and I don't want a bunch of cops stumbling around, slapping his wrist, reading him rights he damn well don't have anymore! He gave them up when he took her! The only right he's got is what I allow him if she's not dead! And if she is . . . well, he's got about as many rights as a cockroach crawling across my kitchen table."

"Jesus H. Christ," he said hoarsely, his voice clotted with exasperation and rage. "Don't you know I'm a cop, boy? I can't listen to this crap no more. You're threatening to kill a man! Kill a man, dammit! Don't you know there's a law against that no damn matter what he's done!"

"There is a better law for it. My law."

"You dumb thickheaded egomaniac! Can't you do it right for once? I promise you . . . no law except me. Just me. Is that too much to ask?"

"It's not your jurisdiction. Sorry."

"That don't . . . that don't matter! I got a badge. That's what's important."

"No way, Homer. I'd just have to fight my way through you, too, and I don't know if I'm up to that."

"Aw, hell! Dammit, Dan . . ."

"I've got it on the recorder tape. His name and why I think it's him. But you'll have to look for it. I don't want to make it too easy or too quick."

"Why you *think* it's him?" He stopped and coughed rackingly. "Dammit, you said you *knew.*"

"I do, Homer," I said quietly. "The same kind of feeling you had when you pulled the blue Caddy over that time. The little girl was in the trunk, remember? You didn't know she was there, but you said you knew without knowing why. Well, that's the same way this is. I know without knowing exactly why except the son of a bitch lied to me for no good reason." I sighed. "That and the look of him."

He was silent for a few long seconds. Then his voice came, weary and dragging. "I sure hope you know what you're doing, boy. I sure hope you do."

"As much as I ever do," I said lightly. "But every so often I'm right."

"Yeah," he said gruffly, "that's when the shit splatters on the ceiling."

I laughed, a short barking sound without much humor. "I'll put the tape where you can find it in an hour or so. That should give me time enough."

His voice was quiet. "Just don't make me go crawling around in that dirty attic of yours."

I laughed again and broke the connection.

* * *

I drove by the gate at a normal speed, then slowed enough to cast a quick glance at the grounds and the distant house. The grounds were lighted, the house dark except for one window on the second floor. My heart fluttered, skipped a beat or two, then settled down again.

She was there, behind that window—or she wasn't. Either way, right now, it made no difference. To find out I had to get beyond that window and to get beyond the window I had to get inside the walls. Elemental.

I parked the car in a turnout a few yards down the road from the gate.

Forcing myself to move slowly, methodically, I checked my equipment. The guns were where they should be, loaded and ready; I had a pocket flash, a small crowbar, a roll of two-inch duct tape, and the ten-foot aluminum ladder tied to the top of the station wagon.

I got out and stood for a moment listening. A dog barked somewhere far away, a night bird twittered in the oaks, and I could hear the faint whispery sound of my own breathing.

I closed my mouth and untied the ladder. I carried it across the road and leaned it against the wall in the dense shadow of an oak.

Sloped for climbing, it reached almost to the edge. Seconds later I was balanced on the top, straddling three strands of barbed wire that reached almost to my crotch. I raised the ladder and lowered it on the other side, then went down swiftly, noisily, the aluminum cracking and popping at every step. But it was too late to worry about that. The sounds wouldn't carry to the house and if the walls were electronically monitored someone was probably already on the way to intercept me.

I shoved the ladder under some bushes and stood at the base of a large elm.

The house was a hundred yards away, the surrounding well-tended grounds crisscrossed with tapering shadows of trees, crosshatched with a latticework of denser shadows created by dusk-to-dawn lights mounted on towering poles. To my left was the gate house, dark and silent. The single light in the window winked at me through the leaves of a huge oak growing a few yards from the house. Nothing moved.

I stepped out from the tree and followed its shadow to where it intersected with another, moving across and up the gradual rise in a cautious zigzag pattern.

It was slow going, and halfway there I decided it was also stupid and useless. If I had triggered an alarm on the wall, they would be scanning the grounds, and a moving figure is easy to spot, even among shadows.

I took a deep breath and stepped out boldly, walking across the lawn straight for the corner of the house.

Nothing happened. No alarm bells, no gunshots, nothing— only the sound of my breathing and the soft swish of my feet in the grass. My skin crawled a little, and I could feel the weight of dark menacing eyes, but I made it to the house, to the shadow of a hydrangea bush by the corner. I stopped again, reconnoitering, expelling my pent-up breath in a soft sigh. Still no sound, no movement. Even the night birds were quiet and the dog had stopped its frantic barking.

I was standing in darkness, but the front of the house was lighted well enough to see the heavy metal grillwork across the windows. All of them, even the second-story ones. My heart sank with a sickening thud. My pitiful little twelve-inch crowbar would be about as effective as a toothpick on a tin of sardines.

Doggedly I struck out again around the side of the house. Somewhere there had to be a garage and maybe a way into the house from that garage.

I walked through beds of flowers, felt a dim satisfaction as the stalks broke under my feet. At the rear corner I paused and peeped around, the satisfaction over the crushed flowers turning into a surge of elation as I saw the low-roofed building attached at right angles to the house: the garage.

The elation was short-lived; the garage doors, four of them, were locked, a single small window in the center of each. Too small for a body the size of mine. The windows were painted white.

But her car had to be somewhere it couldn't be found, and what better place after all than his garage? There was no way around it, I had to know.

I taped the second window, crisscrossed it with the wide duct tape, pressed flat and smooth to hold the glass. I tapped it with the crowbar, a small sound that couldn't have been heard a dozen feet away. Swiftly, my hands trembling a little, I picked out the glass, laid it carefully out of my way.

I stood on tiptoe, poked my hand through the hole with the flash, flipped it on, and found myself looking down on her car.

I leaned weakly against the garage door, a sudden wild rush of adrenaline bringing a sharp bright flash of pain between my eyes.

I squatted on my heels in the shadows, waiting for the dizziness to go away, pondering my next move as best I could.

I had a wild crazy urge to yell, to kick down the doors and howl a challenge to the gutless bastard inside—if he *was* inside. I suddenly remembered the garage, Susie's little car lost and forlorn in all that empty space. No other cars. Maybe she was all alone in there. But maybe she wasn't. This was no time for stupid grandstand plays. Caution. Do it right, as Homer would say.

The rear door was heavy, solid, a wide metal plate with smooth bolt heads in the center telling me it was barred inside. Two others, side doors, exactly the same. I moved around to the front and walked unhesitatingly along the wall to the front door.

Double doors, solid oak, or ash, with heavy bronze mounting brackets. Substantial. I pressed against them gently, felt a slight give, then unyielding resistance. I cursed softly. Nothing short of a tank would do it.

I looked out along the flat concrete apron to the driveway and suddenly I was grinning.

I had a goddamn tank! Or something almost as good. Three hundred and eighty-three wild horses in a steel frame. Even a ball hitch on the back to use as a ram.

I made pretty good time considering the shape I was in, wheezing and gasping by the time I reached the wall, almost too tired to climb it. But I did, managed to get all the way over without ripping off anything important on the wire. I fell to the grass and lay panting for a while before I could make it to inspect the gate.

Flimsy ironwork, more for decoration than restraint, a small chain and a shiny padlock, a ridiculous bit of parsimony considering the elaborate defense of the wall.

I rolled down the Dodge's rear window during the short drive to the gate; I found the hand sledge just where it should be, in the storage space under the third seat.

The lock was a little tougher than I thought; I had to hit it three times. I replaced the sledge under the seat, crawled back into the car and rolled up the rear window.

I pushed open the gate with the car's bumper, drove the curving concrete trail toward the house, my heart beginning to pound again, the solitary glow in the window drawing my eyes like a suicidal moth to a flame.

I drove without lights, the gun in my right hand; and still nothing moved outside the house.

She must be alone, I thought. Alone and waiting. I brushed the chilling alternative out of my mind.

A hundred feet from the house I circled through the trees, reentered the driveway headed outward, thirty feet from the big brown doors. I listened to the throbbing rumble of the engine and fastened the seat belt. I lit a cigarette, took a half dozen quick puffs, and flipped it onto the spotless lawn. I twisted as far left as I could get under the restraint of the seat belt, hooked my left elbow over the corner of the seat—and gunned the motor.

I had to correct only once, a slight swerve to the left—a tendency I have. But I hit the doors square, tail on, the trailer hitch ball catching them first, starting the opening split; the bumper stuck next, ripping the doors out and up, the rear car window bursting in a spray of glass that bombarded my head but missed my eyes, hidden in the crook of my elbow.

I slammed back against the seat supports, felt them give, break away. I lost my grip on the wheel, but I was still able to stab my foot at the brake.

I was inside, the big green machine sliding, careening across a floor slick with polish, glossy with wax, furniture cracking, smashing, flying in every direction.

I glimpsed a stairway and ducked my head in time to miss the banister crashing through the side window, slowing the car, flipping the rear end around with a resounding crash, bringing it to a juddering halt halfway astride a white leather couch nearly as long as the car.

I was out before the car stopped rocking, dazed and shaken, stumbling a little, but halfway up the stairs before the last dish toppled out of a smashed china cabinet.

The gun went up ahead of me, bobbing and weaving, as black and deadly as a cottonmouth closing on a crippled minnow.

There were four exits off the wide hallway, but only one with a tiny sliver of light beneath the door. I hit it running, tested its strength with my shoulder, rebounded, and put two rounds through the lock, then tried it again with my foot before the echoes of the scream inside had died.

It shuddered and cracked and held.

I hit it again with my foot, flatfooted, the way they do it in the cop movies; it exploded inward, bounced off the wall, and swung shut. But not before I was inside, crouched and panting, aching for something to shoot.

But there was nothing, nobody to shoot. Only Susie, crouched on her knees in the center of the big bed, her hands over her mouth, her eyes round with fear, growing bigger as she recognized me.

Pale and drawn, her hair a stringy mess, deep-sunken eyes, and pounds lighter, she was never more beautiful in my memory than at that moment.

"Oh, God, Danny! I knew you'd come! I knew you'd come!"

She was shaking, laughing and crying at the same time, stroking and touching and squeezing, clinging to me, unable to get close enough, the chain that led from her ankle to a large eyebolt in the floor jingling with every movement.

"Jesus, baby," I said, trying to grin, doing some trembling of my own, filling my blurred eyes with her, my aching arms, my empty heart.

She was babbling, trying to kiss me and talk at the same time, her lips salty-sweet, warm and wet and even softer than I remembered.

Finally, I could speak without stuttering. "Are you all right? Did he . . . did he hurt you?"

I watched her eyes as she shook her head. "No, no! I thought once . . . he was going to . . ." She threw herself at me again, squeezing my chest so hard it hurt, her face turbulent with joy despite the free-flowing tears.

"Hey! It's all right. I'm here, baby. Everything's okay now."

I held her until it was over, the heartrending sounds of terror, of anger, and finally, of relief.

"I'll have to go back downstairs to my car. I need tools to get you out of this. I'll only be a—"

Her face contorted with sudden fear. "No! No, please don't . . . not . . . yet . . . please don't leave me. . . ." She clutched me against her, buried her face in my neck again.

"All right," I said, stroking the mass of tousled hair. I pushed her back until I could see her red-rimmed eyes. "Why did he take you, Susan?"

She blew her nose into my handkerchief and shook her

head. "It was terrible, Danny. So terrible and so darned dumb. I tried to tell him it was an accident. That I didn't take his picture. But he wouldn't listen. He smashed the camera, jumped on it, and then . . . and then . . . the girl in the car! Oh, God, Danny, she burned up in the car!"

"I know," I said quickly, trying to forestall another round of sobs. "I know about the girl—his daughter. But why did he take you?"

"His *daughter*?" She repeated it numbly, her face almost ludicrous with incredulity. "I can't believe it! She was . . ." She broke off, her lips quivering.

"She was, honey. Believe me, she was. Now, what happened?"

"My God, Danny! She was doing it to him . . . to her . . . own father!" She shook her head, appalled.

"Out on the road?" Despite what I knew about them, I felt a small thudding shock of disbelief.

"No, no! Not on the road. Back in the trees . . . maybe thirty feet . . . there's a place where people drive back in there to dump things. They were parked in there . . . doing it!" She lifted her head and made a small grimace of distaste.

"But you could see them from the road?"

"No. There's bushes, limbs hanging, weeds, stuff like that. I couldn't see them from the road. Besides, it was dark."

"Please, baby." I wiped the last vestiges of tears from her cheeks. "Now, tell me, what were you doing back there?"

"Oh!" She smiled wanly. "I see what you mean."

"Yeah," I said, and grinned at her. Just seeing her, it was hard not to keep on grinning.

"I was turning around. I was going back to Mickey Conrad's place. I left one of Bucky Deane's cameras there and . . . oh, Lord, I wonder if Mickey's still got it?"

"Okay," I said patiently. "You pulled in to turn around. Then what happened?"

She nodded vigorously. "I pulled in to turn around . . . and there they were . . . in my lights. He was standing on the other side, you know, the passenger side. The door was open. He was just standing there, it looked like at first. I recognized him right away. He was on Billie West's talk show a couple of months ago. I did the preliminary work on that, so I knew him pretty well. Anyway, I knew him, and the first thing I thought was he might be having car trouble of some kind. I stuck my head out and asked him and opened the car door at the same time." She hesitated, winced. "I don't know why in the world I picked up the other camera. But I did. And then, just then, the girl raised her head and I saw what . . . I saw that her blouse was off . . . and he must have stepped back a little . . . because I could see then that his pants were down." She stopped again, then finished indignantly. "I sure didn't know it was his daughter."

"Then what, honey?"

"Well, I got back in the car . . . or started to, at least. I guess that's when I must have pressed the flash button on Bucky's camera. It went off, anyway."

"And he thought you were taking their picture? Did he know who you were?"

"I don't know. I called him by name and the light came on when I opened the door, but I don't think he could see past the headlights. But he did know that I knew him."

She blew her nose into my handkerchief and handed it back to me. She moved her leg and the chain rattled. I lifted her ankle and looked at the chain. Lightweight, yet sturdy, it had small twisted links welded and plated. Heavy enough to require the use of a bolt cutter, it lay in loops and whorls from the handcuff on her ankle to a large eyebolt set into the hardwood floor. Besides the bed, the only other piece of furniture in the room was a small padded chair near the front window.

"At least he gave you plenty of room to move around," I said.

She nodded slowly, obviously reluctant to give her captor credit for even the smallest act of kindness. "He had to. I couldn't have gone into the bathroom otherwise." She began taking up the slack in the chain, looping it in small coils in her left hand. "I could sit by the window and see the cars go by on the road sometimes. I kept watching, but none of them ever came up here ... except him, of course." She dropped the half dozen coils of chain on the foot of the bed, then reached out and gathered one of my hands in both of hers. Her chin quivered. "I knew you'd find me," she whispered, fighting the tears again.

"He's had you chained all this time?"

"Yes," she said indignantly, her chin quivering again.

"Do you know where he is?"

"No. He took that woman, that crazy old woman, somewhere."

"His wife?"

"I guess. I never saw her before a few days ago."

"You've been here, in this room, all the time?"

She started to nod, then shook her head. "No. The first two ... or maybe three days he kept me in another, smaller place. It was close to a road. He kept me tied up, with a gag in my mouth. It was close by. It only took a few minutes to come here."

"The gatehouse. He kept you in the gatehouse because his wife was here. Then when she went to the hospital, he brought you up here. Jesus, I was in that gatehouse the day of the funeral. I wonder ... but no, you were probably already up here. That's why he told me that lie about his wife and all the relatives up here at the big house." I took her hand and kissed the palm. "That was what did it finally. He was lying about his wife and I found it out later but it didn't register. His son told me and I ran him off. Did you meet him? Did he know ... ?"

"I don't think so. But Mr. Markette told me about him. That he was disappointed in him and all that kind of stuff."

"You mean he talked to you about things like that?"

Her head bobbed earnestly. "Yes. He talked to me a lot. He can be really nice when he wants to be."

"Yeah," I said dryly.

She shook her head and made a face of wonder. "I almost felt sorry for him ... sometimes."

"Did he say anything about turning you loose?"

"Yes. He kept telling me he would . . . after his appointment, he said." She stopped and shook her head slowly. "But, I don't know, Danny. I believed him at first, but these last few days, I wasn't so sure. I was beginning to get really scared. He's been acting wild like he did out there on the road."

"Finish your story. What happened after the flashbulb went off?"

"Boy! That set him off but good. He began yanking at his pants and yelling at me. Running toward me and yelling. I got scared. I backed out of there and drove off. But before I got to Lucas White Road he caught up with me. He was blowing his horn, trying to get by me, all kinds of crazy stuff." She wet her lips, looking at me for sympathy. I smiled encouragingly.

"Then after I turned on Lucas White Road he came up beside me, tried to run me off the road. I think we scraped fenders a couple of times. I decided I had better stop. I pulled to the side of the road. He stopped in the middle of the road and jumped out. He ran around on the passenger side of my car and grabbed Bucky's camera and started beating it on the ground. I was screaming at him to stop . . . trying to tell him I didn't take a picture. But he wouldn't listen. He jerked out the film, threw the camera on the ground, and stomped on it. Then he threw it in the car and stood there glaring at me." She shuddered. "Lordy, he looked mad."

"How about the girl? How did that happen?"

She shuddered again. "It just happened. I looked up and saw the car rolling back away from us. I screamed at him, but he just stood there glaring at me. I saw her . . . she was screaming, too . . . and she reached over to grab the wheel. But I guess her hands must have slipped or something. It just suddenly swerved and went over the side of the road . . . just went over backwards." Her fingers came up to her chin, pressed against her lower lip. "Just . . . just a moment later . . . it was awful, Danny! A—a terrible blast . . . fire high in the air. My car rocked and the heat was terrible. If—if we'd been any closer . . ."

Her face was ashen, her fingers trembling. I folded her in my arms again. "It's okay, baby, it's all over." I was kissing the new tears from her eyes when the voice came from the doorway.

"I'm afraid not, Mr. Roman. I'm afraid it's not over, not yet."

There was no chance; he had me cold, the twin barrels of the shotgun lined up with my chest. I cursed my stupidity silently, stared past the twin holes at the cold, handsome face of John Markette. Pale and strained, but with a determined set to the jaw that sent everything in my stomach streaming downward.

I had seen it often enough before: the face of a man who has made up his mind to kill.

I shifted my feet for better balance, lifted my hands slowly toward my shoulders at his command. But he saw the movement and stayed halfway behind the broken door.

"The gun under your coat, Mr. Roman. Lift it out, please . . . two fingers only. Carefully. I won't hesitate to kill you."

"I'm sure you wouldn't. I don't think you'd hesitate at much of anything, Mr. Markette."

He smiled faintly. "Toss it on the chair. Easy. Now, back up . . . until you reach the wall."

Susie was watching us with horror in her eyes, her face beginning to crumble.

"One thing you should know. I left word with a friend of mine, a police captain . . ."

He shrugged. "I doubt it, but it won't matter. I have no intention of trying to hide your body, Mr. Roman. You'll be found dead a few feet from your car, your gun in your hand, a round or two fired for effect. I think the scene will be self-explanatory to the police."

"What about the girl?"

"It's regrettable, but she'll have to disappear."

"And all this because you want to be a big man in Washington for a few years?"

"That's just part of it. The girl saw me . . . saw me committing a sex act with my daughter, saw me stand by and let her die. She's a reporter. Do you think she could go about her business and forget that? And once they start digging it never stops. Then there's my son. I have no illusions about my son. He could never withstand them. Inside an hour he'd be telling them his life story and looking for forgiveness. If only it had been him in that car instead of Charlotte." He spoke quietly, dispassionately, and it was that more than anything that sent a creeping chill of horror through my mind. Susie's head was in her hands, her shoulders shaking, fingers muffling choking sounds of despair, the coils of chain clinking softly.

He shrugged, his tanned face bunching apologetically. "I'm sorry it had to come to this. Believe me, I didn't—" He broke off, glanced quickly over his shoulder as the door swung quietly open.

She stopped silently beside him, an old woman, a face crosshatched with lines, a wrinkled neck, iron-gray hair bound into a bun. As thin and brittle-looking as a breadstick, she nodded politely, as if we had just been formally introduced, her eyes shifting to Susie, gray lips wrinkling in a grisly parody of a smile.

"Martha!" Markette moved sideways to block her entrance, held out his arm and herded her backwards. "Go downstairs, dear," he said quietly, soothingly. "We have some business to discuss. I'll be along presently. . . . Go now, you know you must rest."

I saw bright eyes flick toward the shotgun, the ruined face change expression. Then the sleek gray head dropped, bobbed in acquiescence, and she turned and left as soundlessly as she had appeared, her thin face expressionless, ravaged by time and painful knowledge.

Markette backed into the doorway and waited, his eyes flicking from me to the hallway. I coughed into the deathly stillness and wondered wretchedly if my chance had come and gone. I could see the dark image of the gun in the edge of my vision, feel the small automatic as heavy as a chunk of lead in my boot. I rose on my toes, tensed . . . the next time he looked away . . .

He came back into the room, slowly, carefully, crossed the few feet to the chair. He picked up my gun with his left hand, backed up to the door and tossed the gun into the hall.

He brought something from his pocket and threw it on the bed: a small silver key, shining in the light.

"Unlock her handcuffs, Mr. Roman. Put them on your hands. Behind your back, please."

I shook my head. "No. If you're going to kill us, I'm not making it easy. Try explaining a pool of blood up here."

He shrugged. "It won't matter. I'll just have to spill some of her blood by your body downstairs. It'll be a little more messy, perhaps, but it's not an insurmountable problem. The police won't be coming up here, Mr. Roman. Not when I'll have your body to give them downstairs." He smiled. "A crazy man. Insane because of his missing wife. Drove his car right through our front door, began shooting. Regrettably, but understandably, I had to shoot back. How does that sound, Mr. Roman?"

"It stinks, asshole. You'll never get it to stand up."

He nodded. "In your place I'd say the same." He motioned with the gun. "Now, please, the handcuffs."

I folded my hands across my chest and stared at him. He sighed and shook his head almost wearily, his face turning a pale shade of pink. He was losing a little of his cool.

"You're just making things more difficult for your wife, Mr. Roman. I can make things go . . . easy for her . . . or I can play with her first, make her demise a bit more difficult. I've treated her decently up to now, as I'm sure she's told you."

"That don't buy you anything. You didn't touch her because you probably can't get it up with anyone but your own kid."

His face flamed, then just as rapidly drained of color. "I let you talk to me as if I were filth once before. I won't allow it again." He lifted the gun and I saw his finger tighten around the trigger. I began to wonder if I had pressed too far too fast.

But maybe not. There had to be a kind of terror there inside him somewhere. Killing another human being is an awesome and eternal thing, and I could almost see him weighing the consequences against the gain. The gun sagged slightly.

"Filth?" I made a hawking contemptuous sound. "You'd have to climb up to reach filth. You're a zero. A cipher. Filth is the residue of something of value—" I broke off as he raised the gun again, went up onto the balls of my feet. He was too far away but I had no choice. If I could get under the gun . . .

"All right!" His voice lashed out, raw and rasping. "If I must shoot you here, then so be it. I've heard enough." The wavering barrel steadied, lined up with my chest.

"No! No! No!" It was a scream, yet more than a scream: a hoarse cry of pure savage rage, a primeval shriek of feminine defiance that transcended timidity and fear, and I saw Susie rise to her knees on the bed, the coils of chain gripped in one fist as her arm whipped outward in a looping arc and sent the silver coils snapping and unfurling straight toward the face of John Markette.

Too far, I thought, already dropping toward the floor, seeing him jerk his head backwards instinctively, bringing the shotgun up to guard his face and catching the billowing chain across the barrel, yanking savagely as he saw me coming up with my gun, saw the situation going out of control, already out of control, screaming a curiously feminine scream and jerking the trigger too hastily, showering my hunched shoulders with a hail of pebbled glass as a hanging lamp above my head exploded. A fine mist of plaster dust wafted before my eyes as I stared up at him through the thunderous silence of concussion, the malevolent eye of the short flat gun peering at him from the nest of my clenched hands.

Off balance, he teetered, the shotgun held almost at port

arms, kicked there by its own recoil, held there by indecision and the awesome knowledge of impending death.

I watched his eyes, thinking for one brief second that it had ended when he closed them and grimaced.

And then he opened them again and I felt a curious lilting thrill at the hot licking fire in their depths, the crazy reckless grin.

His feet shifted; his hands tightened; the barrel of the gun began to swing.

I sighed and squeezed the trigger, shot him dead center between the eyes.

Homer showed up right after the Dallas police arrived. Susie and I sat holding hands, ignoring the darkly suspicious glances, not looking at each other too often because the grinning was beginning to hurt and it was too hard not to kiss each time our eyes met. My heart swelled a little more each time, filling my chest, coming up into my throat and choking me, making me wonder if I was going to do something silly like cry.

Homer answered most of their questions, referring others to MacKay of the FBI, as arrogant and arbitrary as an NFL referee. He found time to growl at me once. "That was a shitty trick, hiding the tape behind the scotch."

"I knew you'd wind up there sooner or later, Homer."

Finally they were done with us. I helped her down the stairs, wanting to carry her, afraid I couldn't. Homer clomped along behind us.

The old woman was sitting in a rocker in the middle of her wrecked drawing room, already gone beyond their reach, a string of prayer beads in one hand, her Bible in the other. She was humming, a small pleasant smile on her lips, vacant eyes turned inward to where she had escaped.

A wrecker was standing by to tow my car and I gave him some money and instructions. Then I climbed wearily, thankfully, into the rear of Homer's car and, with the captain of Homicide, Midway City Police, as chauffeur, I took my lady home.

/27/

"Oh, hi, honey!" She threw herself at me, hung from my neck, her lips warm and moist and melting. She was bubbling over, so excited she failed to notice that I didn't return her kiss. I saw the boxes piled in a corner and felt my heart sinking.

I gently disengaged myself and made straight for the liquor cart. I poured scotch into a glass and then set it down with a bang. If I needed false courage to do what I had to do, then I was nothing.

She was watching me anxiously. "What's the matter, honey? I bought your brand."

I shook my head, my eyes going everywhere in the room except toward her. "Haven't you been watching the news, Alicia?"

She stopped in the act of lighting a cigarette, poised, suddenly watchful. "No, Danny. I've been busy . . . packing . . . a few things."

"I've got her back, Alicia."

"Oh . . . well . . ." She turned and slowly sank onto the couch. She held the lighter to her cigarette with an unsteady hand. "I—I'm glad . . . for you, Danny."

"Are you, babe?"

She stared at the cigarette for a moment, then winced and made a face. "No, I guess I'm not." Her voice was low and husky, almost inaudible. "I guess this changes things . . . a little."

"Yes, I'm afraid it does."

She looked up quickly, her face changing, a valiant attempt

at cheerfulness. "Well, we'll just have to do like we said from the beginning." She laughed uncertainly, awkwardly. "I don't mind sharing you—" She broke off, the color slowly leaving her skin as she saw my face and my shaking head.

"Danny?" Her eyes were wide, frightened. "What . . ."

"It just can't be, babe." My face felt as tight and stiff as old sun-dried leather.

For what seemed like an eternity, her gaze held mine, then she lowered her head over the cigarette.

"I see," she said dully. "I should have known better. Miss Goody Two-Shoes comes home and I'm back to being just a whore again. Good enough while she was gone . . ."

"I'll send you a check."

She raised her face, her eyes dark holes in a sun-bleached skull, drenched with rivulets of tears that wrenched at my heart. Then she lowered her head into her hands again. "I hate you for that."

She was silent so long I finally couldn't stand it. "Dammit, don't you even want to know why?"

She looked up, smiled wanly. "Does it matter?"

"Yes, dammit! It matters!" I was suddenly shaking, my nerves snapping like kite tails in a high wind: a stew of anger, remorse, guilt, all mixed up inside and boiling. "You lied to me, dammit! All the damn time you were lying to me!"

She shook her head wearily. "Not really, Danny. I didn't know he had her. You didn't tell me about her for a long time and by then . . ." She crushed the cigarette in a saucer on the table and knuckled at the smears under her eyes. ". . . by then I was in love with you. I was afraid to tell you."

"Oh, Jesus! Afraid? Don't you know you could have saved her two weeks of hell?"

She stared down at her hands. "Maybe I didn't want her to come back," she said sullenly, defiantly. She tossed her head and looked up to me, her chin quivering, her face beginning to dissolve again.

"I wanted you," she whispered, her voice dragging harshly,

raggedly. "I've never really had anyone, Danny. Anyone. Can you understand that?"

"Yes. I can understand that." I moved toward the door. "How much did he give you, Alicia?"

She sniffed, rubbed at the freckles on the back of her hand. "Ten thousand dollars." She stopped, then went on in a rush. "He came back that night at nine o'clock. He told me there had been an automobile accident, that Charley was dead. He said he couldn't afford to get involved because it might come out about her being a call girl and his daughter and cause a scandal that would ruin his chance—"

"And you believed him?"

"Yes," she said miserably. "He said to say he had been here all the time if anyone asked."

"All the time?"

"Yes. He did have a . . . a date with us that night. But his car broke down a few blocks away. He came in all hot and mad about it. Charley was here but she was getting ready to leave on a three-day trip to the coast with one of her special johns. That made him even madder but she coaxed him out of it, told him he could use her car if he would take her to meet her john. She told him she would make it up to him later. She could always work him any way she wanted—"

"You should have told me this, Alicia."

She shook her head miserably. "I didn't know it meant anything, Danny. Not for a long time. By the time you told me about Susie, I couldn't . . . I just couldn't." The tears were coming in torrents, streaming down her stricken face spotted with brown.

With a tight, constricting band around my chest, I walked back to the cart and gunned the shot of scotch. I turned back, my insides crumbling.

She had drawn herself into a tight ball on the couch, knees under her chin, head buried in her folded arms, her shoulders silently shaking. She was beautiful. I wanted to touch her, comfort her somehow, brush away the tears, tell her it would be all right. Instead, I walked firmly to the door, determined to make a silent exit, not look back. But whatever passed for nerve that year failed me. I stopped with the door open, looking back at her.

"I'm sorry," I said. "I didn't mean to hurt you."

She looked up then, and something close to a smile flickered across her face.

"We never do mean to hurt anybody," she said. "Sometimes . . . sometimes it just happens that way."

I left her then. I lit a cigarette and turned back for a moment to look at the light shining out from behind the curtained windows before I got into my car. I had already begun to forgive her. The hard part would be forgiving myself.